KEY LIME GARDEN INN

ANNIE CABOT

CABOT PUBLISHING GROUP

For John who believed in me from the start.

Chapter One

MAGGIE

Maggie Wheeler threw the half-eaten tomato to the ground and studied what remained of her kale and spinach plants. She'd spent the better half of the afternoon, and several hours the day before, installing a fence to protect her garden, and yet nothing seemed to deter the pesky woodchuck.

The woodchuck's hole that began on the other side of the fence extended right in front of her raised beds. If she weren't so upset about losing her plants, Maggie would probably fall in love with the silly animal.

"This is my yard, so you stay over on your side, and I'll stay on mine, and we'll get along just fine."

The woodchuck's large brown eyes stared back at her as if he understood what she was saying.

Waving her hands in the air, Maggie did her best to chase the animal away.

"Shoo. Go. Run. Get going. You're not going to like what I'm about to do."

Maggie watched as the woodchuck came out of the hole,

turned, and ran into the woods. Then, she yelled, apologizing, "I'm sorry, but I have no choice. Don't come back."

Reaching for the bottle in her gardening basket, she remembered what Henry, the owner of Harper's Country Feed and Garden store, had told her.

"If you want to keep the little critter from eating up your vegetables, get a large, plastic bottle and poke holes in it. Then what you do is fill the bottle with cotton balls soaked in the coyote urine, then hang the bottle on your fence. That'll do the trick."

If anyone had told her that she would purchase coyote urine, let alone soak anything in it, she would have thought they were crazy. But now, after days of chasing the woodchuck out of her yard, she was desperate.

Visions of the spilled urine kept her from following Henry's suggestion. So instead, she bought the spray bottle size to keep any liquid from getting on her clothes. And, if it wasn't a windy day, she should be able to avoid smelling like she'd been bathing in it.

Spraying the liquid around the perimeter of the fence, she saturated the spot where the animal entered the yard. The smell was awful, but the more she thought about it, maybe it wouldn't be such a bad idea to reek of the stuff to get out of going to dinner tonight.

Her husband's boss, Richard Patterson, and his wife, Lorna, were hosting the annual office get-together, and it was something Maggie dreaded. Taking another tour of the Patterson's mansion so that their guests could see the latest redecorations would keep Maggie's plastered smile in place for an uncomfortable and possibly unhealthy length of time. She started to laugh, thinking how much fun it would be to secretly sprinkle a little of the urine on Lorna's no doubt expensive and customized sofa.

Richard made Maggie uncomfortable, and she wondered if

any of the other wives felt the same way. There was something creepy about the way he looked at her. As much as she hated going to this dinner, she knew it was a small sacrifice to pay if it helped Daniel's career.

Checking her watch, she started to panic. Even if she rushed, there was barely enough time to shower before Daniel got home. If it weren't so late, Maggie would gladly spend another hour working in the garden. It was the one place that made her feel relaxed, and these days, the only thing she had complete control over. Playing in the dirt was her way of meditating. It was what her friend Chelsea called "tranquil and Zen."

If she'd had the ambition when she was younger, she would have opened a flower shop. Instead, those plans got pushed to the back of her mind as she focused on her marriage and raising their children. Back then, it would have been impossible to run a business and care for her family at the same time. Daniel had always wanted a large family, and so their five children kept her too busy for anything else.

Maggie grabbed her basket and ran back to the house. Inside the mudroom, she pulled off her gloves, hung up her hat, and wiggled out of her boots. She had purchased them from a British catalog the first time she saw Kate Middleton wearing them. If British royalty called the boots wellies, that's what Maggie would call hers. She liked to imagine that she was working in an English flower garden instead of fighting a woodchuck in Massachusetts.

Hearing Daniel's key in the front door, she looked at her image in the hall mirror and rubbed the dirt from her sweaty face. Running to the front door, she slipped past her husband as he walked into the foyer. Taking the stairs two at a time, she yelled to him, "I know what you're going to say. I'll be fast, I promise. We won't be late."

"Don't bother. We're not going."

Maggie was almost at the top of the stairs before she stopped and turned to look down at him.

"What do you mean, we're not going?"

He was sweating and looked as if he'd been hit by a truck. Maggie knew immediately that something terrible had happened. She walked down the stairs and took Daniel's brief-case from him, laying it on the foyer chair, her stomach in knots.

With their son Christopher in the military and stationed in the Middle East, she was constantly on edge, worrying he might be injured or even killed. Their oldest son, Michael, was a police officer. He was married with two children and a third on the way. Maggie was always worried about him as well.

"What's happened? Are the kids all right? Is it Christopher or Michael? Is someone dead? Say something; you're scaring me."

"No. It's nothing like that. The kids are fine. Everyone is fine."

"Then what is it?"

"I quit my job. That's why we're not going to the dinner tonight."

Unable to control herself, she laughed. It wasn't a tiny snicker but a full-blown gut-hugging fall on the floor kind of laugh. By the look on Daniel's face, she could tell he thought she either hadn't heard him or didn't understand the signifi-cance of his words.

"Did you hear me? I quit. No more job. No more money. The end."

Maggie wiped the happy tears from her face and tried to compose herself. Daniel always had a flair for the dramatic. It was obvious to her that this was nothing more than another of his overblown and exaggerated reactions.

She understood what he was saying, but they were hardly poor, and she was confident in time he would be making money at a new job, maybe even more money than he'd made at his old one. Quitting his job was not the disaster he was making it out to be.

"I'm sorry, Daniel. I am. I didn't mean to make fun of this, but I'm glad. I'm surprised you didn't expect me to be happy. I've been complaining about your job for years and have begged you to quit. I finally gave up trying to talk you into leaving."

Daniel's face was red, and he stared at her as if she'd lost her mind. Maggie continued to make light of the situation.

"This is good news as far as I'm concerned. I'm serious. Let's open a bottle of champagne and start planning our future. Maybe we can take that trip to Italy we've been talking about for years. We've got plenty of money in our retirement accounts, and the mortgage is paid in full. Why not take some time before you decide on the next step? I think it will be good for you and us."

Italy—just the thought of going made her heart race. Except for their annual trip to Captiva Island, they never traveled far from home. Day trips with the children and camping seemed to be all the adventures they could manage. Daniel's job kept him working around the clock, so travel was something they had to squeeze into their lives as best they could.

Their children weren't children anymore. They were adults and didn't need them the way they had when they were young. The boys were out on their own, and their oldest daughter, Lauren, was married and had two children. Sarah, their middle daughter, was a financial planner at an investment firm in Boston and seemed very close to an engagement announcement with her boyfriend, Ben. Their youngest daughter, Beth, was a strong, level-headed woman in her final year of law school.

It seemed to Maggie that this was the perfect time to travel before moving on to the next chapter of their lives. She was almost giddy in anticipation of what lay ahead and failed to notice Daniel pacing the floor and wringing his hands. Then, turning her attention to him, she reached out to put her arms around him and was shocked when he flinched and pulled away.

"I'm sorry, I was thinking about how we should celebrate. I didn't let you get a word in. Tell me everything that happened. What was it that made you finally quit?"

Daniel stopped moving and turned to look at her.

"I want a divorce."

If her brain wasn't registering his words, the rest of her body was. Feeling faint, she reached for the sofa. Ten years ago, when she found out that her husband was having an affair, she'd been prepared to hear him say those words. Hearing them now felt like he'd punched her in the stomach. Unable to breathe, she sat motionless, hoping the sofa cushions would swallow her up and she could disappear. When she regained her composure, she took a few deep breaths, and said only one word.

"Why?"

She already knew the answer but needed him to say the words.

He didn't hesitate. "I'm in love with someone else."

Unable to stand, she thought back to the last time he'd cheated. He hadn't wanted a divorce then. Instead, he'd begged her not to leave him. He said he couldn't live without her and the kids and that the affair meant nothing.

Daniel had done everything he could to talk her out of divorcing him. Knowing how much she loved flowers, he'd bring her a new bouquet every week. There were gifts of jewelry and weekly date nights at exclusive restaurants in the city. He was his charming old self and was even able to convince her that she might have had something to do with his wandering eye.

She was always so busy with the kids, maybe she hadn't had time to focus on her husband's needs. She'd heard about men feeling neglected because their wives were too busy tending to the children. The thought that she hadn't been a good wife was constantly on her mind. As soon as she figured out where the cracks in their marriage were, filling them in would be her number one priority.

They did all the things people do to fix things. They regularly met with a marriage counselor and focused on communication. Their children needed them, but they made sure to keep the fires burning in the bedroom.

Learning how to make gourmet dinners and keep the house immaculate, Maggie had worked hard to please Daniel. Hours studying everything she could about the politics of other countries and the price of gold was sure to impress her husband. If she could make Daniel proud of her ability to converse with the people at his firm and keep herself as attractive as possible, he'd never stray again.

Countless hours doing yoga and Pilates, as well as running and dance classes had kept her in shape. Even when she was pregnant, she kept up with her exercise routine and didn't allow herself the indulgence of eating for two.

From the outside, everything about the Wheeler home and family looked flawless. Everyone was jealous of their seemingly perfect life, and that convinced Maggie that everything would be fine. She'd held tightly to that belief, and now it had come back to haunt her.

This time, there was no healing and no plan to work on their marriage. Maggie was hurt but somewhat surprised that she felt no tears forming. As the minutes passed, she realized what she mostly felt was resentment over her years of singular devotion to a man who didn't deserve it.

"Maggie, you and I are still young. Hell, we're not even fifty yet. We got married way too young. I don't think we knew what we were doing. We were babies. We should have been dating all kinds of people before we got tied down the way we did. Listen, you can start a new life. I know it seems hard to imagine right now, but there is so much more adventure in your future. You'll see. Eventually, you'll realize how much you've missed."

Her anger building, she was suddenly sorry she was no longer holding his briefcase. She wanted to hit him with it.

"What am I supposed to say to that? Do you think I should thank you for this opportunity? Out with the old, in with the new? So, you want a new life? The old life doesn't work for you anymore? Now you want a new, probably younger woman? Who is she, anyway?"

She hated how cliché that sounded. Everything about this conversation felt like a scene from a soap opera. She was angry that her husband couldn't be more clever. Was it too much to ask for some originality?

"What does it matter who she is? You don't know her. I know this is difficult, but it can't come as a shock to you."

His last statement did shock her. Maybe to him, it didn't matter if she knew who the other woman was, but for Maggie, it meant worrying if their friends already knew.

Throwing his hands up in the air, he continued, "I swear you walk around with blinders on. You're so busy trying to make our marriage look perfect that you refuse to see just how imperfect it is. I'm sorry, Maggie. I don't know what else to say to you. I know that I don't want this anymore. Not the job. Not the house. Not the marriage."

"How about the kids, Daniel? Do you still want them?"

"Stop it, Maggie. Of course, I want the kids. Might I remind you they aren't children? Divorce doesn't mean we're not a family. I will always be their father, and you will always be their mother. I promise you that our divorce doesn't have to get ugly. I'm going to grab my clothes, and I'll get the rest later. I have a place to stay."

A place to stay seemed like an understatement at this point. Daniel most likely would be going to his mistress. Regardless, he was going, and that meant that this conversation was over. With only a few minutes left to say what was on her mind, she tried to find something more but realized there was nothing.

Daniel went upstairs and Maggie got up from the sofa and walked into the kitchen. Turning, she looked back at the living room and dining room. Was it too soon to feel some comfort knowing that every inch of this house and the three acres of land would belong to her alone? It was a relief knowing they had paid off the mortgage last year. At least that was something.

She was already working on the details of how she would make everything pretty again. She would repaint the kitchen. It needed new paint. Come to think of it, so did the outside of the house. She'd always wanted to live in a yellow house and made a mental note to hire someone to do that right away. She was tired of the gray, and the hydrangeas would look beautiful against the backdrop of the lighter color.

She ran her hands over the pen markings on the trim around the kitchen door. She had drawn a height line measuring her children's growth for each year in different colors, one for each of her children. The memories and milestones in her life came flooding back, and she tried not to cry.

When she felt panic travel up from her chest to her throat, she pushed it back down with more redecorating ideas. She would claim every memory and every celebration in their children's lives as her own and cut Daniel out of each image because she wasn't ready—and had no idea when or if she would ever be—to allow him to claim one more piece of her life.

Chapter Two

MAGGIE

The delicate lace of the curtain moved back and forth, and with it, a breeze that gently caressed Maggie's face. It had been hours since the sun came up, but she had no desire to greet the day. A soft blanket that she pulled up under her chin comforted her, and she wanted to hold on to that feeling for as long as possible.

If she let herself, waves of sorrow could overwhelm her, but she worried that if she allowed that, she wouldn't be able to handle it. Had it really been two days since Daniel's shocking declaration that he was in love with another woman?

The thought of falling into a puddle of tears terrified her. Wasn't there a manual or book that could guide her on how to handle the fallout from a cheating husband? Didn't she read a book years ago about death and dying, something about the five stages of grief? All she had to do was decide which stage of grief she was in. It was a toss-up between shock and denial and wanting to kill her husband. Okay, maybe killing him wasn't one stage, but it made her feel better to consider it. She made a mental note to find that book when she had some time to read it.

The longer she stayed in bed, the worse she felt. Ignoring the buzzing of her cell phone all day yesterday was sure to alarm her daughter, Lauren, since they spoke on the phone almost every day. Although she knew it was probably a mistake not to answer, she was aware that her voice would give away the pain she felt. She was angry but was teetering on the fence between screaming and crying, and the sound of Lauren's voice would probably unravel her composure.

Thursday was a blur, and Maggie knew that staying in bed, although a safe place to hide, wouldn't solve a thing. She had to do something before she recounted the flowers on the bedroom wallpaper one more time. There were at least three cobwebs in the corners of the ceiling that now needed attending to.

Maggie pulled a pillow close and was seriously considering falling asleep again until she remembered that today was Friday and her turn to host her lunch-bunch ladies' get-together. The first Friday of every month with her friends was something she usually looked forward to, but not today. It was going to be nearly impossible to keep an upbeat appearance when, on the inside, she felt like her world was falling apart.

Deciding when and how to tell her children about the divorce was something she knew she would have to deal with sooner rather than later. If Maggie had her choice, later seemed like a good idea, but she knew better. News of the Wheelers' impending divorce would shock their friends, but it was her family that she was most concerned about. As far as their friends were concerned, Maggie would have to grin and bear the condolences that would come.

For now, it was all she could do to focus on her luncheon. There was no way around it; she'd have to get out of bed and as they say, put one foot in front of the other. As luck would have it, the house was immaculate from the thorough cleaning she'd done at the beginning of the week.

She wondered how many times today she would have to

remind herself to "fake it 'til you make it." Even though she preferred to crawl back under the covers, Maggie accepted the fact that she'd have to dress, and act the part of a happily married woman to get through the afternoon.

Taking a deep breath, she sat up and pulled the covers off her body. Today was day one of her new mantra, "One step at a time." Since her lunch-bunch friends usually talked nonstop, Maggie figured at the very least they might distract her from thinking about her situation.

They always made her laugh, especially Rachel, who thought that their group needed an official name and decided on the Nip and Tucks. Rachel said it would be an accurate representation of where they all were in their lives.

It mortified Maggie to think she'd be part of such a group, but she had to admit that the name fit. All but Maggie and her closest friend Chelsea, who had moved to Captiva Island, Florida eight months ago, had undergone some sort of plastic surgery. Even though her right eyelid was starting to droop, and a week didn't pass without her pulling out a gray hair, Maggie decided it was too early to go under the knife.

Each of the women in her group took a turn hosting the monthly get-togethers. Maggie couldn't believe it was her turn. The timing couldn't have been worse. Whether her friends knew her husband had been having an affair, they never let on. Without telling them that Daniel had officially moved out, Maggie wondered how she could probe her friends for information. It was an impossible mess. Her blood boiled the more she thought about how her soon-to-be ex-husband had put her in such an uncomfortable position.

Making it down to the kitchen, her heart leaped at the sight of a rabbit with her baby bunnies hopping around near the back door. Maggie's home was an oasis of peace and calm in the early morning hours. The sunlit screened-in porch showcased the tropical fabric designs of the furniture.

A hummingbird hovered around the hanging petunia just outside the back door. Several years ago, she'd had an attached indoor greenhouse built so that she could keep herbs near the kitchen. Daniel said it was an extravagance, but Maggie endured the lecture so that eventually, he would give in and have it built.

It was a warm day, and the last thing Maggie wanted to do was use the oven, but her love of peach pie convinced her she had no other choice but to light it up. She always had at least one frozen pie ready in the freezer. If anyone had asked her, she would tell them to forgo cake, but not pie.

There wasn't a pie she didn't make. This time of year, summer peaches were perfect for her peach pie recipe. If Maggie knew anything about grief, comfort food was an absolute necessity, and pie was her go-to comfort food. Now, other than the pie for dessert, all she had to do was figure out what to serve for lunch.

Everyone raved about the potato basil frittata she made for Rachel's birthday, so Maggie decided that would be an easy thing to make for today's get-together. She clipped some mint from her window box herb garden for the salad and cut up various citrus fruits for a white sangria. Along with her watermelon, cucumber, and feta salad, the wine would be a perfect pairing.

Maggie loved cooking and baking as much as she loved gardening. Whenever life's difficulties became too much, she would race to either the kitchen or the garden, to either play in the dirt or dig her hands into the dough of a made-from-scratch loaf of bread. Today was no different, and before she knew it, it was getting close to the time for the lunch-bunch to arrive.

After making a pot of coffee, she hung up her apron and ran upstairs to her bedroom to change. Selecting casual pants and a pale pink cotton blouse, she was careful to wear something familiar. There was no reason to overdo it. A dress and extra jewelry would give her away.

Pink was Maggie's favorite color, and with her layered, softly highlighted blond hair, it was a color she wore often. Sterling silver and gold Cape Cod earrings and necklace were the perfect accessories. Pleased with how she looked, she felt ready to greet her guests.

Her cell phone buzzed, and this time she answered, Lauren's concerned voice coming through loud and clear.

"Where in the world have you been? I've been worried sick."

"I'm sorry, sweetie. I guess I had my phone on mute and didn't realize it." A small lie wasn't so bad given the situation.

"Mom, you've really got to keep your phone unmuted. I was about to get in the car and drive over there. Aren't you getting ready to have your lunch today? It's your turn, isn't it?"

"Yes, it is. I made that frittata you love so much. There will be lots of leftovers too. There's plenty for you and the girls if you want some."

Lauren and her husband, Jeff, and their two girls lived only three miles away in the same town. If Maggie had to tell anyone about Daniel, it would be Lauren. If she didn't, there was a good chance Lauren might hear about her father moving out before Maggie could tell her, and that would be worse for everyone concerned.

"Are you still coming over tonight?"

"I'm not sure. Jeff has an overnight business trip to New York. I have to drive him to the airport. It's only for the day. He'll be back tomorrow night."

It had occurred to Maggie that maybe the best way to deliver bad news would be to invite everyone over for a family dinner. She'd have to get in touch with Daniel, of course. It wasn't fair that she would have to be the one to explain the horrid details to their children. All of this was his doing, after all. He should be here to receive whatever hurt and anger the kids might hurl in his direction. She had no desire to protect him from any of it.

"That's okay, Lauren. Maybe tonight isn't a good night. Let's plan to get the whole family over for dinner this Sunday. Do you think you all can make it?"

"Yeah, that would be great. I've been wanting to talk to Sarah about what's been going on between her and Ben. I have a funny feeling that Ben might be proposing to her any day now."

"Really? Why do you say that? Have you heard something?"

Laughter coming from downstairs signaled her friends' arrival. Rachel called out from downstairs, "Hey, Maggie girl, we know you're in here somewhere. The smell from the kitchen is a dead giveaway."

"I'm on the phone with Lauren. I'll be down in a minute. Help yourself to the sangria," she responded before going back to her daughter. "Lauren, I've got to go. The girls are here. Let me call you later, and we can talk more about Sarah. I'm so excited to hear there might be a wedding soon. I really love Ben. This is happy news."

"Okay. Have fun with your friends, and I'll call you when I get back from the airport."

Maggie hung up the phone and ran down the stairs as if she didn't have a care in the world. She was good at pretending to be fine, why stop now? Earlier she'd cringed at the idea of hosting this week's luncheon, but now, she was grateful to see her friends' smiling faces.

Each of the women were incredibly unique and seemed an unlikely bunch to form a group of any kind. It was a book club that had initially brought them together. Over time, they'd become close and spent more time talking about other things than the book they were supposed to be reading.

Jane was petite with short golden blond hair, and since she played tennis several times a week, practically lived in tennis gear. Constantly in white, today's outfit emphasized her toned figure. Maggie was jealous that no matter how hard she worked out, she would never be able to pull off some of the clothes Jane wore. Jane had never married and had zero interest in ever doing so. She often said she was married to her career and that she could always find someone to share her life with as long as it was a temporary thing without commitment.

Rachel's hair was the envy of everyone in the group. It was auburn and wild with ringlets that framed a freckled face with beautiful green eyes. She had a bohemian appearance. An elementary school teacher, Rachel was an artist who loved to paint and sculpt.

The kids in her class were always working on a new project that made Rachel proud. The lunch-bunch never got together without Rachel gushing about a student or two. It was understandable. Rachel had always wanted children, but her husband didn't. Teaching filled that painful hole in her heart.

Kelly was a stay-at-home mom who, when she wasn't taking care of her family, volunteered just about everywhere she was needed. Maggie always wondered how Kelly was able to juggle so many obligations and admired her ability to give so much of herself to others. Her long, light-brown hair was almost always pushed back with a bandana, and her trademark blue topaz dangling earrings brought out her beautiful blue eyes.

Diana raised two children while managing a thriving bakery. She and her husband were starting to travel more as their children were grown and had families of their own. They could never get through lunch without Diana having to take a call or two about work. Maggie admired Diana and was even a little jealous of her impressive career and entrepreneurial spirit.

Chelsea was unlike any of her friends. She had deep wisdom about her and was so well-read, there was hardly a book she couldn't talk about. She was the most educated of the women and had been a professor at the local college.

Easy to talk to, Maggie found Chelsea to be the one person she could go to whenever she needed advice. When life became too stressful, Maggie would call Chelsea, and by the time they were finished with their talk, which usually involved wine, Maggie felt renewed and at peace. After her husband Carl died, Chelsea had retired early and moved to their vacation home on Captiva Island in Florida. Maggie missed her terribly.

Taking a deep breath, she joined her friends in the kitchen.

"Hello, you gorgeous women. How is everyone?"

Diana responded with her usual teasing, "I'm fine, but my husband wants to leave me for you and your cooking. I'm thinking I might give him up to you if you promise to feed me too."

Keep joking and laughing, Maggie. You can do this.

"I may take you up on that. You know how much I love to cook for people."

Pouring the sangria, Jane joined in the teasing. "I don't have a husband to give you, Maggie, but I think my cooking is pathetic enough to hire you to feed me too."

Rachel held up her glass and pleaded, "Me too."

Maggie laughed. "How about you all keep your husbands, and we keep meeting once a month?"

Kelly added her two cents. "I don't blame you, Maggie. Why would you want our husbands when you've got the perfect guy already?"

Certain her reaction would give her away, Maggie turned her attention to the oven. Pulling out the frittata, she placed it on the trivet and searched the drawer for a knife.

Jane, who ran the marketing department at a cosmetics company set up her iPad on the table and dialed Chelsea's number so that she could join them via Zoom. When Chelsea's face appeared on the screen, Maggie felt she had been rescued from the pretense of her perfect life.

She loved each of her friends dearly, but it was Chelsea who had been with her from the start. Chelsea knew about Daniel's previous indiscretion and was never able to forgive him for it. Maggie knew that as soon as Chelsea saw her face, her friend would know that something was wrong.

Trying not to sound too perky, Maggie, knife in hand, jumped in front of the iPad. "Too bad you live so far away, Chelsea. The kitchen smells incredible."

Diana lifted her glass of Sangria. "Here's to you, Chelsea. Since you're not here there's more for me."

With a turn of her iPad, Chelsea served up something even more delicious than the frittata. Whispering, Chelsea teased her friends, "Very funny, you guys. I miss you all, but I can't ignore the handsome hot guy by the pool. Now who's jealous?"

Ever the cautious one, Rachel ran to look at the view and admonished Chelsea, "Shh, he'll hear you."

Chelsea turned the iPad back around. "I'm pretty sure he won't mind. Now update me and tell me everything that's been going on. Maggie, how about we start with you? What's new in your world?"

Startled, Maggie turned and smiled back at Chelsea. "Oh, you know, the same stuff that always goes on around here. The kids and grandkids are fine, I've gained a few pounds, I'm still chasing that stupid woodchuck out of my garden. Pretty soon, he's going to be a dead woodchuck."

Maggie's cell phone buzzed, and she ran to answer the call. She didn't recognize the number, but that didn't matter since she was willing to talk to anyone, even a telemarketer, to divert the focus of the conversation to one of the other women.

The noise from the kitchen was drowning out the voice on the other end of the line, so she moved to the living room.

Maggie placed a finger over her left ear as she held up her cell phone against her right ear.

"Hello?"

"Maggie, this is Mike Driscoll."

"Mike. How are you? We haven't talked to you and Elaine for weeks. Where've you been hiding?"

Dr. Mike Driscoll had been the family doctor for years but had also become a close friend. Daniel and Maggie occasionally had dinner at the Driscolls', and Elaine, although not a close friend to Maggie, was someone she liked very much. Maggie assumed this was a social call, and possibly a request to get together soon.

"Maggie, I'm calling from the hospital. Daniel was brought in about forty minutes ago. He's had a massive heart attack. Maggie, I'm so sorry, but Daniel didn't make it."

There was a brief pause on the other end of the line before Mike continued, "He wasn't alone when he died. Someone was with him in the ambulance. I thought you should know."

Maggie knew instinctively who Daniel was with when he died. A feeling somewhere deep in the pit of her stomach began to turn. She felt light-headed and unable to speak.

The panic that began in her stomach quickly traveled to her head, and she started to sweat. A weakness took over, and she knew she was going to faint. She turned to look at her friends, and tried to speak, but the words wouldn't come.

The last thing she remembered was hearing a woman's voice call her name as she hit the floor and the room went black.

Chapter Three

MAGGIE

The next several days were complete chaos. Maggie's sister, Elizabeth and her brother, Michael flew in as soon as they heard the news. Family members she hadn't seen in years, as well as friends from all over the country came to the funeral.

Maggie had several things that needed to be done, but her mother, sister, and children handled everything. They worked around Maggie as if she wasn't there. They made phone calls, cooked food, or ordered out and made funeral arrangements, keeping Maggie minimally involved.

Her lunch-bunch friends came and, her best friend Chelsea dropped everything to be there for Maggie. She was grateful for their support, but still couldn't find the words to share what was in her heart and on her mind. Truthfully, she still couldn't wrap her head around everything that had happened in the last week.

Maggie knew that soon Mike Driscoll wouldn't be the only person to know the details of Daniel's death. She would have to explain things to her children in time but felt no obligation to run through the awfulness of it with anyone else. It was no one's business but hers. She didn't owe anyone anything. She had already been through the worst trauma anyone could go through in such a short period of time, and somehow, she would have to find a way to not fall apart in front of everyone.

Maggie knew there were plenty of things still left to do, including getting some unanswered questions addressed. She needed time to breathe. Too much had happened, and there was no time to sit quietly and take stock of it all.

Christopher received emergency leave for the funeral but would have to return to Iraq soon. He and Michael now saw themselves as the men of the family, and their mother's protectors. Maggie found their concern sweet but reminded them she could handle her life just fine—even if she didn't believe that herself.

Her sister Elizabeth was older than Maggie. When Elizabeth met her husband, Nolan Chandler, Maggie immediately knew they'd get married and Elizabeth, who Maggie considered her best friend, would move out of the house. She resented Nolan for taking her sister away to live in Maine.

To Maggie, it felt like he might as well have taken her sister to the moon and not a couple of states away. Just as Maggie dreaded, her sister created a new life with new friends and so they gradually drifted apart. That was years ago, and Maggie had made a family of her own. She loved Nolan and was happy to see that her sister and brother-in-law had a good marriage and a stable life.

Her brother, Michael, and his wife Michelle, lived in California. Maggie didn't get to see her brother as often as she wanted but understood that his life was on the West Coast. They stayed in touch as much as they could with video and texting. She was grateful he and Michelle came to support her and her children.

Her mother, Sarah Rose McKinnon Garrison, had always known what Maggie was thinking, even if Maggie tried to conceal her emotions. Growing up, Maggie could never get away with much, and she never understood how, without saying a word, her mother knew exactly what was on her mind. Maggie's father, Edward Joseph Garrison, had died of a heart attack five years earlier. The irony of Daniel dying the same way as her father wasn't lost on Maggie, but at least her father hadn't died in the arms of another woman.

Maggie needed quiet, if only for a few minutes. She climbed the stairs to her bedroom and closed the door behind her. She could still hear voices coming from different parts of the house, but at least she didn't have eyes constantly staring at her, waiting for her to fall apart. Now hiding out in her bedroom, she stood at the window looking down at limos pulling up in front of the house. Her private time didn't last long.

"When did he move out?"

The sound of her mother's voice startled Maggie. Her privacy was interrupted.

"What?"

"When did Daniel move out?"

Tears formed in Maggie's eyes, and she looked down at the rug. Hesitating for only a moment, she confessed what her mother already knew.

"He came home after work and said he wanted a divorce and that he was in love with another woman. He packed his bags and left, obviously taking more clothes than I thought he had. I assumed that he went to move in with her. How did you know?"

"It's not that hard to figure out, Maggie. His clothes aren't in the closet. Nothing in this bedroom suggests anyone but you sleeps here."

Maggie's mother put her arms around her daughter and supported her as she collapsed into the embrace. For the first time, the tears fell. She was glad they were away from the others. She needed the release. To let it all out and cry.

Maggie's mother pulled back and looked Maggie in the eye. "Did you say anything to the children?"

"No. I haven't been able to have quiet time with them. So much has happened so fast that all I've been able to do is deal with the logistics of the funeral. Now that we're talking about it, I'm not sure I should tell them about it at all."

Her mother's face made it clear to Maggie that she had said the wrong thing.

"Margaret Garrison Wheeler, are you out of your mind? Of course, you must tell them. They need to know the truth. I didn't teach you to stick your head in the sand and pretend nothing's wrong."

Maggie looked at her mother in shock. "Didn't you? When was it that you finally admitted to yourself that Daddy cheated on you? And how long did it take for you to tell Elizabeth, Michael and me about it?"

This was not the conversation Maggie wanted to have today. They'd been down this road before. She knew nothing good would come of blaming her mother for Daniel's behavior, but the whole 'stiff upper lip' thing was getting old, and she had no patience for it.

Not wanting to open old wounds, her mother changed the subject. "Do the kids know where he was when he had the heart attack? I assume he was with her when it happened. What did you tell them?"

"They think he was at the office, and someone brought him to the hospital. I didn't have the heart or the guts to tell them the truth. Now that I've had some time to think about it, I'm not sure it's a good idea to tell them. Their father is dead. I don't want them to have any bad memories of him. Who does that serve?"

Her mother knew Maggie well enough not to push. "Well,

let's just get through the funeral. This isn't the time or the place, anyway. The limos are here, and everyone is ready to go to the church."

As they walked to the bedroom door, Maggie put her hand on her mother's shoulder. "I'm sorry, Mom. I didn't mean what I said. I don't know what I'm doing or saying, but I'm glad I told you."

Her mother tapped Maggie's hand and smiled. "I realize you're all grown up, Maggie dear, but you are still my little girl, and you always will be. Never feel that you can't come to me."

They hugged and then made their way downstairs. Maggie's daughter Beth grabbed her mother and pulled her into a hug.

"How are you holding up?"

Maggie looked at each of her children. She was incredibly proud of the people they had become. "Listen, all of you. I'm fine. I appreciate all the support, but everything will be okay. You all don't need to fuss so much. Honestly, I'm going to be just fine."

She wasn't sure she believed what she was saying, but she wanted to relieve the anxious looks on her children's faces. They all made their way out of the house and down the stairs to the driveway. Everyone got into the limousines, with Maggie, Sarah, Beth, and her mother in one, Lauren and her family in another, and Michael and his family following.

The line of limousines made their way to the church. Although Catholic, Maggie had to admit that she hadn't been to church in a long time, and she missed going. She liked the way she felt sitting through the traditions that her family had followed all their lives. Each Sunday felt like a new beginning, a new chance to get it right.

The pallbearers, including her sons Michael and Christopher, carried Daniel's casket into the church and to the front near the altar. The priest rose to the pulpit and spoke of

Daniel's role as a husband and father and how he was such an exemplary member of the community. Maggie had little time to think about Daniel's cheating before she was faced with her newly widowed status. How many who came to the funeral knew of Daniel's infidelities she couldn't tell, and that unnerved her. Were people feeling sorry for her because her husband had died, or was it more likely that they pitied her role as the scorned and clueless wife?

Her daughters Lauren, Sarah, and Beth stayed close to their mother and sat next to her in the front pew. Each of her girls were bereft with grief and did their best not to cry for fear they wouldn't be able to stop. Lauren was the only one of Maggie's daughters who was married with children and so she had her little ones sit close to their grandmother and father during the service.

Maggie heard the priest's first few words before she became lost in thought. She recalled watching funerals on television where family members cried and, in some cases, wailed, throwing their bodies against the casket in uncontrollable grief. She imagined herself doing the same thing, but for a different reason.

A strong desire to throw herself against the casket and cry was overwhelming. She wanted to bang on the polished wood and scream. She knew it was anger, not grief, that made her think such things, and she was ashamed to think that even though Daniel was gone, she still wanted to hurt him.

Daniel had cheated on her. That was the truth. But there were other truths just as important. They had built a life together and had raised five beautiful children. Whatever was wrong in their marriage or flawed in their relationship, there was good in it as well. Looking at each of her children, she was overcome with emotion. Memories came flooding back of camping trips and birthday parties. Her heart grew thinking about the time Daniel had hugged Beth to sleep when she had scraped her knee.

She smiled at the memory of when Lauren was stood up by her boyfriend, and how Daniel made the night special by getting ice cream and playing checkers with her. *Maybe*, she thought, *if only I can keep remembering those moments I can forget about the cheating.* She wanted to forget; she needed to forget to move forward. She needed to forgive. It might not come right away, but for the first time, she believed forgiveness might be possible. The only problem was there were several stages of grief before she could get there, and that was a process she wasn't looking forward to.

It suddenly occurred to Maggie that the woman Daniel was in love with might show up to the funeral. The only problem was that Maggie had no idea who she was or what she looked like. Forgiveness was one thing, but would Maggie be able to feel actual empathy for a person who most likely tried to save Daniel's life?

She had no way of knowing what his final moments were like, but she felt it was important to find the woman and hear the truth of what happened the day Daniel died. She was owed that much after being married to the man for thirty-two years.

When the service was over, Maggie and her children left the church and returned to the limousines to drive to the cemetery, this time followed by a long line of cars. Once at the cemetery and standing on the grassy spot near Daniel's casket, Maggie searched the crowd for someone who might be her husband's mistress. She did see a young woman who was probably no more than Beth's age. Maggie couldn't imagine that her husband had cheated on her with someone so young.

Without letting her children know the details of their father's passing, there would be no way for Maggie to talk to the woman. Maybe it was a friend or classmate of Beth's. She tried to remember if Beth had ever brought the girl home, as she often did, but she couldn't remember ever meeting her. Maggie couldn't be certain who the woman was, so she decided to let it go for now. She had other things to focus on today. When she felt ready, she would talk to Mike Driscoll about the woman who had brought him to the hospital.

Back at the house, guests filled every room, and some even made their way out onto the lawn. The buffet table had more food than they needed, and Maggie was certain when all this was over, she'd have to figure out what to do with it all.

Chelsea moved up behind Maggie and handed her a mimosa. "I'm willing to give this to you, but only if you promise to eat something."

Acting innocent, Maggie said, "I'm eating something."

"Gnawing on a celery stick doesn't count. I'm serious, Maggie, you must eat. That's what I do every time there's something traumatic happening in my life. Food is always the answer."

Maggie took a few sips of her mimosa and grabbed a plate. Not to be deterred, Chelsea followed her around the table.

"So, when are you going to tell me what's really going on?"

Maggie looked away, pretending to be interested in the food on the table.

"What do you mean?"

"Don't try that with me. You know I can always tell when there's something wrong. Haven't I proven that time and again over the years? I always know when something's not right, so talk."

Maggie turned to Chelsea, took a deep breath, and gave her the only answer she could give at that moment.

"All I can tell you is that Daniel said that he wanted a divorce. He came home Wednesday after work and said he was in love with another woman."

Sensing Chelsea's anger building and the possibility of raised voices, Maggie stopped her before she could say a thing.

"Now, before you lose your temper over my buffet table, promise me we will talk about this later. I can't handle it today."

Chelsea's mouth hung open, and her eyes were wide. Staring back at Maggie, she made a promise to be good but only while there were guests in the house.

"Fine, but promise me we'll sit down, and you'll tell me everything?"

"I promise."

Chelsea smiled and did a perfectly Chelsea thing—she made a joke.

"You didn't kill him, did you? I'm sorry, I just had to."

Maggie rolled her eyes and tried not to laugh. It had never entered her mind to be violent. That is, until last Wednesday when she wanted to hit Daniel with his own briefcase. That, and the possibility of dousing him with coyote urine. That day now seemed like such a long time ago, and yet it was little more than a week.

When all the guests had left, her mother instructed Maggie to take a nap and let the family clean up. Chelsea, who was staying with Maggie, agreed.

"Let us handle everything. You go upstairs and rest. It's been a long day."

It was true. Maggie was exhausted and needed time alone, but she wanted to make sure that her family knew how much she appreciated them.

"Thank you all for being so wonderful today. We've all had a terrible loss, and I'm aware that I'm not the only person here who has lost someone. I know it's hard to imagine, but we'll all be okay, I promise. I love you all so much."

Christopher was the first to step toward his mother, immediately followed by the rest of her children, who embraced her in one big group hug. Convinced that each of her children would be able to adjust to the new normal, Maggie looked over at Chelsea and wondered what that new normal would look like. Tomorrow would be the first day, and she was grateful Chelsea was there to support her.

Maggie left everyone to handle the mess downstairs. Once in her bedroom, she looked at the open closet and noticed Daniel had left behind a large sweater. She tried to remember the last time he'd worn it. They often had family football games in the backyard, especially in the fall. She could picture Daniel bundled up in the sweater drinking hot chocolate.

She pulled the sweater off the hanger and sat on the bed remembering the day that she had given it to him.

"I can't believe you made this sweater from scratch, Maggie. It's gorgeous."

Throwing his arms around her, he kissed her. Then pulling back, he looked into her eyes and smiled.

"You take such good care of me. I'm the luckiest husband in the world."

She held the sweater to her face and breathed in the smell, expecting something of him, anything, but there was nothing. What was left now was whatever Maggie was willing to remember, and she knew that over the coming years, that too would change.

Chapter Four

MAGGIE

"Something's missing."

Chelsea removed the coffee cup from Maggie's hands and put it on the kitchen table and pointed to the chair. "Sit."

Maggie did as she was told and grabbed her coffee cup. "I'm not up for a lecture without my coffee, Chelsea."

"I will not lecture you, Maggie, but something is missing, and I'm trying to figure out what has happened to you."

Maggie got up from the table and filled her cup to the brim. "What happened to me? Are you serious, Chelsea? I'm pretty sure lots if you're talking about the last eight days."

"I'm not talking about Daniel's cheating or wanting a divorce or the heart attack. I'm talking about the last time we saw each other in person eight months ago. What happened to my friend? You know, the one who always saw the good in people, the one I used to call Tinkerbell. You used to be a Disney girl all day long. Now you're in a dark place, and I feel like I can't reach you. What's going on?"

It was impossible for Maggie to hide anything from Chelsea. Now that her world had been turned upside down, the disorientation made it difficult for Maggie to get her bearings. She wanted to talk to Chelsea about what she was feeling but doing it without thinking it through first was not something Maggie was comfortable with.

"I don't know, Chelsea. I know there's been something holding me back from really being happy, but I'm not sure I know what that something is. You're right about something being missing. It feels like that something is me. Does that make sense?"

"Of course, it does. I've been telling you for a long time that you seem to be going through the motions but are not really living. I know you love your family and this house, and whether he deserved it or not, your husband, but what about you? I know you have dreams, but I think you won't allow yourself to admit that. If there ever was a time to think about yourself, that time is now."

"Think about myself? I'm not sure I know what that means. I'm a grandmother, for heaven's sake. I'm in love with those kids. My children might not be children anymore, but I love the fact that they seem to be content with having me in their lives. I talk to Lauren just about every day, and I think there might be a proposal happening soon for Sarah. That means wedding preparations and you know how much time that can take. I'm here for the boys when and if they need me. Beth is just starting out in her career, and there are so many exciting things coming her way. I don't want to miss a minute of what's going on in their lives. I hear what you're saying, but I have everything I want and need."

"But?"

Maggie wanted more for herself but didn't feel the right to complain. Admitting that something was missing in her life seemed ungrateful. But if she said that aloud, she might be asking for too much.

Chelsea didn't wait for an answer and sat back in her chair with an enormous smile on her face.

"I have an idea. Why don't you come to Florida with me? A change of scenery would do wonders for you, especially now. You don't have to stay long, just long enough."

"Long enough for what?" Maggie asked.

"Long enough to figure things out. I sometimes think that you've let your role as a mother and wife define you to such an extent you won't listen to your own voice. Not that those things aren't super important, they are, but those things are only part of who you are, Maggie. Maybe until now, you haven't taken time to honestly find out who you are and what you want out of life. The kids are grown, and Daniel is gone. What do you want your future to be? When you think of your life five years from now, what does it look like?"

Maggie could barely imagine what the next week would look like, let alone five years from now. What she did acknowledge, however, was that Chelsea was speaking the truth, and it frightened her. Maybe taking some time on Captiva would give her the space and the quiet she needed to ponder these things. The idea of sitting at the beach with her toes wiggling in the sand was appealing until Maggie remembered what time of year it was.

"It's crazy hot in Florida right now, Chelsea. I know you love the heat, but it's too much for me. I'll come down, I promise, just not in the middle of summer."

Chelsea gave Maggie her "not-taking-no-for-an-answer" look.

"It's two days away from September, Maggie, summer's over. Stop looking for an excuse not to go. It's a great idea, and you know it. Come, hang out at the beach, and enjoy a drink with an umbrella in it. It's the perfect place to unwind and relax. Just come for a few days at least. You can come back here any time you wish. You need this, Maggie. Besides, I miss you. We can have a girls' week and catch up."

Maggie couldn't argue with her. Captiva Island had been

the place where she and her family would travel to every year. In the early days of their relationship, before they were married, and before there were children, Captiva was where she and Daniel would go to unwind and reconnect. The memories were both wonderful and bittersweet.

"I don't know. Let me think about it, and at least run it by Lauren. It's possible she and the girls might need me. I watch my grandchildren sometimes, so I've got to see if she's got anything important on her calendar coming up."

Chelsea got up from the sofa and topped off her coffee.

"Check with Lauren. She'll tell you to go and to have fun. Promise me that if she does, you'll stop making excuses and start packing."

There was nothing left to do but to promise. Maggie suspected that Chelsea was right about Lauren approving of the idea. It was the first glimmer of joy after such a difficult and unhappy eight days. The only thing she had to worry about now was whether she could fit into her swimsuit.

Lauren was over the moon when she heard the news.

"Don't tell me you're considering not going, Mom. I think it's a great idea. If I didn't have the girls and school starting, I'd join you. I'm so excited for you. I know you'll have a great time."

"Are you sure you and the girls don't need me? I can always go to Captiva another time, you know. It doesn't have to be right now. It's awfully hot there, anyway. It's almost better to go when it's winter here. And besides, there is still so much to do with your father's estate."

"Mom, stop. You are just looking for an excuse not to go. I can help Sarah handle all that up here, and if we need you, we can video conference or text or email. It's impossible not to handle things remotely these days with all the technology. Besides, you couldn't get a better person than Sarah to handle the financial papers while you're away. She knows this stuff better than any of us. I think even Beth could help if we have a legal question."

Maggie was running out of excuses and felt like the cards were stacked against her. It was difficult to refuse Chelsea, but now, with Lauren supporting the idea, Maggie knew she couldn't fight them both. In the mood she was in, dealing with Daniel's estate was the last thing she wanted to do anyway.

Maggie was very adept at handling finances herself, and she often worked with their family accountant and attorney. She felt confident, especially with Sarah's and Beth's help, that they could deal with anything important during her absence. After all, she would only be gone a few days at most.

Calls to the rest of her children followed. Not that she needed their permission, but somehow hearing their individual opinions made her decision easier.

Michael was first. "I think it's a great idea, Mom. It's been a while since you've done anything for yourself. It's a perfect time to go, and Chelsea is such a blast. I can only imagine what fun the two of you will have."

Maggie called Sarah next, and she confirmed what Lauren had said about the legal papers.

"Mom, you know I can take care of all of it. Just give me Chelsea's address and number in case you don't answer your cell phone. Otherwise, go and enjoy yourself. Leave everything to me."

A call to Beth sealed the deal.

"If you don't go, you'll regret it. You've got to get out of here and think about something other than Dad."

Something other than Dad. Maggie wondered if that was even possible.

With her children's blessing, she began to get excited about the trip. Chelsea made the flight arrangements and insisted she and Maggie go shopping for a few new things first.

"I honestly don't need anything new, Chelsea."

"Nonsense. Everyone uses a vacation as an excuse to buy new clothes. Besides, when was the last time you went shopping for yourself? I think you spend so much time in that garden of yours, the idea of getting dressed up is the last thing on your mind."

Shopping at the local mall was not what Chelsea had in mind when she suggested they buy new clothes. Instead, a trip into Boston's Back Bay was her idea of the perfect retail experience for their mission, and she wouldn't let Maggie argue with her about it. The shops in this part of town were high end and not the typical clothing stores that Maggie usually shopped at. They spent the morning going into small boutique stores as well as larger ones inside Copley Place. By lunchtime, they each had several bags to carry into The Capital Grille for lunch. It was perfect weather, so they decided on an outside table to enjoy the scenery.

Maggie looked over the menu and chose the seared salmon with avocado, mango, and tomato salad, while Chelsea ordered the Caesar salad with shrimp. Two glasses of Pinot Grigio arrived, and it was Maggie who raised her glass first.

"To my best friend, Chelsea. I don't know what I would have done without your support these last few days. Thank you for everything."

"We've only just begun, Maggie. Here's to a wonderful vacation and time away for you. You won't regret it, I promise you."

Waiting for their food, Chelsea pressed Maggie to talk about Daniel.

"Is it too soon to look at what happened, Maggie? I mean, did you have any idea that Daniel was cheating on you? After all, he did it once before. There must have been signs. Anything?"

Maggie took another sip of her wine and shook her head. "No. Nothing. That's what worries me the most. How could I not see it? Daniel said something to me the day he asked for the divorce. He said I was so busy trying to make our marriage look perfect that I didn't see how imperfect it was. Maybe he was right. I don't know."

"Maggie, while there might be some truth to your not wanting to see what was really going on, you can't let Daniel's words make this about it being your fault somehow. It makes me furious to think he felt you were somehow to blame for his infidelity. There are ways to deal with marital problems but falling into the arms of another woman shouldn't be one of them. If he really wanted to stay married and fix things, he should have come to you, and the two of you could have gone to see a marriage counselor. It's not like you haven't been down this road with him before. He knew what he was doing, and what he was choosing."

The women stopped talking when the waiter placed the food in front of them. Once he walked away, Maggie looked up at Chelsea and asked the question she needed an answer to.

"Do I try to make everything perfect? I mean, forget about the marriage for a minute. Do I do that with other things as well? Be honest with me. I need to understand this if things are going to change. I'm starting to think that I've been lying to myself for years, and I hate that I was so blind to it all."

Chelsea had a mouthful of food when Maggie asked the question. Chelsea swallowed and then put her fork down.

"Maggie, I don't call you Tinkerbell for nothing, you know. You like to see the good in everything. You want to be happy, and I get that. There's plenty of ugly in the world, and I think you work hard to make everything pretty. I think you're not comfortable with confrontation and so, rather than fight, you sweep things under the rug. We all tell ourselves little lies. I call it self-preservation. You haven't invented anything new, trust me."

Maggie knew the truth before Chelsea answered her, but it was important to hear her friend say the words out loud. Ignoring the truth had cost Maggie so much, it didn't make sense to keep avoiding it. The food on Maggie's plate looked delicious, but she suddenly had no appetite for any of it. Instead, she took another sip of her wine and tried to hold back the tears that were begging to be released.

Chelsea reached for Maggie's hand and tried to comfort her.

"What happened with Daniel was not your fault, Maggie. He made his choice without regard for your feelings or the trust you had built again after what he did to you all those years ago. You must lay the blame where it belongs. Don't take this on yourself, because if you do, you'll spend the rest of your life living with a tremendous regret you can never resolve. It won't do you or your family any good going down that road. You and Daniel built a family, and now you have them for the rest of your life. Let Daniel rest in peace and leave this behind you so that you can move on."

Maggie smiled, knowing Chelsea was right, but she also knew that to find closure, she would have to do more. She wasn't sure at this moment what that something was, but she was determined to find it. So much unknown lay ahead of her, but she took comfort in knowing that she wasn't alone and wouldn't have to go through all of it by herself. She was scared and excited at the same time. Looking at Chelsea, she was convinced adventure was just around the corner.

"What I do know, Maggie, is that I'm going to have to keep hounding you to eat. As long as I've known you, there hasn't been a moment when food has not been the answer to any problem. This 'new you' isn't going to work. There's lots of delicious food waiting for you in Florida. So, eat up."

Her appetite returning, Maggie enjoyed her salmon and was grateful she had a friend who was willing to tell her the truth. Her lunch was delicious, and she smiled thinking about Chelsea's comment about food always being the answer for any question. A perfectly prepared meal, shared with people she loved, always made Maggie happy. Her extra pounds were proof of that. Soon, they'd be on Captiva Island where tropical plates prevailed and walking around barefoot all day long had the power to melt away any worry and stress.

Chapter Five

SARAH

Sarah Wheeler closed the door to her office and faced the man sitting on the leather sofa.

"I'm not sure you understand the problem, Scott. You are in way over your head at this point, and I'm trying to help get you out of the mess you've created for yourself. You can't keep spending the way you are and expect to have any kind of return on your investments. At this pace, you'll be broke by the end of the year."

The man ran his fingers through his hair in frustration.

"It's my wife. I can't get her to cut back or to follow a budget. You and I both know this has been going on for a long time. Clearly, I don't have the influence with her to make any difference. She's out of control."

"I think you need to bring her in here so that I can talk to her. If she refuses to look at the situation, then I'm not sure I can help you. The truth is that this is more of a marriage problem than a financial one. Have you considered a marriage counselor?"

Looking dejected, Scott looked up at Sarah and shook his head.

"Well, perhaps it's time you do. Talk to your wife about seeing someone professionally, and let's get you and your wife on my calendar for next week. Don't lose hope, Scott. There's always a chance things will turn around now that there is a plan for communication. The problems develop when people stop talking. You're not there yet, at least I don't think you are. Stop by my assistant's desk on your way out and book a time one morning next week."

Scott Abbott walked out of Sarah's office as if he had just come from the principal's office for being in trouble with his teacher. His situation was dire but not hopeless, and Sarah had to admit that he wasn't the first, nor would he be the last to struggle with marriage and money at the same time. She was convinced that she could make a real difference in the Abbott marriage. Sarah laughed at the thought of raising her prices to cover their therapy sessions as well as being their financial advisor.

Kristen, her assistant, knocked on the door.

"Ms. Wheeler, Ben just called and left a message not to disturb you but to let you know that he would be coming by in about thirty minutes to take you to dinner."

"Thank you, Kristen."

Sarah grabbed her purse and headed to the ladies' room. Going out to dinner was the last thing she wanted to do. The day had been a long one and she was exhausted. Although Sarah enjoyed being with her Ben, tonight wasn't a good time. They had seen a lot of each other recently with Ben taking her out to lunch several times in the last two weeks. He gave Sarah something to look forward to, even during her most difficult workdays. It was hard to put her finger on exactly what was bothering her, but she couldn't ignore the fact that lately, things between them seemed strained.

Sarah and Ben had been dating for almost two years. They got along well together except for those moments when the talk of marriage crept into their conversations. At least once a week, Ben mentioned either marriage or having children, and although Sarah was usually able to sway the conversation in another direction, Ben managed to find a way back to the subject.

It annoyed Sarah because as much as she loved Ben, she never felt ready to marry him. She loved being with him but didn't like the inevitable discussion about taking things to the next level. Getting married, felt like a prison sentence, and she wanted nothing to do with it. Perhaps it was time to make that clear to Ben. She realized she could lose him, but wasn't it unfair to make him think they eventually would marry and have children if that was the furthest thing from her mind?

Passing the elevators, Sarah ran into Ben just as his elevator reached her floor.

"Hey, gorgeous. Perfect timing. How was your day?"

"If I didn't have to meet with one client this morning, I don't think I would have bothered coming in. It feels weird going back to work after the funeral. It's so strange that this time last week my dad was still alive."

Ben wanted to put his arms around Sarah, but he remembered the last time he did that in her office building, Sarah was annoyed and requested that they not get too affectionate in front of her co-workers.

"Well, that's why I'm here. To take you to dinner and make you feel better. Do you care where we eat because I have a place in mind?"

"Honestly, Ben. I'm so tired I'm not sure I can do more than grab something to go. I want to get back home, put my pajamas on and climb onto the sofa with a big fluffy blanket. I might even consider eating right out of the Ben and Jerry's Cherry Garcia ice cream container."

The look on Ben's face made Sarah realize she had said the

wrong thing. She didn't want to disappoint him since he'd made the effort to see her.

"I'm sorry. If you want to go to that restaurant, I don't mind. I can always relax when I get home."

"No. It's not that. I was planning to make reservations at Deuxvae for tonight. I know so much has been going on, and I should have considered after everything you've had to deal with in the last week that you wouldn't be up for going out tonight. We can do it another night when you're feeling better. Why don't you get your things and I'll walk you to your car? You should get home and rest."

"Are you sure?"

"Yes, I'm sure. Come on. Let's get your things."

They walked back to Sarah's office to get her bag and explain to her assistant what her plans were for the remainder of the day. It was hard for Sarah to ever be upset with Ben. He always put her feelings first ahead of his own, and she loved him for that, but she also knew that Deuxvae was such a romantic restaurant that the owners had a special table in the back, dedicated for those who planned a proposal. Everyone knew about the restaurant's reputation for romance and that there was, on average, one proposal a week at that table. Sarah couldn't help but feel that she had possibly dodged a bullet.

Sarah couldn't wait to get into her pajamas and snuggle up on the sofa. Her apartment in South Boston was only two miles from the Financial District, and it took no time at all to get home. Normally, she could take the bus or a taxi or even walk down Summer Street if the weather was good, but because she had been assigned a dedicated spot in the garage at Rowes Wharf, she couldn't resist taking her car into the city.

Her cell phone buzzed, and she saw that it was her brother Michael calling.

"Hey, what's up, big brother? How's Brea feeling?"

"That's why I'm calling. This one isn't like the other two, sis. She's really struggling with this pregnancy. With the first two she had morning sickness, but it didn't last too long. This time, she's got morning sickness, afternoon sickness, and night-time sickness. She's having difficulty getting the fluids and nutrition she needs for herself and for the baby. She's got something called…wait a minute. I had to write it down because it wasn't something I've ever heard before. Hyper-emesis gravidarum. You ever hear of that?"

"Yeah, actually isn't that what Kate Middleton had with her pregnancies?"

"I don't know her. Is she a friend of yours?"

Sarah laughed. It had never occurred to her that her brother wasn't up on the latest royalty news.

"You know. The princess in England, the future queen? Anyway, never mind. What are the doctors telling you?"

"I've got to bring her into the hospital. They say she needs fluids and shouldn't be there for more than a couple of days. I can't leave the girls, and I've got no one to watch them. Can I drop them off with you just long enough for me to check Brea in and get her settled? It would only be for a few hours at most."

Even though Sarah didn't want any children of her own, she loved being an aunt to her nieces. Michael and Lauren had two girls each, and it was Aunt Sarah who spoiled all four of them regularly.

"Of course, you can drop them off here. I left work early anyway, so this is perfect timing."

'Thanks, I'll see you in about thirty minutes. I didn't feed them dinner yet, so maybe…?"

"I got it. No worries. I can make them something here. Just come along and don't worry about a thing."

Michael managed to get to Sarah's apartment in record time. Quinn and Cora brought toys and crayons and Cora's security blanket that was never far from her fingertips. Michael said Cora held it while eating dinner and while sleeping, and it was starting to look like it needed a serious washing. Sarah laughed when she remembered the time her brother had waited for Cora to go to sleep before he was able to pull the blanket out of her arms so that they could wash and dry it before quietly placing it back next to her.

Sarah wasn't a very good cook. Growing up, her mother tried to teach her how to follow a recipe, but Sarah wanted instead to climb trees and throw a football with her brothers. She was a tomboy right from the start, and while her sister Lauren learned the secrets of the kitchen, Sarah was content to read a book or follow her brothers around. Now, with two little ones to feed, the best she could come up with was macaroni and cheese. Fortunately, both girls loved it and ate every bit on their plates.

As soon as her four nieces started visiting her apartment, Sarah had immediately subscribed to the Disney Channel. It was a good thing too, as it filled the time when she ran out of ideas to entertain them.

"What do you guys think? Should we watch *Frozen*?"

Both girls yelled in unison. "*Frozen!*"

"Okay, *Frozen* it is."

They were able to get to the end of the movie before Michael arrived back at the apartment, but Cora looked like she was about to fall asleep.

"Everything okay with Brea?" Sarah whispered.

Michael seemed relieved. "Yeah, she's going to be fine. They say when you get sick like this that the baby is healthy, so that's a good thing. It's just hard to see her looking so exhausted and pale all the time. I think the fluids will help. She was really dehydrated from all the vomiting. I hope you never have to go through that when it's your turn."

Sarah looked stunned at Michael. "I can't believe you said that."

"What did I say?"

"In case you didn't already know this about me, I have absolutely no desire to ever get pregnant."

"What are you talking about? That's just fear talking. When you have your own child, it's the best feeling in the world. I'm always so surprised by how much you love them before you even meet them. It's the most awesome thing being a dad. And Brea is the best mother. You'll change your mind."

Sarah looked Michael in the eye and with an expression as serious as she could make it, responded with, "No. I won't."

Michael looked sad as if somehow Sarah had injured him in some way. "What about marriage? Do you plan to get married?"

Sarah looked uncomfortable and couldn't make eye contact with her brother. She didn't answer him. Sarah thought she might hurt him more with her response, so she said nothing.

"Does Ben know how you feel?"

Sarah was taken aback. "We haven't talked about it. At least not seriously."

Michael didn't mince words. "Sarah, you've got to tell him, and I mean right away."

It suddenly occurred to her that Ben might have confided in Michael about his plans to propose.

"Michael, since when are you in the business of telling me what to do with my dating life? What exactly do you know? Has Ben said anything to you?"

Now it was Michael's turn to look uncomfortable. It was obvious he didn't want to say anything, but it was written all over his face.

"Oh, God." Sarah pulled her sweater close, and sat on the sofa, putting her head in her hands. "He was going to take me to Deuxvae tonight, but I was too tired after the events of the last few days. I just needed a break."

"You are just like Mom, you know that?"

Sarah looked up at him. "What does that mean?"

"It means you run from things. You stick your head in the sand and hope that whatever unpleasantness comes it will just go away. Life isn't like that, Sarah. Not only that, if you don't stop doing it, it'll be the way you handle everything in life. You've got to confront things head on."

"And you think Mom doesn't do that? Where do you get off saying that? I mean, I can't believe you think that of Mom. I've never seen anything to signify what you're suggesting. Is there something specific you're talking about, because if not, I think you better take that back."

Quinn and Cora were both asleep. Michael walked over to Sarah and knelt in front of her.

"All I'm saying is that if you don't want to marry Ben, you need to tell him. Let him find someone who does. You can't let him keep thinking there's a chance. That is if you're absolutely certain he's not the one."

Sarah figured since they were already talking about this, she might as well go all the way.

"It's not that I don't want to marry Ben. It's that I don't ever want to get married to anyone. Ever."

Michael looked like Sarah had punched him in the stomach. "Not ever?"

"No."

"Is this because of Luke? I know how upset you were when that ended."

"That's a bit of an understatement, don't you think? More like devastated. But no. It's not because of Luke or Ben or anyone specifically. It's just that I'm not sure I'm the marrying type. You wouldn't understand. It's different for women, Michael, especially if you have children. It's so hard to juggle the commitments of family life and a career. And don't get me wrong, I love being an aunt and I love my nieces, but I've never felt a strong pull to have a child of my own. I'm starting to think I should go with my gut and stop punishing myself for not wanting marriage and babies. Not every woman does, you know."

"Sarah, I'm not so stupid to think that marriage is for everyone. I know it isn't. But please give it some time. You're still young, and you have plenty of time to build a career. I don't ever ask you for anything, but I'm asking you to please not close the door on the possibility, at least for now. Would you do that for me?"

Michael practically had tears in his eyes, and his words were so sincere Sarah had no choice but to agree. If she couldn't embrace the idea of marriage, at least she could give her brother a bit of hope by doing this one thing for him. She took a deep breath and gave in, even if it was just to placate her brother temporarily.

"You're such a romantic, you know that? Brea is pretty lucky to have you for a husband."

Quinn was awake now, but Cora was still asleep. Michael lifted Cora off the sofa and held Quinn's hand, whispering, "I'm glad you think so, but right now, my lovely wife is cursing me for getting her pregnant again. I think she might have even called me a few names when her head was in the toilet. She forgets she was the one who wanted to have a third child. Seriously, I'm worried about this vomiting. Apparently, it can go on for quite a while, even past the first trimester."

Sarah hugged her brother. "I'll stop by the hospital tomorrow during my lunch break and check in on her."

Michael was relieved by Sarah's offer. "Would you? That would be great. I'm going to try to get there during the day if I can, but I might not make it until later. Thanks, sis. I've got to get these little ones home and in bed. Thanks again for watching them for me. Brea's sister is coming over in the morning and will get them to school and stay with us until Brea comes home."

She opened the door for her brother and smiled. "Any time."

Sarah watched from the window as he drove away. She was happy that he had such a wonderful marriage and that her sister Lauren was equally blessed in hers. Although Sarah had promised her brother to leave the door open to the idea of marriage, she knew the truth. No amount of wedded bliss as evidence of marital happiness could sway her opinion on the matter. For now, she decided to keep that bit of information to herself.

Chapter Six

LAUREN

L auren pulled her long blond hair back into a messy bun and took a deep breath. Most of these books and toys she had picked up off the floor just yesterday were now strewn around the room once again. She was already tired and grumpy, and the day had barely started. Truth be told, her frustration wasn't really about the mess they had made. Lauren Wheeler Phillips, former top real estate sales manager, was now dressed in her bathrobe and slippers, wiping a mustard stain off her T-shirt, wishing she was dressed in heels and showing a house.

She blamed it on her star sign. She was a Gemini, and since that was the sign of twins, she knew that a Gemini's personality traits suited her perfectly. She wanted to have children and be a stay-at-home-mom when she was working, and now that she was home with her children, she wanted to be back in the office. Lauren laughed when she briefly entertained the idea of "having it all" and doing both things. Maybe for some women it was possible, but she felt she didn't have the energy or the drive to be able to accomplish it. She worried that if she tried, she'd only be marginally good at both things but would never excel at either one.

There were moments since her father's heart attack when Lauren dissolved into a puddle of tears, but most of the time, and especially for the sake of her children, she remained almost stoic about it. Among her siblings, she was the closest to her father. She'd always felt a tremendous need to defend him whenever any of her brothers and sisters complained about him. She considered herself Daddy's little girl and remained so even after she was fully an adult. She couldn't put her finger on it, but she assumed her father favored her because she was his firstborn.

Her sister Sarah worked hard at gaining their father's approval. She'd entered the finance industry and worked long hours to impress him. They talked about investments and venture capitalism, and it seemed to Lauren that no matter how hard Sarah worked to get their father's approval, his attention was never enough for her. Lauren could see the disappointment on Sarah's face when their father didn't give her the right amount of notice. It was painful to watch, but they never talked about it. It was something Lauren didn't want to bring up and so she never did.

Her siblings were close in age, as well as loving and supportive of each other, and their bond made it easier on their parents. There were occasional squabbles, but all in all, the family was a close-knit one.

A few years earlier, however, Lauren noticed that something had changed in her sister Beth's demeanor. Lauren recognized a chill in the air whenever Beth was in the presence of their father. Beth almost always disagreed with anything he said, and it was beginning to look like she was constantly trying to pick a fight with him. When Lauren confronted Beth about it, her sister was defensive.

"You think he's so perfect. Why don't you open your eyes,

Lauren? You've never been objective when it comes to him. You've always been Dad's favorite. Admit it, you know it's true. Nothing he does ever seems to upset you. Well, he's not perfect."

"I never said he was perfect, Beth. But do you always have to be so combative? I know everyone has a bit of rebellion in them growing up, but sometimes it feels like you go out of your way to be argumentative. You don't have to agree with him, but you could just walk away. Don't engage. The way it is now, you can cut the tension with a knife every time the two of you are in a room together. I'm not his favorite. Dad loves all of us equally. You're impossible to talk to, you know that?"

The last blowout forced Beth to stay away for longer periods of time. She would remain at school where she was happy. Even breaks during the holidays, Beth always made excuses about not coming home. Finally, in law school, although busy, Lauren figured Beth could no longer use those same excuses and watched her sister begrudgingly participate in family time. It was obvious to Lauren that Beth seemed distant and couldn't wait to get back to her apartment. Lauren hated that she had no control over her sister's actions but was more upset that Beth wouldn't reach out to her and share what was going on in her life.

Now that their father was gone, Beth seemed to have a sadness about her that worried Lauren. She knew it might not do any good, but a talk between the two of them was needed, and soon. It was possible that their father's death had made Beth feel guilty over the way she'd treated their dad. It was hard to tell. Lauren was willing to do whatever it took to help her sister.

Lauren's cell phone rang, and she saw that it was Beth. "Hey, I was just thinking about you. What's up?"

"Getting a bit nervous over the next few months. I'll be doing a trial court in the fall, and I'm scared to death. I guess I should have thought about my public speaking phobia before I decided on law school."

"Uh, yeah, that might have been something to work through. It's a sink or swim situation now. No time to back out. I think you're going to be an awesome lawyer, Beth. You don't have a thing to worry about."

"Listen, Lauren, I know we didn't get much time to talk at the funeral, but I thought maybe we could get together over coffee or dinner. I've had something on my mind, and I wanted to talk to you about it."

"Absolutely. Why don't you stop over tomorrow morning? Once I drop the girls off at school in the morning, we'll have plenty of private time here at the house."

"Oh my gosh, I forgot. It's their first day of school tomorrow, and Lily's first day of first grade. Maybe I'll come by early so I can see them leave for school. I bet they're really excited."

"They both have been talking nonstop about it for days. Everything is about school and what things they're going to do there. Olivia has been very specific about what she should wear. It's a big deal. I'd love for you to be here to see them off. How about getting here at 7:30? I'll make breakfast for us, and we can talk once we drop the girls off."

"Sounds good. I'll see you then."

The timing couldn't have been better. Now, Lauren would finally find out what had been bothering Beth, and perhaps she'd be able to help her sister through whatever it was.

Olivia and Lily were so excited about school it was going to be impossible to get them to go to bed. Lauren figured she'd tell them the faster they went to sleep, the faster the morning would come. That usually worked when they had something to look forward to. Once she got them settled down, Lauren found Jeff in his office, going over papers.

"Are the girls finally asleep?"

"It didn't take long this time. I used the old 'tomorrow

won't come until you're asleep' story. You look frustrated. Lots of work still to do?"

"It isn't the abundance of work, it's the work itself. I've been pushing these papers around for the last hour, and in about five minutes I think I'll give up and throw them in the trash."

Jeff had been struggling at work, and tonight wasn't the first time he had mentioned his concerns about his job. Jeff was a wonderful husband and father, and it pained Lauren to see that he wasn't getting any pleasure from his career. He was one of the top advertising executives in his firm, but the accolades that had propelled him to his position didn't seem to bring him any joy.

"Maybe it's time you forget about work and come sit outside on the patio. It's a beautiful night with plenty of stars. How about I get us a glass of wine and we relax outside? Tomorrow things will look different. They always do."

Her husband smiled and got up from his desk. "You're not going to use that line that tomorrow won't come unless I close my eyes and sleep, are you?"

Lauren laughed as her husband put his arms around her.

"Nope. At least not for another couple of hours."

"Hold still. I can't get the knot out of your hair unless you stop moving around."

Lily and Olivia had already had their breakfast and were almost ready for school. Olivia had pulled out a princess dress to wear on her first day, and Lauren had to convince her that her princess dress needed to be washed and wasn't ready for school just yet.

Fortunately, there were no temper tantrums from either girl. The only person ready to cry was Lauren. Her babies were growing so fast, and today would be the first day that both girls would be gone for a full school day. When Beth arrived, Lauren looked like she was ready to burst into tears.

"Can you believe how fast they're growing? It feels like just yesterday when I brought Lily home from the hospital, and now she's in the first grade."

Beth laughed at her sister. "I understand, but for heaven's sake, it's not like they're going off to college. Trust me, you have plenty more years before they leave the nest. Get a grip."

Lauren knew Beth was right but seeing both girls anxious to get to school made her weepy, nonetheless. Lauren was glad that her husband wasn't away on a business trip. Lately, his job was keeping him from home more and more, and she worried that he was missing out on some of the major events in their daughters' lives. Today, he was able to see the girls off before he left for work. Kissing his daughters, he grabbed his brief-case, and then kissed his wife goodbye.

Beth called out to her brother-in-law as he made his way to his car.

"Play nice with the other kids, Mr. Phillips."

Olivia was confused. "Daddy doesn't play with kids when he goes to work, Auntie Beth."

Beth laughed and tried to explain, but Olivia shook her head, insisting her aunt didn't know what she was talking about.

They all piled into the car, and since both girls were at the same school, there was only one drop-off location. Lauren and Beth watched as Olivia and Lily, along with their teachers, walked into the school. Lauren pulled the car away only after the last child had entered the building.

Beth rubbed her sister's shoulder. "You going to be, okay?"

"I will be. Let's get out of here before I make a scene."

Laughing, Beth couldn't help but make fun of her sister. "Yeah, don't worry, sis. Before long, the girls will be embarrassed to be seen with you and will be asking you to drop them off about a block from the front door. And a couple of years after that, they'll be driving themselves to school."

"Stop. You're making me depressed."

They drove back to the house, and Lauren ran inside to make them breakfast. "Coffee is already brewed, so help yourself. I'll get these eggs done fast, and we can sit and talk. I have a coffee cake that I made yesterday. It's Mom's recipe, you know the one with the sour cream in it? I couldn't help myself; I had a piece already this morning. It came out really good this time."

Beth poured herself a cup of coffee and sliced a piece of the coffee cake which had been under the cake dome on top of the counter. Lauren was as good a cook as their mother. Their brother Michael always insisted that Lauren and their mother should have their own cooking show on the Food Network.

Beth took a few bites of the cake.

"It's delicious, Lauren. Just like Mom's."

Lauren plated the eggs and cut up a cantaloupe. A side of bacon and some hash brown potatoes completed the spread. After she poured herself a cup of coffee, Lauren sat across from Beth and waited for her to say something.

Although Beth seemed anxious to talk, Lauren could tell her sister was having a hard time finding the words.

Taking a deep breath, Beth started. "I can't believe I've waited all these years to talk about this. Do you remember when I was in high school, and Dad and I were always arguing? I was so angry at him."

"I remember. None of us fought with Dad or Mom very much. At least not more than the usual arguments that happen when you're a kid. You and Dad went at it all the time."

Beth couldn't look Lauren in the eye; instead, she played with the food on her plate and continued.

"I saw Dad with another woman."

"What do you mean?"

"I mean, I saw him kissing another woman. I remember because it was my sixteenth birthday. I was so excited to take the commuter train into Boston with Jessa and Molly. We'd never done that before and thought we were so grown up because we were on our own with no adults. We walked around downtown Boston and went on the swan boats at the Public Garden. We got ice cream cones and spent some money on makeup. When we were on the boat, I looked up and saw Dad on the bridge kissing a woman. It was the kind of kiss that made it clear they weren't just friends."

Lauren thought it best to keep a level head and try to understand what Beth was saying. She thought it possible that this was the imagination of a young teenager. It was so many years ago; perhaps Beth was mistaken.

"Beth, if you thought it was Dad, why didn't you go to him and confront him with what you saw? He could have cleared things up at that time and the two of you wouldn't have had to have all those years constantly fighting. You should have given him the chance to explain. Maybe what you saw wasn't really…"

Beth cut Lauren off with one statement.

"Dad cheated on Mom then, and he did it again recently."

Lauren quickly got up from the table and walked away, a mixture of anger and shock driving her emotions. She turned and looked at Beth. "How do you know he did it again?"

"I know because I followed him."

Her heart racing, Lauren pressed her sister for more. "You followed him? What are you talking about?"

"You remember my friend Lara from school? I introduced her to everyone a year ago. Remember she joined us at Thanksgiving because she didn't have a place to go since her parents were in Italy?"

"I remember her, yes."

"Well, she saw Dad with someone, and she told me about it. A few months ago, she was at a restaurant in Cambridge, and she saw him. She said she was reluctant to say anything but felt it was the right thing to do. I believed her of course, knowing what I knew about Dad all those years ago. I have to assume that he cheated on Mom more than these two times, but I can't prove it. All I know is I started following him. I saw him go into the hotel with a woman about six weeks ago. Once I saw that, I stopped following him because I was so sick to my stomach about it, and I didn't want to keep seeing what was obviously happening."

Neither Beth nor Lauren had the stomach for breakfast, and so the food sat getting cold.

It would have been easy to believe that Beth was mistaken about their father all those years ago, but something about Beth's words told Lauren that her sister was telling the truth, and yet, she felt the need to defend their father. It was more denial than anything else. She didn't want to believe their father was capable of such things.

As much as Lauren didn't want to believe it, she knew all of it was true, and her reaction was immediate. She threw her arms around Beth to comfort her. Being the oldest, Lauren felt tremendous regret that she couldn't protect her baby sister from this pain, a pain they both would now share.

Lauren looked into her sister's eyes. "I'm so sorry you had to go through all this by yourself. You should have come to me or Michael or any one of us. We could have dealt with this as a family. What a tremendous burden you've been carrying."

Beth addressed the elephant in the room. "How much do you think Mom knows?"

Lauren shrugged her shoulders. "Good question. It could be not at all or some of it or all of it. Can you imagine what she must have gone through if she knew any of it, especially this latest indiscretion?"

"Do you think we should talk to her about it? I mean, I have no idea how we would do that, but it feels like that discussion has to happen at some point. Although I'm not sure what good it would do."

Lauren sat back in her chair and took a sip of her coffee. "Mom is off on an adventure right now. We need to wait and think about this for a bit. She deserves this time away and to feel some sense of peace after Dad's death. Let's let her enjoy this little vacation and think more about what to do."

Lauren could see the tears forming in Beth's eyes, and her heart ached for what her little sister had suffered with all these years. She reached for Beth's hand and tried to comfort her. Beth looked back at her sister and hesitated before she said what was really bothering her the most.

"I don't know whether to be angry at Dad or if I should forgive him and let it all go. If I'm angry about anything right now, it's that there will never be a chance to confront him and talk about it. There will never be closure for me. How do I live with that?"

"You live with it the same way all of us will, especially Mom. You make peace with it. Dad wasn't a perfect human being. He made mistakes, but I know one thing. We always knew we were loved, Beth. Most of your life you believed Dad was the best guy in the world, didn't you? I think we need to remember him that way. Do you think you can?"

Beth twirled the curls in her hair, a habit she'd adopted around the sixth grade. She looked at Lauren and shrugged her shoulders.

"I don't know. I guess I can try."

"At least now you don't have to be the only one dealing with this. I'm glad you told me, Bethy. I'm only sorry I couldn't have been there for you all those years ago. Promise me you'll come to me whenever you need to talk. That's what big sisters are for, after all."

Lauren couldn't help but wonder how many choices in their lives were impacted by the actions of their father, and what might happen in the future because of those choices. She worried that ignoring the problems in her parents' marriage had colored every decision she and her siblings had made over the years. Confronting them now might not produce the outcome they hoped for.

What Lauren was certain about was that death wasn't always closure, and opening old wounds had the potential to harm as well as to heal. Only time would tell which direction their new choices would take them.

Chapter Seven

MAGGIE

No matter how many times Maggie traveled over the Sanibel Bridge on her way to Captiva, she was always amazed at the immediate calm she felt. This was her oasis, and the warm sun hitting her face as Chelsea's convertible passed over the ocean was a reminder that she was home, once again. She was glad she didn't have to take a taxi or rent a car. Maggie always felt that the best way to travel around Florida was in a convertible.

Chelsea laughed when Maggie raised her hands above her head as if to reach for the sky. "Happy you decided to come?"

"This place always makes me happy. The colors, the smells, the sun on my face, the salty air, all of it."

"I know what you mean. That's why I came and never left."

"Yes, well, not everyone does what you did, Chelsea. I mean, have you any idea how many people talk about moving to the place where they vacation? Happens all the time. Until reality hits and they realize they have a life back home with plenty to keep them from actually doing it."

"Well, you know me. I'm not one to let things like that tie

me down. Life's too short. I don't want to miss out on anything and one day find myself sick and unable to do anything that I want, or worse, dead."

The words were barely out of her mouth when Chelsea realized what she had said. "Oh, Maggie. I'm sorry. I wasn't thinking. I didn't mean…"

"Stop. Don't be silly. I know you didn't mean anything by that."

Once over the bridge, Chelsea changed the mood by suggesting they stop for lunch before they unpacked.

"How about a piña colada? I've been in the mood for one ever since our plane hit the ground."

"That sounds great. I'm ready for something tropical. I'm starving too."

Chelsea's home was on Andy Rosse Lane, a busy tourist location. She pulled her car in front of her house and helped Maggie with her luggage. Climbing the stairs to the beautifully decorated front porch, they dropped their bags and headed to the restaurant. By the time they reached Captiva, it was getting late, and most of the restaurants were packed. They were lucky to find one open table in the corner of the outdoor seating area.

She had forgotten how much she loved this street. It wasn't just the fresh seafood that drew people in, it was also the live music and the barefoot tourists with tanned faces that kept things festive and upbeat. It didn't have the same sea of Solo cup spring break vibe as Ft. Myers beach. The island was mostly a family-oriented and older crowd.

A young man with a guitar sitting on a stool at the far end of the outside dining area was playing a Jimmy Buffet song. He smiled as they approached their table. The hostess handed them menus and took their piña colada orders.

"I'll probably say this several times this week but thank you so much for being such a good friend and suggesting this trip. I think it's just what the doctor ordered."

Chelsea smiled at Maggie and agreed with her friend's assessment. "Go ahead and thank me as many times as you like. I don't mind. Seriously, you needed this. I'm glad your kids convinced you to come."

The area, known for its grouper, boasted several recipes for anyone who loved the fish, and Maggie almost always had at least one grouper meal when she was on the island.

"I'm having the grouper sandwich, how about you?"

Chelsea loved salmon more than any other fish and so she chose a salad topped with it.

When their drinks came, they raised their glasses to toast to a wonderful and relaxing vacation.

The tropical pastel colors of pink, yellow, coral, and aqua dominated the buildings on Captiva Island and matched the equally gorgeous bird of paradise, hibiscus, and periwinkle. It was the kind of place that most people traveled to in their dreams, but Maggie and her family had been lucky enough to visit here often.

Maggie grabbed a piece of paper that someone had left near their table. Having already spent many years visiting Captiva, she was knowledgeable about the island; however, the article mentioned something about the island that Maggie didn't know. Reading aloud, she shared the information with Chelsea.

"Did you know that Anne Morrow Lindbergh used to visit Captiva? Apparently, she wrote a book while she was on the island. I guess that was years ago when the only way to reach Captiva was by boat. The book is titled *Gift from the Sea*. The author certainly gave the book an appropriate title. This island is indeed a gift. I have to find that book. I want to know more."

"I bet you can get the Kindle edition and maybe an audio-book as well."

"Great idea. I brought my headphones with me. I'd love to sit on the beach and hear her perspective on the island. I'm putting this on the top of my 'to do' list. I promised myself on this trip there would be no 'to do' lists, but this is a fun one, and those are allowed."

Maggie imagined the coming days as lazy and carefree, and it was exactly what she needed. She envied the people who lived here year-round and wondered what her friend's day-to-day life on the island looked like. When Chelsea's husband Carl was alive, they had enjoyed the island together. Since his passing, Chelsea didn't lack for company. She attended parties and events on the island and even hinted that there were plenty of men her age that showed an interest in her.

"So, Chelsea, tell me, how do you keep busy? You haven't told me much about life down here, other than the handsome guy you teased us with last week. What else have you been doing?"

"Well, as if that guy couldn't keep me busy around the clock, I'll be honest, I've made a few friends, and don't make fun of me, but I'm on a pickleball team. We play a couple of times a week in Sanibel. It's keeping me in shape, and it gets me out of the house. There are a few women who live here year-round, but most are down here for the winter and then they go back north. I'm never at a loss for activity. There are plenty of things to do, and plenty of people to do them with, some even handsome. And, of course, there's my painting. That keeps me pretty sane."

Maggie was happy for her friend. Chelsea had found a life for herself after the trauma of losing her husband after years of caring for him. Carl had been a lovely man, and he'd adored Chelsea. He was an orthopedic surgeon and loved his work. But he loved Chelsea more, and it was heartwarming to see the way he looked at his wife. Before Carl's illness, they'd traveled often and bought the house on Captiva Island several years ago. They traveled to Florida every winter for vacation with Chelsea sometimes staying on Captiva for an additional week or two. She was always trying to get the lunch-bunch ladies to come down for a visit, but it never happened.

Although she was happy to be on the island, Maggie had a brief moment of sadness that washed over her. A person could almost see the pain in her eyes if they chose to—Chelsea could see it, but she did everything she could to ease her friend's pain and sadness, and Maggie was grateful for her care. It was a comfort to her that Chelsea didn't judge her but instead listened patiently as Maggie tried to untangle the thoughts that were so distracting.

"This looks delicious, and the piña colada is almost like a dessert. If this is how I'll be eating all week, I'm going home with several more pounds on me than I had when I arrived."

"That's what vacations are for Maggie. I don't own a scale, so you won't know how much you've gained until you get home. By then, you'll be too far away to blame me."

"You know, Chelsea, you've got a point. I'm here to enjoy myself, and I'm not going to care one bit about calories."

As the women enjoyed their dinner, Maggie looked past her friend to the end of the street. People walked in the middle of the road as if there were no cars driving around. She watched as couples walked arm in arm toward the beach. An older woman with a walker making her way toward the Mucky Duck nodded her head hello to everyone she passed. Young girls in bikinis were laughing and carrying beach chairs, probably on vacation themselves.

There was an aroma in the air that reminded Maggie of the frangipani fragrance her daughter Sarah had bought for her on her last trip to Bermuda. Maggie knew that life went on after death, but how to do it well was what she needed to learn. On Captiva Island, she thought she might be able to forget the pain of losing Daniel, not once but twice in two days. If there was any possibility that this island had magical powers, Maggie hoped she would find them on this visit. She worried that if she didn't, she might not be able to deal with the reality of her life once she returned home.

"Penny for your thoughts." Chelsea's voice caught Maggie off guard.

"Oh gosh, I'm sorry, Chelsea. It's possible my thoughts aren't really worth that much."

"I'll be the judge of that. Come on, spill."

"I don't know. I was just looking around at everyone, and it always amazes me how life goes on no matter what. I remember when my father died. Lauren was pregnant with Olivia at that time. She gave birth only one day after he passed. It was so poignant the way life and death happened within a day of each other. We were all sad, of course, but exuberant when the baby came. Our emotions were all over the place that week. I guess that's where I'm at right now. My emotions are all over the place, and I've no idea what's going to happen tomorrow, but sitting here, it doesn't seem to matter at all. Life just keeps moving along, and I've got to keep moving along with it, don't I?"

"Yes, you do, my friend. I know what you mean about life and death. I thought when Carl died, my life was over. I could barely put one foot in front of the other. I didn't want to get out of bed, I didn't want to eat, and all I seemed able to do was sleep. That I could do. But if I remember correctly, a dear friend showed up at my house and pulled me out of that bed and made me eat a delicious piece of her homemade lasagna, and a slice of her chocolate cake, even though she preferred to make pies. It still took a while before I could see a brighter future for myself, but my best friend never left my side and basically nursed me through the worst time of my life."

"I'm glad I was there for you, Chelsea. You and Carl had a good marriage. At least you have that to remember him by. My memories will forever be a mixture of confusion and regret. I feel like there is so much I'm never going to understand about Daniel and me. I mean, it feels like he lived a separate life from the one I thought we had. I hate to even think like this, but what if these two affairs weren't the only ones? What if there are more women I don't know about?"

"Maggie, you are going to drive yourself crazy thinking like this. I know this is difficult and probably much too soon, but at some point, you're going to have to make peace with this. If you want to move on, there's really no other way."

Maggie put her hands to her face and shook her head. "Oh, I'm sorry, this is supposed to be a fun and relaxing week, and I'm already such a downer. At least for this week, I've got to shove all this negative thinking to the back of my head. There will be plenty of time when I get home to deal with it. I came to Captiva to get away from thinking about Daniel, not obsess about him, and that's exactly what I'm going to do."

They finished their dinner and walked back to the house to unpack. Maggie loved how colorful the homes were on Captiva, and Chelsea's house was no different. A mixture of pale pastel colors of lime green and yellow adorned the outside, and on the inside, a tropical oasis of light coral and teal dominated. The steady movement of cool breezes and ocean waves surrounded the house, and Maggie with it. So much of the area felt like she'd fallen into paradise. It was impossible not to be stress-free in such a place.

Chelsea made a pot of coffee while Maggie walked onto the lanai. When the coffee was ready, Chelsea carried and placed it on the table along with a plate of homemade choco-late chip cookies. Marveling at the view, Maggie took a deep breath of ocean air.

"Chelsea, you've really managed to find yourself a piece of heaven on earth."

"Well, Carl and I bought this house when the prices were

so much cheaper. I don't think I'd be able to buy this place if it were on the market today. We really lucked out buying when we did. Everything down here is untouchable these days. Even rentals are fairly steep."

"I guess that lets me off the hook."

"Off the hook?"

"Yeah, no way you'll pressure me to buy something down here and stay."

"Oh, that. Well, I must admit you're right, I was thinking about you staying here more than just a week. It may seem a bit selfish of me to expect you to ever consider it, but I'm not thinking about myself, I'm thinking about you."

"Me? What do you mean? You think moving to Florida will help erase all the bad memories? Is that what you think? Don't forget, Chelsea, I've got many more good memories with Daniel than I have bad ones. We couldn't have stayed together if I didn't."

She sounded defensive, even to herself. Maggie could tell her friend had more to say about that, but she was tired of the subject and wanted to forget about everything, at least for a little while. She wondered what it was that made people think they were experts on everyone else's life but their own. Trying not to be rude but wanting to make it clear she was in no way in the mood for such introspection, she did the only thing she could think of.

Stretching her arms above her head, Maggie yawned. "I think I'm ready for bed. It's been a long day."

Chelsea nodded and said, "More like a long couple of weeks. Get some rest. You deserve it. I'll see you in the morning. I think I'll sit out here for a bit. Nothing better than Captiva nights. The stars are abundant."

Maggie got up and walked over to Chelsea, giving her a big hug. "Thanks for everything, BFF. I'll see you in the morning. Good night."

Both women knew Maggie had stopped their conversation in mid-stream on purpose, and they both also knew that deflection would only work once. There would be plenty of time to talk, but for now, sleep was the only thing Maggie could manage.

Chapter Eight

MAGGIE

The smell of freshly brewed coffee wafted through the house, and along with the sound of the ocean, Maggie found it impossible to stay in bed. Putting on her robe and flip-flops, she walked downstairs and saw a delicious display of scones and her friend Chelsea scrambling eggs.

"Good morning. How did you sleep?"

"I don't think I've slept that well in months. There must be some magic in that salty air. It's magnificent. Not to mention that I feel refreshed and energized. Seriously, someone needs to bottle this stuff and sell it to people as an alternative to sleeping pills. They'd make a fortune."

Chelsea laughed and filled two plates with eggs. "I hope you like scrambled eggs. I was in the mood for them myself. I didn't buy bacon, though. I'm not a bacon person, but I was thinking that you might want some to go with your eggs. I can always run out and get some if you want."

"No, thanks. I'm just one step away from being a vege-tarian anyway. I won't miss the bacon. The scones look amaz-ing, though. Don't tell me you made them."

"Guilty. I got up early this morning and thought you'd love

them right out of the oven. They're always better when they're warm."

"I always said you should open a bakery, Chelsea. You're an amazing cook. I remember the birthday cake you made for Beth. It was incredible. I don't know where you get your ideas from. Do you belong to some baking club or something? Your cakes rival the Bubble Room ones, except your portion sizes are smaller."

"No. You know me. I'm just a foodie at heart. I watch all the cooking shows and collect tons of recipes everywhere I go."

"I guess that explains all the torn pages in the magazine I was looking at last night."

"Oh dear. Sorry about that. I should probably replace them with better magazines. So, Maggie. What's on the agenda for today? What do you want to do? We could just chill at the beach or check out the shops."

"I was wondering, if you wouldn't mind, I'd love to just take a walk on the beach. It's early, and the crowds haven't arrived yet so this might be the perfect time. Of course, you're welcome to join me."

"Maggie, honey, you should make this vacation exactly as you want it to be. If you want to be alone, be alone. I'm here for you, but I knew this wasn't going to be a girls' trip, even though I didn't say as much. This is your time. Spend it the way that you want."

Maggie didn't want to be rude, and she loved being with her friend, but she needed some time alone to think and was grateful that Chelsea understood.

After breakfast, Maggie got dressed, putting on something light and comfortable. There was a bit of fog over the ocean, and it made the air cool, so she took a sweater just in case. This time of the year, a morning like this one was unusual, so she was thrilled to enjoy the cooler temps, even just for a few hours. She was pleased there were no other people either on the road or the beach, but she knew that wouldn't last. It wasn't tourist season, so that meant she would have the beach to herself for a while at least.

Taking her flip-flops off, she let her feet get wet and stayed close to the water until she found herself farther down the beach and near the road leading to the beach parking lot and shops. She passed only one other person on her walk and was lost in her thoughts. This beach had meant different things to Maggie over the years. Her first visit to Captiva had been with her parents when she was only thirteen. Jumping over waves and collecting seashells made the vacation fun, and it was the beginning of a lifelong hobby of shell collecting.

Captiva Island was where she and Daniel had honey-mooned. Moonlight walks, star gazing, and collecting seashells that would forever represent their romance and their future together made the island theirs alone. Once the children came, they would rent a cottage and come as a family to the island as often as they could. Watching her children collect seashells made her heart full. The island, and specifically this beach, had been an important part of her childhood and growing up. To be able to share it with her children and watch them love it as much as she did was everything.

Now, in the middle of her life, the beach had a new meaning for her. One that, as beautiful as the ocean was, filled her with sadness. There would be no collecting of seashells or anything else this time. She wondered if she could retrace the steps in the sand, the steps that had led to today, what would she do different? She was terrified to live a life of regret, and yet she had so many. Realizing she would drive herself mad with these thoughts, she pulled her sweater close and wiped the tears from her face. It was almost more than she could take, and so she decided to walk back to the house, composing herself by taking deep breaths along the way.

Maggie knew every store, every house, and every business

on this road, but there was one property that she had always wondered about. A wall covered with drooping bougainvillea framed either side of an iron gate. There was so much land-scaping it was hard to see beyond the beginnings of the long crushed-shell driveway. She had passed this property before and had even asked Chelsea about it. No one knew much about the owner except that it was not abandoned but once belonged to the Johnson family. The only descendant of the family lived there year-round but was something of a recluse.

Maggie decided to follow the property's wall along a different path. She hoped to see more of the garden, and as luck would have it, another gate, slightly opened, convinced her to sneak inside. Although worried she might come upon a No Trespassing sign, she saw none. There was nothing to keep her from walking farther into the garden just beyond the gate. Her love of flowers made her appreciate the variety of colors that lay before her. Unique to the area were an abundance of fruit trees, which included lemon, mango, and key lime.

She was surrounded by the most beautiful flowers. Clearly, someone carefully nurtured these plants and not only provided water, sun, and necessary plant food, but love and care for every detail. Maggie felt like she had walked into a secret garden, but she knew better. As much as she wanted to explore the area further, she didn't want to anger the owner or create any kind of disturbance.

Maggie was about to turn back to leave when a voice from within the garden called out to her.

"Hello? Who is it?"

"I'm sorry, I didn't mean to bother you. I was just admiring the garden. I'm very sorry to trespass. I'm leaving right now."

"No. Please. Come in."

Maggie followed the voice around several croton bushes. A petite, frail-looking older woman sat under a pergola. She sat at a small table with four chairs surrounding it. Maggie couldn't help but continue to apologize and explain her presence on this woman's property.

"I honestly don't usually trespass on other people's property. It's just that I was out walking and felt drawn by the flowers, I guess."

"Please, you don't have to apologize. I'm not surprised that you were pulled into this little oasis of mine. I don't know what I would do if I didn't have all of this to hide behind."

"You're hiding, are you?"

"Well, isn't that what everyone says about me, that I'm a recluse?"

Maggie didn't want to insult the woman and had no other information about her as a reference. Staying quiet seemed the only proper way to respond. The woman sensed Maggie's reluctance to speak and so she offered a chair to her.

"Won't you please sit down? Perhaps you'll join me in having a cup of tea?"

"Oh, no. I should be getting back home. I'm staying with a friend, and I'm sure she'll be worried if I'm gone too long."

As if Maggie hadn't said a word, the woman called out to have someone bring another cup. "Ciara, can you please bring another cup for my guest? I'm sorry, I didn't get your name."

"It's Maggie, Maggie Wheeler, and you are?"

"Lovely to meet you, Maggie. My name is Rose Johnson Lane. Please call me Rose."

Maggie sat next to Rose and thanked the woman who brought her teacup. "Well, Rose, your place is magnificent. I've walked by your gate many times over the years and always wondered about it. Have you lived here a long time?"

"My parents bought this property in 1934. Of course, it was a much smaller cottage but the same amount of acreage. In those days, you could only get to the island by boat. My family lived in Connecticut, and that's where I was raised. We would come to Captiva every year and stay for several months.

I know today homeschooling is very popular, but in those days, it was almost a necessity for families like ours who kept two homes or traveled often. My family built up the place, and now I'm afraid it's rather too big for me."

"It's wonderful that your family has kept this property all these years. I imagine it's been difficult to push back against those who would want it for tourism."

"Well, I have had several issues with the island about that over the years. There are a few people who would love to get their hands on this land. Many years ago, my family decided to turn the place into an inn. There are six bedrooms, so it seemed natural to share the property with others who wanted to find a place so close to the water. Everyone loved the Key Lime Garden Inn; people came from all over the world to stay here. Of course, as time passed, I did everything I could to keep the inn running, but it was too much for my husband and me. Our son helped us for a while, but, well, he was sick for a long time, so that made it difficult."

"I hope you will be able to keep the property forever. I've no doubt your children must absolutely love coming here. You needn't worry, they'll preserve it and their children as well."

A sadness that wasn't there before suddenly appeared on the woman's face.

"I'm afraid I'm the last of my family. My husband passed away three years ago, and my son only last year. You're not supposed to outlive your children, but only God can decide what is best about that."

Maggie suddenly felt that she had ruined the woman's morning with her snooping. As much as she appreciated Rose's hospitality, she wanted to turn and run as fast as she could back to Chelsea's house and leave the woman alone.

"I'm so sorry, Rose. I didn't mean to pry."

Rose smiled and tapped Maggie's hand. "Don't be silly. I'm happy for your company. Why don't you tell me about you?"

"Oh, trust me. You don't want to hear about my life. I thought maybe we could talk about something that would cheer us both up. Like, tell me how you have managed to create such an amazing garden. I would kill to have a garden like yours."

"Ah, well, I used to be very involved in every aspect of this yard, but now, especially with my arthritis…"

Rose pointed to a man at the end of the garden.

"I can't manage it anymore. It's all Paolo. He's truly a blessing. He helps me with everything, but especially the garden. His sister, Ciara, cooks for me and helps with house-cleaning. When they lived in Italy, Paolo worked a vineyard and had years of experience with plants. Somehow, he managed to make his way to Captiva and runs an incredible nursery not too far from here, closer to Sanibel. My husband hired him to take care of our property, and he's been doing it ever since. He's a real treasure."

"I'm fighting with a woodchuck back home. He's always eating my vegetables, and I honestly am at the point where I should give up and make him a little garden of his own that he can eat from. I truly don't know what to do about it."

"Perhaps Paolo can help you. You should talk to him. He has a wealth of knowledge on gardening. Stop by his nursery when you have a chance, and I'm sure he can help you. It's called Sanibellia. In the meantime, I am very interested in you, Maggie. Please, tell me—I see that you're married. Do you have any children?"

Maggie had forgotten that she was still wearing her wedding ring. At no time in the last two weeks had she even considered taking it off. Now, it was wrapped around her finger like a lie.

"Yes. I have five children, three girls and two boys."

"Five. Oh, my goodness. Just like Anne. You know about Anne Morrow Lindbergh, don't you? She used to come here a long time ago. She was around my mother's age, and they were friends. I was already out of the house with a family of my own when they were together here on the island. I have several shells that belonged to my mother—gifts from Anne."

Maggie remembered the piece of paper she'd found the day before on the history of Mrs. Lindbergh's time on the island.

"You know, Rose, even though I've been coming to Captiva all these years, I've never spent much time reading about its history. I had no idea until just yesterday that she visited Captiva. I must admit, I didn't really know much about her except about her first baby that had been kidnapped and killed. I think that's mostly what people remember about her."

"Yes, that's true. It's unfortunate because she was so much more than that story. She was truly an incredible woman. Anne was a wonderful writer as well as a loving mother and devoted wife. I have all her books in the house. Would you like to borrow one that I highly recommend now that you're here on the island? *Gift from the Sea*. You will love it. Let me get it for you."

Rose struggled at first, but when she regained her footing, she used her cane to walk to the stairs leading to the porch and front door. Considering her instability, Rose was quick to return with the book. She handed it to Maggie and returned to her chair.

"Here you go. You will love this one. I promise you."

Maggie took the blue colored book and could see that it was well-worn from being read more than once. She couldn't be certain, but something made Maggie feel that Rose had loaned the book to others before her. Maggie opened the book to the first page and saw that it had been autographed by the author. While looking at her new friend, Maggie's eyes met Rose's.

"She signed it."

Watching Maggie, Rose smiled as if she had kept that little secret until the very last minute, a gem to share with her new friend.

"She did. All of Anne's books inside the house, are signed. It was a gift to my mother. I think they found they had much in common and stayed in touch over the years. I know they spent many hours talking about motherhood, marriage, and the struggles of being a woman in those years. Their friendship was really the gift."

Maggie gently held the book so as not to tear the delicate pages. *Gift From the Sea, An answer to the conflicts in our lives.* She thought for a moment if only it could be as easy as reading a book. How could a woman in 1956 know anything about what Maggie was going through? Turning to the back of the book, she saw a picture of the author with a gentle smiling face, a ruffled blouse, and a cameo at her neck.

"Are you sure you want to lend this book to me, Rose? I mean, you don't know me from Adam. Thirty minutes ago, you had never even met me. How can you let me borrow something so special?"

"Because, Maggie, I know you'll be back. I know you will return the book to me. I'll be here when you do."

Standing, Maggie pressed the book to her chest and felt tears form. She had no idea why the gesture should move her so deeply, but it did. Rose was a petite woman, no more than five feet tall. Maggie bent down and gave her a hug.

"Thank you, Rose. You're right. I will be back. I promise."

Maggie was almost to the gate when Rose called out to her, "Don't forget to go see Paolo about that woodchuck."

Smiling, Maggie waved back at her new friend, grateful she still hadn't learned how to mind her own business.

Chapter Nine

SARAH

Pulling into her mother's driveway, Sarah parked her car and slipped the folder that held several copies of her father's death certificate into her briefcase. Without a power of attorney, there was only so much she could do, but she would defer any non-urgent issues that needed attention to the following week when her mother would be home. Her job, at least for this week, was to get organized and prepared for what lay ahead.

Picking up the stack of papers her mother had left on the dining room table was the last thing she needed to do before heading to the hospital to visit Brea. Her phone buzzed, and even though the number was not one that she recognized, she decided to answer it.

"Hello, Ms. Wheeler, this is Arnold Kragen. I'm your father's attorney and am trying to get in touch with your mother, Mrs. Wheeler."

"I'm sorry, Mr. Kragen, but I don't know you, and I'm not in the habit of giving out people's information. If you are trying to reach my mother, then you should have her information already. Nice try."

Sarah hung up the phone and was disturbed by the call. She knew the family attorney, and it wasn't Arnold Kragen. It wasn't unusual for scam artists to show up after a family member had died. Scouring obituaries was the pastime of sleazy attorneys trying to make a buck off vulnerable families. They were akin to ambulance chasers, and it disgusted Sarah that somehow this man had her cell number.

Once inside the house, she found it difficult to stand in the quiet of the living room where once the noise of children and at one time, two dogs, a cat, and several guinea pigs filled the space. Everyone was gone, but beyond that, a sense that nothing would ever be the same for the Wheeler family overwhelmed her.

Standing in front of her father's chair, she was once again a little girl, her bare feet on top of his size twelve shoes, dancing across the living room. As she grew older, her father continued to see her as a child. Feeling very small, she struggled to find ways to make him proud of her and her choices. It was the reason she'd gone into the finance industry. She knew the more money she made, the more impressed he was with her. It angered her and made her sad that he didn't know her at all. Now that he was gone, she would never have the chance to change that.

The papers her mother left for her were neatly piled on the table with sticky notes labeled on the top of each folder. Sarah smiled at her mother's organization—a habit Sarah inherited. Her mother hated clutter. Every countertop and table were kept clear except for the legal documents. She knew that her mother would never be able to enjoy a vacation if she thought there was anything unattended to back home. Even one glass in the sink was enough to keep her mother from sleeping.

Several watering cans covered the back patio, and since Sarah promised her mother that she would water the plants, she filled two cans and set about pulling off dead leaves from the greenhouse plants, even talking to them just as her mother had done for years.

"Don't worry, you guys. She'll be home before you know it."

She turned on the hose and soaked what was left of her mother's vegetable garden. She remembered her mother having a fit over a woodchuck, and now Sarah understood why. Teeth marks and brown leaves were all that was left on most of her plants.

Once the outside pot plants were watered, she filled the cans again and gave each indoor plant a drink. Fortunately, the woodchuck had no control over what happened inside the house, and so her mother's indoor plants had thrived. Careful not to get any water on the leaves of the African violets, she was amazed at how vibrant the colors were. Purples and pinks and a few white flowers made the windowsills around the dining room full of color.

One last look around the house and then she'd be off to drive over to the hospital to see her pregnant sister-in-law. She climbed the stairs to the second floor to look in on all the rooms just to make certain that there wasn't anything else that needed attending to. Inside her parents' bedroom, she noticed something seemed off. The closet was opened and almost all her father's clothes were gone. She knew that her mother hadn't had enough time to remove them from the house, nor would she so soon after his passing.

Her curiosity growing, she opened drawers to his dresser, and except for a few old shirts and a large sweater in the closet, his clothes were gone. Sarah went into their bathroom and opened the medicine cabinet. The only items there belonged to her mother. She was beginning to worry that there was more to her mother's behavior than she was aware of and ran down the stairs to her father's home office. Looking for signs of something, anything that might explain what had happened, she opened drawers and file cabinets. She turned on the computer, hoping to find clues that would explain things. Nothing in her father's office looked out of place.

For a man with so much important and proprietary information at his fingertips, security and computer login information would make it difficult for Sarah to penetrate anything of value, except one thing. His Gmail account was open, and his personal emails were accessible. This was not his office email account, but rather his personal one, the one he communicated with family from.

Sarah searched for anything that might be a clue as to her father's last days, and she found it. An email to someone named KellyLv00xx. It wasn't recent, however. This was an email from about four months ago, but it was still something she could follow up on. It was plans for a lunch between the two of them. It seemed casual and intimate, but there was nothing about the email to suggest anything untoward. Who was KellyLv00xx and how could she find out?

Sarah sat at the dining room table for ten minutes before she made a phone call to her sister Lauren.

"Can you come over to Mom's house? I need to talk to you about something, and I'm a little shaken."

"Absolutely. I don't have to pick up the kids for another two hours. I'll be right there."

Sarah's cell phone buzzed, moving on the table. She saw that it was Ben and thought once again that his timing couldn't be worse.

"Hey, Ben. What's up?"

"I thought maybe we could make up for our missed dinner. How about tonight? I'd love to spend some quiet, quality time just the two of us?"

Sarah wanted more than anything to find time to talk to

Ben, but tonight wasn't going to work since she had no idea where this latest development would lead her.

"Oh Ben, I'm so sorry. I really can't tonight. I'm at my mother's house, and I have to do some things here. Lauren is heading over because we need to work through some estate stuff together. I promised Michael that I'd check in on Brea at the hospital. Can I take a raincheck?"

"Of course. I realize you have lots going on right now. How about we try for next week instead of pushing for this week? Too much has happened lately, and it feels like I'd be putting unnecessary pressure on you right now. Promise to get in touch if there's anything I can do? How does that sound?"

Sarah was grateful that Ben was so considerate. She felt a bit guilty for pushing him away lately, but there was too much on her plate and she couldn't imagine adding one more thing, even if that one thing was Ben.

"You're a sweetheart. Thank you for understanding, and yes, I promise to call you if I need anything. Honest."

Just as she hung up the phone, the front door opened, and Lauren ran inside, worried by the look on her sister's face.

"What is it? You've got me scared to death. Are you all right?"

"I'm not sure."

"Well, that doesn't tell me anything. What's going on with you? You look as if you've seen a ghost."

Sarah turned to Lauren, grabbed her hand, and pulled her up the stairs. "Come with me."

Once inside their parents' bedroom, Sarah opened the closet doors. "This. This is what's wrong."

Lauren was shocked to see a partially empty closet with no sign of her father's clothes. She remembered her conversation with Beth earlier and was afraid she understood the implication.

Sarah once again pulled open the drawers to her father's

dresser and then stormed into the bathroom to open the medicine cabinet as further proof of her father's absence. Lauren sat on the edge of the bed, afraid to look Sarah in the eye.

"You know something, don't you?"

There was no way around it, Lauren was going to have to tell Sarah about her conversation with Beth. How to explain to Beth why she couldn't keep this information a secret from their siblings was something she'd worry about later. This was too important to put off, not to mention they needed to come to a decision about how they would approach their mother about it. Telling Sarah about their father's cheating was probably going to come as a serious blow to her, and Lauren had no idea how to begin.

"Let's go back downstairs. I feel like making a cup of tea."

Sarah followed Lauren down the stairs to the kitchen but couldn't resist reminding her of how much she was like their mother. While growing up, everyone said Lauren was the spitting image of her mother. Her mannerisms and voice were so similar, people often mistook the daughter for the mother whenever she answered the phone.

"Lauren, you are just like Mom. She always made a cup of tea before she sat us down to talk about anything serious. Making tea is a sure sign you're about to tell me something I don't want to hear."

"Everyone says that I'm like Mom, but I'm not so sure. Mom was content to stay at home and take care of the house, Dad, and us kids. She never seemed interested in going to work outside the home. Her whole life was in this house. That's not me."

Lauren set out her favorite teacups for the two of them and grabbed the milk from the refrigerator.

Sarah laughed at her sister, thinking she must be joking. "What are you talking about? You live for Jeff and those girls."

"Of course, I do. That's not what I meant. It's just…"

Lauren voice trailed off to a whisper, as if saying how she felt was betraying her family in some way. "I don't know, Sarah. I have days when I wonder if I don't use my brain, will it go to mush? I mean, I don't feel challenged in any way. I'm not looking for excitement. That's not what I'm talking about. I just feel like there's something more inside me that's screaming to get out."

The tea kettle whistled, and Lauren turned off the stove, grabbed an oven mitt, and poured the hot water into their teacups.

Sarah knew exactly what Lauren was trying to say. It was the very thing that kept her awake at night. The thought of marriage and children scared her, and she knew that the reason rested squarely on her fear of losing her autonomy. For now, those thoughts had to wait. Lauren knew something about their father, and Sarah needed to hear what was going on.

"I think you've stalled long enough, don't you?"

Lauren took a deep breath and looked at Sarah. "Dad has been cheating on Mom for years, and I think they were separated when he died. That's why so much of his stuff is gone, I suppose."

"You suppose? What does that mean? When you drop such a big bomb like that, you need to follow it up with certainty."

"It means I don't know for certain that they were separated, but it seems likely, given the facts."

"What facts?"

For the next few minutes, Lauren shared everything that Beth had told her earlier the day before.

The two women sat in silence for several minutes, Lauren waiting to see how Sarah would take the news, and Sarah waited to hear that it was all a terrible mistake, a misunderstanding somehow. Neither would come easily, but for Sarah, it was as if her lifelong hero, their father, had died all over again.

Through tears, Sarah found the strength to accept the fact that her father was not the man she'd thought he was. As hard as that was to admit, the idea that their mother had endured more than she'd ever let on was heartbreakingly cruel. Sarah looked at her sister and asked the obvious question. "How much does Mom know about these other women?"

Lauren shook her head. "I asked Beth that, but I don't think any of us know, and I don't think we'll be able to find out without confronting Mom about it. I don't know about you, but I'm not that willing to go there, at least not yet."

Sarah's face turned to anger.

"Are you kidding me? I want to know. We all should know exactly what happened here. I mean, he lied to us, to all of us. I think that deserves a bit of investigation, don't you? I'm not willing to just let this hang over us like that. We've got to find out exactly what happened when he died. Mom said he was in his office, but I don't buy that. What if he was with 'her'?"

Lauren was getting equally mad.

"Don't you think that Mom might already know that? I realize you think you had this special relationship with Dad, but he wasn't perfect, and their marriage wasn't perfect. If he cheated, he cheated on her, not on you."

Sarah felt as if she had been slapped in the face. The sting of Lauren's words would stay with her for a long time. If her sister hadn't quickly pulled her into a hug, she probably would have stayed angry at Lauren, and at everything that her father had done. Instead, she fell into her sister's arms and wept for the loss of a man she'd trusted to always take care of her, no matter what.

Sarah knew the anger would come again, probably in waves, because she would once again have to confront the very thing that kept her from opening her heart fully. She would fight the anger, but she knew she would lose because she had yet another reason not to trust, and to lose faith. That her father had taken those things away from her was unforgivable.

It was a forty-five-minute drive from her mother's house to the hospital, and Sarah was glad for time alone in the car. Everything Lauren had told her was swimming in her head. She badly needed a distraction and was glad she'd promised her brother to visit Brea at the hospital. She wondered if she should stop and pick up flowers or a gift for her but then remembered that her brother had warned her about smells and how everything made his wife sick.

Even though her sister-in-law was sick from the pregnancy rather than giving birth, her room was still in the maternity ward. Sarah thought it would probably make Brea happy to see other pregnant women and to hear the cries of the newborns. Not far from Brea's room, people were standing in front of a glass wall watching the newest family members swathed in pink and blue cloth. Sarah stopped for a minute to look at the babies. Some were sleeping, but there were a few that were crying, obviously missing their mothers already.

Sarah walked past the babies and turned the corner to her sister-in-law's room, her name visible on the door.

"Well, look at you with your private room. Who do you have to know to get a sweet deal like this?"

Brea smiled but not for long. With a swift grab for the plastic container near her bed, she bent over it to vomit. Her sister-in-law tried to avoid forcing Sarah to watch, but she didn't turn away fast enough. Wiping her face with a cool, wet face cloth, Brea sat back against the pillow and apologized to Sarah.

"Stop apologizing. I'm just so sorry you're going through

this. Can I get you anything at all? I feel like I should maybe get a nurse."

"Would you, please? I want to visit with you, but it's not so much fun with a plastic bucket of…"

Sarah walked to the nurses' station and asked someone to come to help clean up. A nurse came right away, and once Brea was able to calm down and settle her stomach for a bit, she felt better.

"Do you have any idea how many commercials there are about food? I had no idea, but now that I can't eat anything, all I see are food commercials. It's cruel, and do you want to hear something strange? Even though most of the day, I'm nauseous, I still have cravings. It's the weirdest thing. This morning I craved a strawberry ice cream soda, so they brought me one. Of course, it stayed in my system all of ten minutes, but it was a glorious ten minutes."

"Oh, Brea, that sounds awful. I'd never be able to deal with what you are dealing with right now. I'd die if I couldn't eat."

Her sister-in-law laughed. "You do what you have to do to win the prize at the end of it all. You get to take home a beautiful little baby. I love this little one so much already. It's a small price to pay for him."

Sarah tried to understand how anyone could love someone so much as to suffer like this. She was so preoccupied with Brea's troubles that she almost didn't hear that they knew the sex of the baby.

"A boy? Oh, my goodness, Michael must be over the moon. We've got so many girls in this family; I think he never thought there would be another boy. I'm pretty sure we all gave up on that possibility. Congratulations. I'm so happy for you both."

Sarah hugged Brea and could see she had tears of joy in her eyes. To know that kind of love made Sarah envious. It wasn't jealousy, but something else. She was confused about her feelings but was happy for her brother and sister-in-law.

The day had forced a rollercoaster of emotions on her. Sarah had to admit that today was one of the strangest days she had ever experienced. One minute she'd felt as if the world was ending, and the next, elation and complete joy. Both feelings involved her family and a future that she could only imagine.

Chapter Ten

MAGGIE

Chelsea finished washing the dishes and folded the towel, placing it on the kitchen counter.

"What are your plans today? Any interest in coming with me to the farmers' market?"

Maggie remembered what her new friend Rose told her about Paolo and his nursery. "I'd love to join you. I understand there is a beautiful nursery near there that I want to see."

"Oh, I know that place. I purchased a few plants from them a couple of months ago. It's a lovely nursery, and I must admit, the help isn't hard on the eyes either. If I remember, there's a handsome Italian guy that works there. He helped me find the plant I was looking for. He's got the most gorgeous blue eyes. Maybe we'll get lucky, and he'll still be there."

"You must mean Paolo. He tends Rose's Garden. He does all the landscaping for her. I think she really depends on him and his sister, Ciara. She takes care of the cooking and the inside of the house, I guess."

"So, you saw him?"

"I saw him from a distance. He was working at the far end of the yard. Besides, Rose and I were deep in discussion about

Anne Morrow Lindbergh. I really didn't have time to notice much about him. By the way, if he's so gorgeous, how come you haven't pursued him? I've no doubt that's where your head is at right now."

Chelsea laughed. "I admit I've thought about the handsome Italian. Maybe I'll get a chance to talk to him today. I say let's get in the car and go see Mr. Blue Eyes."

Maggie rolled her eyes and laughed. Her friend had come out of a difficult time, and Maggie was truly happy that Chelsea seemed more than ready to begin dating again. If she could once again find the kind of love she'd had with her husband, Maggie was more than willing to play her wingman at the nursery.

Chelsea insisted they drive with the top down, and she'd get no argument from Maggie. Driving to Captiva from the airport did interesting things to Maggie's hair, so this time she decided to wear a baseball hat to keep it in place.

The sun felt invigorating, and the blue, cloudless sky had a clean healing effect on Maggie. It was going to be hard to go back home and begin the inevitable routine of fall baking, holiday decorating and Christmas shopping. In Massachusetts at least, Christmas always seemed to come before Thanksgiving, in part due to the holiday decorations in every store. As soon as the Halloween candy corn came off the shelves, Christmas decorations replaced them. Maggie usually looked forward to this time of year, but she understood this holiday season would be like no other.

There were several shops along the road to the farmer's market, and Maggie wanted to stop at them all, but since the market was the farthest, they decided to stop there first, hitting the shops on the way back.

"I want to make a delicious dinner for the two of us tonight. I always try to do something elaborate for dinner on farmers' market shopping day. Even if I'm alone, I still put out the fine china, a crystal wine glass, and polished silverware. I don't care who thinks I'm nuts; it makes me happy."

"I think it's wonderful, Chelsea. After all the kids don't want any of those things. When I think how my mother saved Hummels and so many collectables, I cringe. You have no idea how much stuff my mother has in that house of hers that I'm going to have to get rid of when she passes away."

"She's not ill, is she, Maggie?"

"Oh, no. Not at all. Hopefully, she'll be with us for many more years. I'm just saying that it's great that you're using your things and not letting them collect dust. At home, I'm famous for making tea and using my English tea kettle and teacups. The girls always say that there has never been an important event in our family where I didn't pull out the tea kettle and make everyone have a cup of tea first."

"You are lucky to have your children, especially now."

Chelsea and her husband had never had children. It wasn't something Chelsea liked to talk about. This was the first time that Maggie sensed a touch of sadness in her voice about it.

"I am happy to have the kids nearby, but I never thought about having children so that they'd be around to take care of me when I'm old. My children are wonderful adults, and I love them all, but I'm not old, and I don't intend to be a burden to any of them, now or when I'm an old lady. I appreciate all their concerns for me, but they each need to get on with their lives and let me get on with mine."

Maggie stopped, realizing that there had been a bit of frustration in her voice. "I'm sorry, Chelsea, I sound like I'm angry about something, and I'm not. Of course, I want the best for my children and grandchildren, but I need some space, a chance to breathe. To find my place in this crazy world. I need time to figure things out, and sometimes the kids' meddling can be suffocating. There, I said it. Does that make me a bad mother?"

Chelsea parked the car and turned to Maggie. "All perfectly normal my dear. You need to take as much time as you need. There are no rules, except the ones you make for yourself. Now let's go buy some delicious food."

The women filled their bags with freshly made French bread, wine, cheese and an assortment of olives, capers, tomatoes, and spices. Wherever possible, they purchased organic, but everything looked so fresh it didn't matter if it was.

Maggie couldn't wait to bite into a ripe peach. With the juices traveling down her chin, she talked with her mouth full. "I swear, everything looks more appealing at a farmers' market than at a supermarket. This peach is unbelievable."

Chelsea laughed at her friend and handed her a napkin. "You know, I hadn't thought about it, but if you want, we can have a nice lunch after we shop for plants. We could go over to the Island Cow. They've got a great crab cake there."

"That does sound good. It seems like I just ate breakfast, and yet I'm hungry again. It must be all the fresh air."

Once everything was placed into the trunk, they headed out of the parking lot toward the nursery, which was only five minutes away.

"*Sanibellia.* What a beautiful name for this place."

A blue and gold macaw in a cage at the entrance to the nursery welcomed customers as they walked past.

Chelsea stopped to try to get him to talk.

Laughing, Maggie teased her, "I don't think he likes you, Chelsea. Maybe you shouldn't try so hard. Ignore him, and I bet he'll say a few words."

There were so many winding paths throughout the nursery, it was hard to decide which way to go. Maggie wanted to see everything and not miss one plant. She felt like she had stepped into an enchanted forest, much like the way she had felt when she walked through the gate on Rose's property.

"So, you decided to visit Sanibellia. Mrs. Lane told me you might be stopping by. I'm glad you could come."

The slight Italian accent was a dead giveaway. Maggie knew it was the man who cared for Rose's property. She didn't remember him looking her way when she had been sitting in the garden with Rose, but it was clear that although they hadn't been formally introduced, he recognized her.

Chelsea extended her hand. "Hello. I'm Chelsea, and this is my friend Maggie."

Paolo turned his attention from Maggie to Chelsea. "Paolo Moretti. Pleasure to meet you."

Paolo looked back at Maggie and reached to shake her hand as well. He took her hand in his and stared into her eyes. The exchange made Maggie feel awkward, as if she was doing something wrong. His eyes were ocean blue. Maggie had never seen eyes so blue before. Against the tan skin and black hair, he was an incredibly handsome man. Maggie pulled her hand back and cleared her throat before talking.

"So, you own this nursery?"

"Yes, my sister Ciara and myself, actually. We have several workers here, and many have much experience with gardening and plants. If you have any questions at all, there are many here with the knowledge to help. I can help you find what you're looking for if you'd like. Is there something specific you are shopping for?"

"Looking for something specific? Um, no. not really. We just came from the farmers' market and thought we'd stop in to see your beautiful plants."

Chelsea interrupted their conversation, her voice jolting Maggie, taking her by surprise.

"Mr. Moretti, we were just about to have lunch at the Island Cow. Perhaps you could take a break and join us?"

Paolo didn't hesitate. "I'd love to. Thank you. Let me just

talk to my assistant to let him know I'm leaving for a bit. I'll be right back."

As soon as Paolo left the women, Maggie turned to her friend. "What was all that?"

"All what?"

"We never talked about inviting him to lunch with us. I know you want to get to know him better, but I'm feeling a little uncomfortable. I didn't expect you to move so quickly. I'm going to feel like a third wheel."

"Maggie. We're getting older by the minute. Do you have any idea how hard it is to find a good man these days? We're not kids. When you see someone you like, you move on it."

Since looking for a man was not something at the top of Maggie's list, she was no expert on this topic. She'd promised to be Chelsea's wingman, and it looked like there was no time like the present. Paolo returned within what seemed like thirty seconds, and they were off.

Maggie could tell that Paolo wanted to open the door for both women, but the car being a two-door convertible meant that he had to sit in the back and had to get in first. She was happy that the restaurant was not that far from Sanibellia. Small talk was getting hard to instigate, and she hoped that Chelsea would soon dominate their conversation over lunch.

They chose an outdoor table in the corner, which gave them privacy to talk.

"Rose tells me you have a problem with a woodchuck in your garden at home."

"Yes. That animal and I are engaged in a war. Sometimes I win small battles and sometimes he—or she—wins. Ultimately, I'm losing the war. Most of my vegetables are going to the woodchuck instead of feeding me and my family."

"Tell me about your family, Maggie. Rose tells me you have five children."

Maggie was shocked that Rose and Paolo had talked about

her after she left them. She supposed that Rose had every right to talk about her; after all, she did trespass on the woman's property.

"Yes, and I'm a grandmother as well. I've got four grandchildren and another one on the way. I'm very lucky to have them. They're all good kids, happy, healthy. I have a lot to be grateful for."

"And if you don't mind my asking, why is it that your husband didn't come with you to Captiva?"

The question seemed invasive somehow and forced Maggie to look down at her hands, once again playing with her wedding ring.

"My husband recently passed away. My friend here thought it would be good for me to get away and visit Captiva for a while."

Now it was Paolo's turn to look uncomfortable. "Please, Mrs. Wheeler, I apologize for asking. It was none of my business. I am so sorry for the loss of your husband. Please, I ask that you forgive me."

"No. Paolo, first, please call me Maggie. You don't need to apologize. You couldn't have known. You did nothing wrong."

She could tell that her words comforted him and thought a change of topic might be in order. "Can you tell me more about you and your sister working for Mrs. Lane? How did you come to work for her?"

"Ah, Mrs. Lane is a wonderful lady. My sister met her first. You see, in addition to Ciara working for Mrs. Lane, she works at the Coastal Community Outreach in Ft. Myers. She oversees many of the non-profit departments within the organization. Mrs. Lane is an important benefactor for the food pantry and soup kitchen. As part of her involvement with my sister, Ciara would make sure that a delivery of food came to Mrs. Lane. As they became friends, it was clear that the woman had much money, but not much in the way of time and mobility to shop. She certainly didn't need the donation of the food. I think she just wanted company, and that was the only way she could think to have visitors. No matter how much money someone has, it's the connection with others that brings happiness. It's been very sad for her since her son died."

It was clear that their conversation did not lend itself to Chelsea flirting with Paolo. Maggie tried to think of a way to engage her friend. "Chelsea, didn't you used to volunteer at Andover's food pantry for a while?"

By this point, Maggie was starting to feel a strain in their discussion. Almost forced, Chelsea had no choice but to smile at Maggie and nod her head. "Yes. Thanks for remembering that. I did volunteer."

Trying to be polite, Paolo smiled at Chelsea. "It's a wonderful thing to donate your time to people who aren't as fortunate."

And then he turned his attention back to Maggie.

"When do you return home? How long are you staying here? Do you think you will visit again with Mrs. Lane before you travel back home?"

"I'll be leaving on Wednesday, so I'm here a few more days. Yes, of course, I plan to visit with Rose once more before I go. She was very kind to loan me a book, and I plan to spend the next couple of days reading it before I return it to her. I will probably come by on Tuesday. Do you think Tuesday is a good day for her?"

Paolo seemed pleased with her answers. "Yes. Tuesday is a very good day to visit with her. I will let her know that you'll be coming by that day. Perhaps you can come around lunch time. My sister Ciara can cook for you. She is a very good cook."

Not to appear as an afterthought, although it was too late to avoid that impression, he added, "Please, Chelsea, I hope you will come as well. I'm sure Mrs. Lane would love to meet you."

Chelsea nodded her head and thanked him. They spent the rest of lunch talking about the island and about Rose. Nothing Maggie could do would help Chelsea gain the kind of attention she craved from the gorgeous Italian with ocean blue eyes. As guilty as she felt, Maggie was pleased that Paolo seemed interested in her, and hoped she would see him again on Tuesday.

Chapter Eleven

MAGGIE

It was unusual not to find Chelsea in the kitchen cooking breakfast when Maggie came downstairs the next morning. When she couldn't locate her inside the house, she walked outside onto the lanai and found her friend, a large canvas in front of her. Chelsea had always enjoyed painting but had stopped when Carl needed care. Maggie was thrilled to see that her friend had started painting again. Hues of pink, peach, turquoise, and cream covered the canvas, and the beautiful flowers behind a cottage were taking form.

"I'm so happy you're still painting, Chelsea. That's beautiful."

Chelsea put her paintbrush down and turned to look at Maggie.

"Me too. I can't tell you how much pleasure sitting out here on the lanai and creating something from nothing brings me. It took a while, but after Carl died, I dug up some of my old materials and started to paint again. I've been so busy these last couple of weeks, I put everything away again, but I hate a blank canvas staring at me every morning when I get up. I figured if I wasn't going to paint, then it had no place out here.

I changed my mind last night after looking at so much beauty at Sanibellia. I wanted to capture some of the flowers before they left my brain. So, what's the plan for today?"

"I'd like to take some time to just sit on the beach and read. Care to join me?"

"Would I be a terrible hostess if I decline? I honestly want to keep painting. You know how it is when the feeling strikes you and the lighting is just perfect."

Maggie nodded. "Of course, I don't mind. I need to read the book that Rose gave me so that I can return it to her before I leave. Paolo says Tuesday would be a good day for me to drop by. Would you like to come with me then? It would give you another opportunity to see him."

"Seriously, Maggie? That man couldn't be less interested in me if he tried. Paolo only had eyes for you at yesterday's lunch. Tell me you know that, right?"

Once again, Maggie felt like she had done something wrong. Instead of acknowledging Chelsea's words, she turned away.

"Maggie, listen to me. I know you feel uncomfortable thinking that a man could be attracted to you. And I also know that Paolo isn't the first man to admire you."

Maggie shook her head. "What do you mean by that?"

Chelsea sighed. "What I mean is that I've seen several men over the course of our friendship check you out. You're a beautiful woman, and there's nothing wrong with liking the way that makes you feel."

"Chelsea, the truth is I don't know how I feel about anything. I loved my husband. I loved being married. I loved the life we built, but now it's all gone. I know it wasn't perfect, but no marriage is."

"Maggie, I know you loved those things, but enjoying another man's attention doesn't take away from that. I've said it before, and I'll keep saying it until you get it. Life goes on, and you must get on with it. It's fine if you aren't ready to date someone. All of this is very new, and you're trying to make sense of it. I get that. But trust me when I say this: You are much more than a wife, mother, and grandmother. What in heaven's name is wrong with admitting that?"

Wanting more than what she had always made Maggie nervous. Her life was filled with so much privilege she felt it wasn't right to ask for more. She suspected it had something to do with her father. Always looking for ways to give back to his community, Maggie's father constantly reminded her and her siblings about those who were less fortunate. "People would do anything to have your life, Maggie. Don't you ever forget it."

Years of volunteering for various causes her husband chaired and making herself available for every school event that her children needed her to organize had convinced Maggie that she had done her part, and yet she still felt something was missing. As it was now, she wondered if she was being punished for her private pain. It was confusing to feel tethered to everything and nothing at the same time.

Voicing her concerns was not an option. Keeping to herself seemed her only choice. If she had to consider who she would confide in, Chelsea would be at the top of her list, but her friend had enough to deal with when her husband was so sick. Maggie never wanted to burden her, and now it would seem that her dear friend understood more than Maggie had realized.

Maggie rushed to Chelsea and pulled her into a hug. "I'm trying, Chelsea. I am."

Chelsea squeezed her friend and did what she always did: She lightened the mood. Grabbing a small white decorative bucket, she handed it to Maggie.

"Here, take this. Collect lots of seashells. I know you want to read, but you won't be able to resist taking a few shells home. I know you. You can't come to Captiva and not go home with a bag full of shells. I bet you'll find some gorgeous ones. By the way, I'd kill for your body. That swimsuit looks fantastic on you."

Maggie laughed, gathered her beach chair and umbrella, and stuffed her towel, book, and water bottle into her large, pink-striped beach bag. She couldn't wait to quietly sit by the ocean and read. It was one of her favorite things to do when she needed to relax. Back home, she had her garden, but she longed for private time sitting with a good book listening to the ocean waves at the closest beach to her house. Most of the time when she'd gone to Cape Cod, it had been with her children, and reading was a luxury she couldn't manage with five kids.

There were more people at the beach today, and Maggie walked as far away from the entrance to The Mucky Duck as she could. A tourist attraction, the restaurant had a steady stream of cars vying for parking spaces. The area was filled with picnic benches, and the large lunch crowd of people made it impossible to have the quiet Maggie needed to read her book.

Nestled next to a brush of green vegetation and beach grass, Maggie was able to place her chair into the secluded spot and still have a perfect view of the water. She dug into the sand with the base of the umbrella and secured it, pushing her bag up against the pole. It was still early, and there was no need to open it just yet.

She sat back and looked up at the sky. Not a cloud to be seen and the warmth of the sun along with the salt air helped her meditative spirit. She imagined Anne Morrow Lindbergh sitting in this very spot filling her journal with contemplative observations. After reading several articles and snippets of Anne's writing, Maggie was convinced that Mrs. Lindbergh had moments where putting pen to paper was her only chance to say what was truly on her mind.

Halfway through the book, Maggie rummaged through her

bag and pulled out her Kindle. *Gift from the Sea* intrigued her so much that she needed to know more about the woman who had so much to say about women and their place in the world. Anne spoke of marriage and motherhood, and Maggie found that the issues women had been dealing with in Anne's time were not so different than the difficulties Maggie struggled with now.

Needing to understand Anne better, she downloaded a book by Susan Hertog. *Anne Morrow Lindbergh: Her Life* was a large book, and Maggie knew she'd be reading it long after she left the island. Anne had lived such a diverse and busy life. Maggie knew about her husband's flying but didn't realize his wife would fly with him for many trips, often leaving her children in the care of family. Maggie wanted to know more, and if this book didn't provide all the information essential to understand the woman, she would continue her research through other books and online.

A large lightweight beach ball rolled in front of Maggie, followed by a little girl, no more than five years old. Maggie smiled, remembering similar moments with her children on this very beach. Piles of seashells back home from the many trips to Captiva made her less interested in adding to her collection on this trip, no matter what Chelsea said, but after reading *Gift from the Sea*, Maggie was curious to see if she could find some of the seashells that Anne mentioned in the book. Maggie pulled her coverup over her head and grabbed the white bucket Chelsea had given her.

The wet shells and rocks always looked shiny, but Maggie knew that to truly appreciate their beauty, she needed to look beyond the water to drier spots. She found several shells that had the potential to make their way back to Massachusetts. Among the pile in her bucket, a whelk shell was the largest. She looked up and noticed that she had traveled far from her chair. The bucket was getting heavy, and she laughed at how silly she had been to collect so many. She would have to leave several of her shells with Chelsea, or maybe even return them to the sand.

Maggie walked back to her chair and took several gulps of her water. She was starting to get hungry but didn't want to walk to the Mucky Duck, so a granola bar and an apple would do for now. Once she was done eating, Maggie opened *Gift from the Sea* and compared her large whelk seashell to Anne's.

The snail-like creature, the whelk, had left its home, and the shell remained in Maggie's hand. She ran her finger along the ribbed edge of the shell and read Anne's words.

"I turn the shell in my hand, gazing into the wide-open door from which he made his exit. Had it become an encumbrance? Why did he run away? Did he hope to find a better home, a better mode of living? I too have run away, I realize, I have shed the shell of my life for these few weeks of vacation."

Is that what Maggie had done too? She didn't think that her time with Chelsea was running away, but Anne's words resonated. The thought of leaving Captiva in a couple of days depressed her. Maggie being Maggie, she felt guilty about that. Her children and grandchildren probably missed her, but as much as Maggie missed them too, she didn't want to leave the island. Although she didn't own any property on Captiva, the island had always felt like a second home to her. Once back at the house, it was Chelsea who instinctively sensed Maggie's dilemma.

"I think we should stop at Royal Shell tomorrow and see what's for sale on the island."

Maggie was surprised. "What would you do with a second property?"

"Not for me, silly, for you. I think you should buy something down here. I can tell you don't want to go home."

Maggie smiled at the suggestion, but thought the idea was crazy. "Chelsea, I would love to come down and stay much longer than I did this time, but there's no way I could buy a property and stay here for months at a time. The kids need me, and…"

Chelsea jumped at the obvious pause in Maggie's voice. "And what? What else is there that's keeping you in Massachusetts?"

Maggie didn't want to be rude, but the fact that Chelsea never had any children made her perspective poles apart from Maggie's. Rather than focus on the kids, Maggie tried to think about what else she had in her life but couldn't. It was a topic for another day. There was only so much introspection she could handle and holding a magnifying glass up to her life was not something she was willing to let Chelsea do on this trip.

"How about we put that idea on hold for the time being? I've promised Rose to return her book tomorrow. I don't want to drop the book off and run, so I think the polite thing to do is to spend a bit of time visiting with her. I can tell she's lonely and probably doesn't have many visitors. Would you like to come with me?"

"Thanks, but no. I think it would be better if you went alone."

Maggie wondered if she had hurt Chelsea's feelings by not wanting to buy a property on Captiva. Just as soon as that thought entered her mind, her friend did what she always did. She lightened the mood and laughed.

"What's so funny?"

Chelsea put her arm around Maggie and gave her a squeeze. "Maggie, my dear, you constantly amaze me how clueless you can be. You know darn well that Paolo will be working at Rose's. Have you already forgotten the impression you made on him?"

Maggie turned to her friend and looked her in the eyes. "Chelsea, I am going to return the book and spend some time with Rose before I leave the island. I don't really expect to ever see Paolo again."

Maggie failed to convince her friend. Chelsea's smile made it clear she wasn't buying it.

"Whatever you say. Listen, when you get back from visiting with Rose tomorrow, why don't we go out for a gourmet dinner? Have you ever been to the Thistle Lodge at Casa Ybel on Sanibel?"

Maggie shook her head. "No, but I hear the food is amazing and the ambiance and views are really beautiful."

"Great. We should have a special dinner on your last night. I'll make the reservations. In the meantime, how about you hop in the shower, and we can run over to Sweet Melissa's in Sanibel for dinner tonight, and then come back here to watch the sunset?"

"Sounds perfect. After the day at the beach, I need to wash the sand off me. I won't be long."

Maggie was pleased they were talking about something other than her buying a property on Captiva. The idea was enticing, and she might even consider it if her children supported the idea. To suggest a move to Florida would garner protests. Maggie knew exactly how they would react to the idea. Beth, Michael, and Sarah would think she was losing her mind. Lauren was an unknown, and Maggie's always supportive son, Christopher, would think it was a great idea.

Maggie had watched each of her children's successes with great pride, but she could tell that there was something troubling her oldest daughter. So far, Lauren hadn't felt ready to talk about it, and Maggie didn't press. She knew in time Lauren would come to her to talk. She always did. Everyone said they were two peas in a pod, and they were right. Maggie knew she was right about Lauren having something on her mind. It was only a matter of time before she found out what it was.

Along with Daniel's estate, Maggie expected there would be other, more pressing issues to deal with when she arrived home. Not the least of which was deciding what to tell her children about their father's indiscretions. She couldn't avoid the truth forever. Her own mother was able to figure out what was going on without Maggie saying a word. Her children, especially her girls, were just as intuitive. For the first time, she considered that her trip to Captiva was indeed running away. There were only two days left before she would have to return to her life in Massachusetts, and it frightened her that she had no idea what that life looked like.

Chapter Twelve

P eering out the window at the ocean below, Maggie was overcome with sadness. This would be her last full day on the island, and her heart was heavy for leaving. Her days on Captiva Island had been filled with sun, sand, music, delicious food, and new friends. Rose, Paolo, and Ciara were lovely people, and Maggie was grateful to have added Anne Morrow Lindbergh to that list as well. She knew that once she returned home, these people would continue to be with her, even if only in her heart.

She gathered her things and headed downstairs to find Chelsea. As usual, she found her friend on the lanai, her bone china teacup and saucer by her side. She had been painting for hours, and the canvas was now filled with deeper colors contrasting against the lighter ones. Maggie used her cell phone to take a picture of Chelsea.

"I envy you your talent. There's something quite serene about this spot. Sorry, but I had to capture the image so I can look at it when I'm back in Massachusetts."

Chelsea put her paintbrush down and turned to look at Maggie.

"I promised myself I wouldn't push, but don't completely rule out moving down here. I'm worried that once you get home, your life there will keep you just busy enough to forget how happy you were on the island."

"Honestly, Chelsea, I don't think I could ever forget how wonderful this trip has been. I needed time away from all the craziness. You know I'll be back. I just don't know when, but I will come back. I promise."

"How about some breakfast? I know how much you love your tea. I could make more."

"No. Thanks. I'm not exactly sure why, but I have zero appetite this morning. My stomach isn't feeling that great. I'm nervous about saying goodbye to Rose. I know she's not well, even though she didn't tell me anything about her health, but I can just sense something isn't right with her. I'm worried today might be the last time I see her. It's so strange to feel this close to someone I've just met. It feels like I've known her forever."

"If you'd like, I promise to look in on her after you've gone."

"Oh, Chelsea, would you? That would make me feel better. I'd like to know how she is getting on. I'm not sure what kind of technology, if any, she is familiar with, but I'm sure she has a landline phone. I'll get her number for you and for me. I want to stay in touch with her when I get home. I'll give her my cell phone number as well."

Smiling, Chelsea picked up her paintbrush and turned to her canvas. Without looking directly at Maggie and unable to see her reaction, she teased her friend.

"I think that's a great idea. That way Paolo can get in touch with you too."

Maggie ignored the comment and put her sunglasses on.

"I'm not sure how long I'll be at Rose's, but I'll be back as soon as I can. I'm looking forward to our dinner tonight."

Chelsea had to make her point with her answer. "Ciao, Bella."

Maggie hoped that Chelsea would finally understand her reluctance to discuss Paolo and leave the subject alone. The teasing was getting old, and although she didn't want their last night on the island to be anything but relaxed and fun, she realized there was a strong possibility that she'd have to set Chelsea straight about her need to focus on herself, rather than dating. It was a topic that continued to make her uncomfortable. Her husband had only been gone a couple of weeks. The traumatic developments surrounding his life and death were still very much on Maggie's mind and heart.

Approaching Rose's home, it suddenly occurred to Maggie that entering the garden from the beach area wasn't going to work this time. She looked for the box next to the gate and pressed the button. Expecting someone to answer her call, she was surprised when the gate opened on its own. As soon as she stepped onto the property, Paolo came running to meet her.

"I'm so glad you could come today, Maggie. Rose has been looking for you for the last two hours already. She keeps asking if you've arrived yet. She asked that I bring you into the house as soon as you got here. She's waiting in the front room. It's her favorite spot since it has so many windows that look out onto the ocean. Come, I'll take you to her."

Maggie was happy that this time she would be able to see more of the house. The garden was overwhelmingly beautiful, but she had to admit, she wanted to see beyond its borders to the far side of the land and inside the home as well.

Rose was sitting in a chair near a window that had not only a view of the ocean, but a part of the garden that had a bird bath, bird house, and two feeders. A butterfly bush planted just beyond the bath gave the birds a front row seat to a daily ballet of butterflies dancing to the sound of the waves. It was a perfect spot to sit and be alone with one's thoughts. Rose was clearly frail, but the look on her face gave her complexion a healthy glow.

"Hello, Rose. I've come for a visit and to return your book. Thank you for lending it to me. It was the perfect book at the perfect time, but somehow, I think you knew that already."

Rose smiled, and the twinkle that had been in her eyes the first time they'd met returned.

"I'm so glad you came to see me again, Maggie."

Pointing to the bookcases across the room, she said, "Please, go and look at my books. This is my favorite spot to read."

Rose had an eclectic assortment of books, and Maggie could understand why Rose spent many hours in this room. The peaceful nature of the property extended to this spot, and Maggie imagined Rose sitting in her chair reading into the night with the sound of the waves just beyond the house.

After looking over the assortment of books, Maggie found others by Anne Morrow Lindbergh, and returned *Gift from the Sea* to its rightful place among them, then she sat in the chair across from Rose.

"I'm jealous of your spot here, Rose. I'd love nothing better than to sit for hours and read. My life seems to be filled with lots of to-do lists, so I never have time to myself. The children and now the grandchildren need me, and, well, I don't think I mentioned to you that my husband died almost two weeks ago. My trip to Captiva was a chance to get away and try to figure some things out."

Rose was quick to respond.

"You thought a week on an island would give you the answers you needed?"

Maggie started to laugh but then realized what she wanted to say wasn't funny at all.

"Not really. They say you can't know where you're going until you know where you've been. I'm not so sure I know where I've been all these years. My marriage wasn't what I thought it was, or maybe it was. I don't know. You see, Daniel had a life I didn't know about. There were other women. As a matter of fact, he died in someone else's arms. I knew about his cheating many years ago, but I'm afraid if I look closer, I'm going to find out there were many more affairs that I didn't know about. How can a woman be married for so many years and not have a clue about the man she married?"

Rose smiled. "I suppose it's because the man doesn't want her to know."

Maggie laughed. "Oh Rose, I love how you get right to the point. I think you're right, though. Daniel let me know what he wanted me to know, and it's as simple as that. It feels absurd to say this, but somehow, I've been allowing myself to take some of the blame for his actions. I know it doesn't make sense, but I've been focused on my being so blind instead of his cheating. It's as if my not knowing who I was married to for so many years made me culpable in some way. How crazy is that?"

"Maggie, dear, whether you knew your husband or not is not what's important. What truly matters now is whether you know yourself. Do you know who you are? Do you know what you want? These are the questions you should be asking yourself. Until you can answer them, you won't have closure on the life you had with Daniel. And you won't be able to be there for your family. You've taken the first step by just finding some time for yourself here on the island. Don't stop that journey when you get home. It's time to ask yourself who is Maggie Wheeler?"

It was as if Rose had slapped Maggie in the face. Rose's words were a much-needed shock to Maggie's body, but she wasn't sure why the words hit her so hard. Hadn't Chelsea been saying the same thing in her own Chelsea way?

The color drained from Rose's face, and she looked as if she was in pain. Maggie got up and ran to her side.

"Rose, are you all right? Can I get you anything? Should I call Paolo or Ciara?"

"I think I'd better lay down for a spell. I'm sorry I can't visit with you longer, Maggie."

"Don't be silly. Let me help you to your bedroom."

Maggie called for Ciara, who was in the kitchen, to come help them get Rose onto the bed. Once she was settled, Ciara left the women alone to talk.

"Rose, I should probably go and let you rest."

"No. There are a couple of things I want to say to you before you leave. Come sit by my side."

Maggie did as Rose asked and took the woman's hand in hers.

"I have several journals that I've written over the years. They're in the bookcase in the front room. I was inspired to write them because of Anne and her journaling. If I could advise any woman who is searching for meaning in her life, I would recommend writing down her thoughts. There were times I didn't know what I would write. I would sit in my chair with a blank page in front of me for an hour before my pen would move. Some days I wouldn't write a thing, but I left tears on those pages. You can still see them today. Those are the wrinkled pages. Sometimes that's the way it goes."

A lump formed in Maggie's throat because she knew exactly what Rose was saying.

"A woman's path isn't a straight line, Maggie, but if you stop resisting, if you stop fighting against the changes and let them come, you can ride an amazing wave."

Rose's pain seemed to intensify, and she closed her eyes for a moment, then opened them again and smiled, only to close her eyes once more.

Ciara came into the room with some pills, a glass of water, and a cup of tea. Whispering, she said, "She'll rest for a while now, Maggie. I'm sorry the visit couldn't have been a longer one."

Fighting back tears, Maggie nodded and left the room. Paolo was waiting for her on the porch.

"Thank you for being such a good friend to Rose, Paolo. I don't know what she would do without you and your sister."

Paolo walked beside Maggie as they headed to the gate. "She's been like a mother to both of us. We've been blessed to have her in our lives. She was there for us when we came to the island, and of course, when the cancer came, we made sure to be here more often. These days, we don't bother to go home for very long. The doctors say it won't be more than a month or two."

"What's going to happen to this property when she passes? I hate the thought of it getting bulldozed to the ground. They'll end up putting retail stores and businesses here."

"Rose wants to leave the property to me and my sister. She even has suggested we update the place and reopen the inn."

"Oh, Paolo. That would be fantastic. She told me about the Key Lime Garden Inn and how she and her family couldn't manage it anymore. I could tell there was sadness in her voice about it. Do you think you'd be able to reopen it?"

"We've turned her down, Maggie. It's impossible for us to manage the nursery, be in Ft. Myers handling the Coastal Community Outreach, and run an inn. It's just too much. It's also difficult to imagine what else we would do with such a big property. When we said no, she said to sell it and take the money. She said we could give it to the families who need it. But we can't make money from this home. We just can't do that."

Maggie could appreciate his dedication to Rose but felt terrible that without Paolo and his sister, such a beautiful place might be destroyed, and the Key Lime Garden Inn would stay nothing more than a memory of a time long gone.

"I know this is none of my business, but you can't let anything happen to this place. Its history alone is of tremendous value to the island. My heart breaks at the thought. Won't you both please reconsider?"

They stopped just before the gate and Paolo took Maggie's hands in his, his blue eyes meeting hers. The strength of his callused hands was comforting to her, and she didn't pull back.

"Maggie, I will talk to my sister. I can only promise that. I will do that for you if you promise me that you will return, and soon."

"Thank you, Paolo. It means a lot to me. Of course, I'll come back. Captiva feels like home to me."

She remembered that she'd wanted to leave her information with Rose, so that they could stay in touch.

"Paolo, do you have a pen? Let me give you my address and cell phone. I'll also give you my friend Chelsea's information. Please let me know how Rose is doing."

"Of course. I will give you my cell phone as well. It's the best way to reach Rose. She never answers the landline anyway."

After they exchanged numbers, Paolo opened the gate. Maggie walked through and turned back once more and waved before walking toward Chelsea's house.

Chelsea had made dinner reservations earlier for the Thistle Lodge for seven o'clock. The grounds of the resort were expansive and beautiful, and the women were given a table where they had a view of the sunset.

Raising her wine glass, Chelsea said, "Here's to a wonderful vacation and a promise that you will return soon."

Maggie said, "I'll drink to that."

Glasses clinked, and they opened their menus.

As much as Maggie loved seafood, she'd had her fill on this vacation and longed for something different, so she selected the filet mignon this time.

"I'm so sorry about your friend Rose, Maggie. She sounds like an amazing woman. I'm sorry I don't know her."

"She is a lovely person, and I'm heartbroken that I won't get to know her better. I wish I could stay because honestly, I think I'd sit with her for hours for the rest of her days and learn everything I could about her. She's a woman with a life-time of wisdom."

"Well, as I promised you, I will see if I can check in on her after you've gone. Maybe I'll get to spend a little time with her."

"I think she'd love that, Chelsea. Thanks."

Something about their exchange earlier in the day must have given Chelsea a warning that talk of Paolo was off limits. Throughout the night, her friend steered clear of the subject, and Maggie was relieved. The last thing she wanted to do was to have any sort of confrontation with Chelsea on their last night together.

The dinner was delicious, and after their meal they took a short stroll on the beach before heading home. Maggie still hadn't packed her suitcase, but she didn't want to take her feet out of the sand. It surprised her how much she had come to see this place as her home instead of a vacation spot. She assumed years of traveling here was the reason, but this time, and especially because of her new friends, the island had new meaning for her. Maggie had much to deal with when she returned to Massachusetts, and top on her list was figuring out how soon she could return to Captiva Island.

Chapter Thirteen

LAUREN

The plan had always been that Lauren would pick up their mother at Logan Airport, but with everything she and her sisters had discovered while their mother was away, it was decided that all three girls would be there to welcome Maggie home. Beth and Sarah chose to stay back at the house to clean and make lunch while Lauren would be the one to drive to the airport.

Maggie's face was all Lauren needed to see to know that her mother was rested and happy. She pulled the car up to the baggage claim exit so that her mother would see her. Security made it clear that she couldn't stay there for more than a few minutes, so Lauren jumped out to help her mother get her luggage in the trunk.

September in New England was generally warm, but the last two days in Boston had been colder than usual. Pulling her sweater close to her body, her mother was clearly feeling the change in temperature.

"How was your flight?"

"The flight was fine, but I'm already sad to be in Boston. It feels like October, not September."

Lauren laughed and after closing the trunk, ran to the driver's side and hopped into the car. Fortunately, she had the heat on, so her mother felt better once inside.

"Sorry, Mom, I'm afraid your vacation is over and it's back to New England's unpredictable weather. It won't be that bad the rest of the week, though. I think it will be back in the seventies."

"Well, it seems like a sign to me. A sign I should go back to Florida."

"I assume you had a good time. You look rested."

"Yes, it was wonderful. I honestly didn't realize I needed a vacation until we landed in Florida. You know Chelsea, there was no way she was going to take no for an answer. I don't always take her advice, but this time she got it right. It was exactly what I needed."

Because of the traffic, it would be at least an hour before they made it home. Lauren wondered how much she should say before they made it back to Andover. She was always protective of her mother and was concerned that she might feel bombarded the minute they walked in the door. Lauren had explained to her sisters that they needed to give their mother some space before hitting her with a million questions, but they wouldn't listen, insisting that they needed to get to the bottom of what was going on between their parents and that their mother had had more than enough time away. It was time to deal with whatever fallout was coming.

"Mom, while you were away, Sarah and Beth came to me and wanted to talk about you and Dad."

"What about your dad and me?"

"Well, Sarah was at the house, and it looked like a lot of Dad's stuff was gone. The closet was practically empty, and nothing of his was in the bathroom. They thought I might know what was going on, so they came to me. I told them I had no idea and that we could talk to you when you got back. I said that there was probably a good explanation. There is a good explanation, right?"

Lauren expected her mother to tense up when confronted with this, but instead her mother came right out and said exactly what Lauren suspected.

"Your father moved out of the house Wednesday night. He came home, announced he'd quit his job, wanted a divorce, and was in love with someone else. He packed up his stuff, and left the house. I'm sorry to shock you, but there it is."

Her mother's demeanor was what shocked Lauren. Maggie had confessed a major traumatic event as if she was reading her grocery list. What had happened to the woman who for most of her life tried to protect her children from experiencing the slightest unpleasantness? For Lauren, not looking into her mother's eyes at this moment was impossible and so she pulled the car over to the side of the road when it was safe to do so.

Turning off the engine, Lauren turned to her mother and searched for tears or any emotion, but there was none.

"Mom. I'm so sorry. That must have been a terrible shock."

Her mother nodded her head and then took a deep breath.

"Yes, that's an understatement. I guess it was a shock, but I'm trying to understand why I didn't see it coming. I don't have an answer to that, at least not yet."

Her mother placed her hand on Lauren's face.

"I didn't have a clue how to tell you about your father and still preserve whatever good feelings you have for him. He wasn't perfect. I'm not perfect. None of us are. I can tell you this with certainty, though. He loved all his children. He was a good father, and I have no doubt that whatever was missing in his life, it had nothing to do with any of you kids. He adored you all. You can be sure of that."

Tears fell on Lauren's face, and she grabbed her mother's

hand and pulled her close. They hugged and then her mother asked how much Beth and Sarah knew.

"I'm going to let them tell you what they know and how they feel. They've prepared a nice lunch for you. Let's get home, and you can talk to them. I know they're all grown up, but right now they're acting like little kids. I think we've all felt that way ever since Dad died. You might as well know that we've packed a few clothes and are planning a girls' sleepover. If you thought you'd get some time to yourself tonight, you can forget it."

Lauren pulled the car back onto the road.

"How is Brea doing?"

"Much better. She's home from the hospital."

"I'll have to stop over for a visit. I'm sure they've got their hands full."

Lauren was quick to keep her mother from doing too much. She knew that she had a hard time saying no.

"Brea's mother helps them a lot, so they're not struggling, in case you were planning to offer your time."

"I didn't say I was going to watch the girls; I said a visit."

"Uh-huh. Whatever you say, Mom."

Her sisters welcomed their mother home with smiles and carefree attitudes. Nothing of the previous week's observations were mentioned, and it was obvious the more they talked over lunch that Sarah and Beth were heeding Lauren's words about not approaching their mother right away. Unfortunately, it was hard not to address the elephant in the room, and their mother decided to take control of the situation.

"I'm going to say what I need to say, and then we are all going to enjoy the evening and talk about other things. Agreed?"

Seeing them nod in agreement, their mother began to explain what had happened before Daniel died.

Lauren couldn't hold back any longer.

"Mom, we all already knew about Dad. I'll let Beth explain."

The room was quiet except for Beth sharing the events leading up to their father's death. The pain on their mother's face was difficult to watch. Lauren wanted to go to her mother's side and hold her, but instead waited for Beth to finish.

Maggie leapt off the sofa and ran to her daughter. She held Beth close, and soon all three girls were part of a group hug.

"My darling Beth. I can't imagine what this has been like for you. It pains me to think you couldn't come to me. I know it would have been hard, and I'm furious with your father for having put you in such a difficult position."

"Dad didn't know I knew, Mom. I never told him. I saw him, but he never saw me."

Lauren still couldn't get over how brave her sister had been all these years. The idea that her sister carried such a weight was hard to accept. All they could do now was to be there for Beth and for each other. There was no way to make right what had been done in the past, and it was beyond their ability to even make sense of it. It did, however, explain something else that was going on in Beth's life.

A few months ago, Sarah had mentioned to Lauren that Beth was seeing someone new. It wasn't until recently that the sisters found out who that someone was. Beth had been seeing a much older man, one of her professors. Was it possible that relationship was influenced by Beth's difficulties with their father? Lauren was no psychiatrist, but it seemed to her that Beth's attraction to him might not be a healthy one.

Lauren made a mental note to find out more about this professor, and she'd have to do it without Sarah's involvement. Her sister was less than subtle when it came to things like this.

She had no idea how she would do it, but something had to be done. What Beth had gone through these past years was enough to convince Lauren that professional help might be required.

The four women agreed to table this conversation for another time. It wasn't as cut and dried as her mother expected. There would need to be further discussion, but now wasn't the time. What they all needed was to have a good time together. Movies, popcorn, pizza, and pjs was the only plan for the night. They spent hours laughing and painting their nails. Talking about life in general and the latest gossip about people they knew.

Beth pressed Sarah about Ben, and everyone in the room could tell it wasn't something Sarah wanted to talk about. That didn't stop Beth.

"Come on. Spill. Michael told us anyway, so it's not like it's any big secret."

"What are you talking about? What does Michael know about Ben and me?"

Beth continued, "Well, for one, he knows that Ben was going to ask you to marry him recently."

Sarah looked uncomfortable as her mother's face lit up.

"Sarah, is that true? Did Ben propose?"

"No. No, he didn't propose, and I have no idea how Michael would know about it anyway. I haven't said a word."

Beth shot back. "Ben told Michael, Sarah. He was going to take you to dinner and ask you. You know that romantic restaurant Deuxvae? Everyone gets engaged there. It's practically a thing. If you've got reservations at that restaurant, and you don't get a ring, something's seriously wrong."

Sarah made a face at her sister. As usual, Beth didn't know when to stop talking. It was as if she was trying to upset Sarah on purpose. It was only natural for Sarah to fight back.

"Right. Because you're such an expert on relationships.

Why don't you tell us about your boyfriend, Bethy? How about it? Wouldn't we all like to hear about Beth's boyfriend?"

Their mother looked at Beth in anticipation.

"You've been seeing someone, Beth? Who is he?"

Now it was Beth's turn to squirm.

"It's nothing. He's…it's not serious."

Sarah wouldn't stop.

"It's her professor. Don't they have rules about that? Isn't it inappropriate for a professor to date his student? Especially a married professor."

Beth's face was red, and she looked like she was about to pounce on Sarah.

Lauren turned to her sister in anger.

"Sarah, explain yourself. How do you know he's married?"

"Because I went to the trouble of looking into it when I found out Beth was seeing him. It wasn't that hard to research. I had my assistant look into it and then I did a bit more snooping."

The look on Beth's face made it obvious to Lauren that Beth hadn't known any of this. Her professor had lied to her, and instead of coming clean, she had to find out from her sister. Lauren knew her sister. Especially after what she knew about their father, there was no way she would knowingly date a married man.

Lauren looked at Sarah and shook her head in disgust. Sarah understood for the first time that she had done something to intentionally hurt her sister, and all because she'd panicked when Beth had asked about Ben and marriage.

As soon as Sarah realized what she had done, she apologized.

"Bethy, I'm so sorry. I should have known you wouldn't date a married man. I feel awful. I should have told you before in private. I snooped because I was concerned for you. I was waiting for the right time. Obviously, this was not the right time."

Beth's words were a whisper.

"Oh, I don't know, Sarah. Maybe this was the right time. I don't think I would have wanted to be alone when I found out. I'm glad you all are here with me. It makes it easier somehow."

Lauren was happy to hear Beth say those words. It was true; all four women had gone through so much. It warmed her heart to know they had each other's backs no matter what.

It was an opening, albeit a small one, but Lauren hoped her sister Sarah might share what was in her heart about Ben. There was only one way to find out.

"Sarah, what about Ben? What's going on between the two of you?"

"To be honest, I'm not sure. I don't know what it is that's holding me back. Ben is great. He's always been there for me, and you all love him. I know he's a great catch and I'm being stupid if I turn him down, but I don't think I can see myself married to him. I feel terrible about it. To be honest, I'm not sure I ever want to get married or have kids."

Their mother said what no one had suggested up until now.

"You don't love him, Sarah. At least not that way. I'm not sure it's marriage that you don't want, or children. I mean it might be. I'm not saying it's not possible. My gut reaction is that you aren't in love with Ben."

Lauren nodded her head in agreement.

"I agree with Mom. Ben just isn't the one. The only problem is that you're going to have to tell him that, and soon. I think you should tell him before he gets on one knee. Don't put him through that."

The landline phone rang, and their mother got up to answer it. The sisters continued to talk until their mother came back into the living room.

"Who was that on the phone?"

"Someone named Arnold Kragen. I've never heard of him, but he says he was your father's attorney. We've never hired an Arnold Kragen that I'm aware of. Sarah, have you seen anything in the paperwork I left you about him?"

"No, but he called me the other day. He said he was trying to get in touch with you. I told him that if he was Dad's attorney, then he'd already have your information. I thought it was a scam. What does he want?"

"Well, girls, I'm not sure why this surprises me, but your father had a new attorney, one that I didn't know about. I've agreed to meet with him in his office tomorrow morning. Apparently, your father drew up a new will that I was unaware of."

The girls were shocked, and Sarah was worried. "I'm going with you."

The frustration on Lauren's face showed, and she was concerned that there was more to learn about their father than they'd thought. Why would their father create a will with an unknown attorney? What new secrets would they learn, and how would those secrets change their lives going forward? It was impossible to know, but Lauren felt that spending the night bonding with her mother and sisters would be the last time they could pretend to be certain about anything.

Chapter Fourteen

MAGGIE

Arnold Kragen's office was close to the North End of Boston. Maggie always loved this part of the city. The Italian restaurants and strolling through the streets stopping into Mike's Pastry for a cannoli was an annual tradition in the month of August that she and Daniel had never missed. Maggie expected that for the rest of her life old memories like this one would pop up at random times. She would have to get used to that and not push them away.

Sarah was able to get a parking space on the street and paid the meter using an app on her cellphone.

Arnold Kragen's office was on the third floor, and the elevator looked old and frightening to the women, so they took the stairs. A lightbulb flickered in the hall, and there were cobwebs in the corners of the stairwell.

Maggie was getting nervous as they got closer to his office.

"This doesn't seem like the kind of place your father would have come to find an attorney. Do you think this guy is legit?"

"I have no idea, Mom. This whole thing seems weird to me. Maybe we should have called Samuel Cohen. He's the family attorney, right?"

"Yes. I should have called him to have Arnold Kragen checked out. It's too late now."

They reached the office, and the attorney met them at the door.

"Mrs. Wheeler, please, come in."

"Thank you. This is my daughter, Sarah. Mr. Kragen, I have other appointments, so I'd appreciate it if we could get right to the point. I might as well confess that I was unaware of my husband drawing up a new will. We already had our wills done by our family attorney a few years ago. You'll forgive me if I'm a bit skeptical about all this. Exactly when did my husband create this will?"

"Yes, I understand your concern. Your husband hired me to draw up this will for him about six months ago. April 10th, to be exact."

Maggie couldn't understand why Daniel would do such a thing, and with this attorney of all people. If he wanted a new will, all he had to do was go to their attorney and have a new one made. Hiring this man meant that Daniel didn't want either their attorney or Maggie to know of it, at least until after his death.

The lawyer handed a copy of the will to Maggie, and she and Sarah looked it over. Everything about this will looked exactly like the one they had drawn up with their family attorney, with one exception. All of Daniel's assets were to go to his wife with one exception. Daniel had made provisions for a woman named Emily Wheeler.

"According to this document, someone named Emily Wheeler is to receive an inheritance. I don't know anyone by that name."

"Yes. Your husband requested that a distribution of one hundred thousand dollars be left to his daughter, Emily."

"My husband has three daughters Mr. Kragen, and none of them are named Emily. There must be a mistake."

"No. There is no mistake. Ms. Wheeler lives in Hull, Massachusetts with her mother."

Maggie sat back in her chair for support. Under any other circumstance she would have questioned the document. But this was Daniel's doing, and by now, Maggie had come to expect a constant discovery of secrets where he was concerned. That he would have sought out a new attorney to update his will made perfect sense. She would, of course, show this new will to Samuel Cohen, and they would make certain it was a legitimate claim, but Maggie knew in her heart that every bit of it was true.

Sarah was not so accepting.

"This Emily Wheeler needs to be vetted. None of us have ever heard of this person, and with all due respect, we don't know much about you either."

Arnold Kragen was nonplused.

"Of course. I would expect nothing less. Here is my card. Please understand that it is my responsibility to make certain that Mr. Wheeler's wishes are adhered to. I need to move quickly to resolve his estate. Please get in touch with me as soon as you possibly can."

Before Maggie and Sarah left the office, Maggie had one question.

"Mr. Kragen, there is something I don't quite understand. Why did you get in touch with me about this? What have I to do with this will?"

"If you've read the document closely, you'll see that Mr. Wheeler asked that you be informed upon his death, and that you be given a copy of the will. There is nothing more for you to do except receive a copy of this document as he wished."

Stunned, Maggie couldn't image what Daniel was thinking to involve her in this except to make her aware that a significant amount of money would be taken from his estate and might upset her and his other children. She chose to think that was his reasoning; any other explanation seemed cruel.

"Thank you, Mr. Kragen."

Maggie and Sarah got up from their chairs and quickly left Arnold Kragen's office. Sarah complained the entire way to the car. All Maggie could do was listen. Once they got on the road, Maggie called Samuel Cohen and asked if she could meet with him as soon as possible. He had an appointment but would be free in an hour, so the women drove to his office immediately.

"Sarah, I know this is a shock. It's a shock to me as well, but there's no reason to get worked up about this until we know more."

"Mom. There is no way that I now have a half-sister somewhere about to collect money from Dad's estate. Isn't it possible that some woman he broke up with is getting back at him? I mean, don't we need a paternity test or something? You just can't claim to be someone's daughter without proof."

"Sarah, don't you think Emily's mother would have had to prove this to your father when she gave birth? I mean the will doesn't say the money goes to her mother, so Emily must be over eighteen years old. If she was a minor, then her mother would inherit the money. Come to think of it, there is no mention of the mother at all, so I have no idea what kind of relationship your father had with Emily. Did he see her regularly? Did he never see her and therefore felt some regret or responsibility to give her some money? I never saw money going to anyone on a regular basis that would have indicated child support. You kids will inherit everything equally when I pass away, but this woman wouldn't receive a thing because I wouldn't know about her. Your father did this of his own free will."

By the time they reached Samuel Cohen's office, Sarah had calmed down. The attorney brought them into his conference room and looked over the will.

"First, Maggie and Sarah, I want to offer my condolences on the death of your husband and father. I'm sure this has been hard on the whole family."

"Thank you, Sam. I appreciate it."

"Let me also say that I know Arnold Kragen. He's a good attorney. He's fairly old school. I'm sure you got that from his no frills office décor and the way he dresses. He's been around a long time. I think he even worked with my father years ago. So, I hope that alleviates any concern you might have had about his credibility."

"Yes, that does help. You can understand my concern though. I'd never heard of the man before yesterday, and of course, to put it delicately, the contents of this will were kept from me."

"I understand. Looking over it, however, it looks perfectly legitimate. Everything about the will is standard. As you probably have already noticed, the will is almost entirely drawn to the exact specifications of the will I drew up for you and Daniel when you came to see me a couple of years ago. The only difference is the mention of Emily Wheeler."

"So, this new will is the one that should be enforced?"

"Yes. As you can see at the beginning of this paragraph, and which is standard, this new will makes any previous wills null and void."

"I see."

Sarah's anger was forming again, and she questioned the attorney.

"What about proving that Emily Wheeler is, in fact, my father's daughter?"

"Are you asking whether you can contest this will?"

"Well, yes, I guess that's what I'm asking."

"Of course, you have that right. Is that what you want to do?"

Maggie stopped Sarah from continuing with this line of questioning.

"No. It's not. I don't want to contest it."

"Mom. What are you saying?"

Maggie looked at her daughter and put her hand on her arm. "I don't want to contest this will. I want to move on."

Maggie didn't want to discuss it further, and certainly not in front of Sam Cohen. She got up from her chair, and Sarah followed. She extended her hand to say goodbye to Sam.

"Thank you, Sam. I appreciate you looking this over."

"Of course, Maggie. If there is anything else I can do, please don't hesitate to call me."

The women got in their car and didn't say a word for the entire drive home. By the time they reached the driveway, Sarah couldn't stay silent any longer.

"Mom. I understand this is all very overwhelming. I bet you'd like nothing more than to hop on a plane and go back to Captiva and pretend none of this is happening, but you can't stick your head in the sand anymore."

Maggie turned to her daughter and knew it was time to set her straight.

"Sarah, my love. I love you very much, even when you act too big for your britches. I know you are a very smart woman. You've had the best education money can buy. You're in charge of many people in your firm, and everyone looks to you for answers. You are a problem solver. You always have been, even when you were a little girl. So, I'm going to say this with all the restraint I have in me. This is my life. Not yours. I will do exactly as I see fit, whether you approve or not. Now I'm going into my house and I'm going to get the fireplace going, make myself a lovely cup of tea, and sit by the fire. I suggest you go home and tend to your own life."

Maggie got out of Sarah's car and went inside the house, leaving her daughter to sit in the driveway. She figured her daughter needed a few minutes to get over the shock of her words. She had no doubt that the woman who just stormed into the house didn't look anything like the mother Sarah was used to, and that was perfectly all right with Maggie.

The fire and the tea were soothing to Maggie's spirit. It was impossible to think that only forty-eight hours ago she had been wiggling her toes in the warm sand on Captiva Island. True to her life these days, anything could happen and usually did in a very short span of time. How many more hits did she think would come her way? Would she be able to stand strong against them?

What was it that Rose had said? *"A woman's path isn't a straight line, but if you stop resisting, if you stop fighting against the changes and let them come, you can ride an amazing wave."* Maggie wasn't sure about the amazingness of her wave, but she could appreciate the end of resisting. Daniel had another daughter. This was true no matter what she thought or did. It would be something to deal with but nothing that could harm her. Of that she was certain. For her children, she wasn't so sure. Having a half-sister wasn't anything Sarah was open to, but she didn't know about the others. It was possible none of them would ever encounter Emily. The money would be deposited into her account, and that would be the end of it. Whatever was going to happen would play out in time. For now, she was content to settle into her chair and enjoy the quiet.

Before Maggie could relax, she had to examine her plants both around the house and inside the greenhouse. Several of them needed attention, and so she set about to watering them and giving some plant food. The leaves of an azalea plant were limp but would return to their perky, strong state within an hour of watering. Considering she hadn't been away that long, most of the plants were fine. Once she'd completed that task, she was ready to settle down on the sofa and relax.

The warmth of the fire and a blanket was all Maggie needed to enjoy the rest of her day. Soon rain hitting the window joined the other sounds and the room was filled with a sense of peace that Maggie had craved since returning from Florida. She thought about reading, but her eyelids grew heavy, and before long, she was asleep. She was able to rest for a few hours before the phone rang. She debated whether to answer, but it was Chelsea, and Maggie was anxious to hear news from Captiva.

"Hey. How's the weather up there?"

"Very funny. It's not hot, that's for sure."

"So, do you miss me yet?"

"Of course, I do. I hate to ask, but how's the weather there?"

"You don't want to know. Sunny and hot. Anyhow, I'm calling you about something else. Are you planning on attending the next lunch-bunch get-together?"

"Oh man. I forgot about that. It's next Friday, right? Whose house?"

"Yes, it's at Jane's house, or at least it *was* at Jane's house. According to Rachel, Jane's been acting weird lately. She isn't answering her phone. She hasn't talked to anyone in the group since Daniel's funeral. That's the last time anyone has seen or heard from her. So, I got worried and decided to call her. You know, just to make sure she's alive. She is, but when I was talking to her this morning, she seemed different to me. She asked about you, of course, but then I swear she either has a cold or she was crying."

"Oh, no. That doesn't sound like Jane. She's always so upbeat. I can't imagine what could get her down. Maybe I should just drive over to her place in the morning and check on her."

"I was hoping you would suggest that. She did say that she can't host the lunch-bunch, so I think Rachel is next on the list."

"Did she say why she couldn't host it?"

"Nope. She didn't give a reason, just that she couldn't do it and asked that someone else do it. Also, she said she wouldn't be attending this time. Something's not right. Call me tomorrow after you check on her. I'd love to know what's going on with her. Everyone seems to confide in you, Maggie, so if you can't get anything out of her, I'll be shocked."

"It's a lot harder to ignore someone when they're standing at your front door. I'm not going to call her; I'm just going over there. She won't be able to push me away that easily. Thanks for letting me know. I'll see what I can do. In the meantime, send me a picture of tonight's sunset across from the Mucky Duck. Maybe a video instead so I can hear the waves. I'll talk to you tomorrow."

"Will do. Maybe I'll even send you a picture of my piña colada just to rub it in."

"What a good friend you are. Love you."

"Love you, too. Good night."

Chapter Fifteen

MAGGIE

It had been about six weeks since Maggie had been to Jane's house. It was much larger than it had any right to be considering Jane was the only one living there. It was in a very upscale part of Andover, although everyone would say that the town in its entirety was upscale. Jane's job took her all over the world, and Maggie loved listening to stories of Jane's travels whenever they got together. With no husband or children, Jane was free to come and go as she pleased, and every woman in their lunch-bunch group was jealous of her freedom.

Never one to complain or have a negative attitude, it was hard to imagine what might be upsetting Jane so much that she would be crying. Chelsea was always very intuitive about such things. If she thought there was something to worry about, she was probably right.

Maggie reached the front door and rang the bell. She had to ring it a second time before Jane answered.

"Maggie. Hey. You're back from Florida. How'd it go?"

It felt awkward, but Jane didn't invite Maggie inside.

"It was great. Thanks. I just thought I'd stop by and see how you are. We haven't had much time to talk since the last lunch-bunch get-together. I'm sorry we didn't talk much at the funeral. So much was going on, and it all seems like a blur to me now. Is this a bad time? Can I come in for a bit?"

Jane hesitated before answering, "Yes. Of course. Please, come in."

The house was dark and smelled of incense.

"So, how've you been? I heard that you won't be hosting the next lunch. Are you traveling?"

"No. I'm not going anywhere for a bit. I haven't been feeling well, so I'm taking some time. I guess they call that mental health, right? I'm taking a mental health month off. Just need some time to rest. I've been traveling a lot, and the job can get stressful at times. I think people occasionally take a mental health day here and there, but I needed more than that, so I came up with a mental health month. Seems appropriate."

"Of course. You must do what's best for you and your health. Is there anything I can do for you?"

"No."

The response was curt and abrupt. It even bordered on angry. Chelsea was right. Something was very wrong with Jane, and she needed to drag it out of her. There was no way Maggie was leaving without helping her friend.

"Jane. Listen, something is obviously bothering you. So much so that this house feels like a tomb. This isn't like you. You're lemons and sunshine all the time. Talk to me. What is going on?"

"That's what you think? That my life is a bowl of happiness 24/7? Do you ever really look at things, Maggie or are you just so content with your little world that all you can see is your perfect life and perfect family? Did you ever think that maybe I wanted a family too? Maybe I wanted children?"

"Okay. You need to calm down and tell me why you're so angry with me, because I'm starting to think that what's going on with you has to do with me somehow."

Jane started to cry. She moved to the sofa and put her head in her hands. All Maggie could do was sit next to her and wait until the sobbing stopped. Whatever it was that was hurting would come out if she sat quietly with her friend. As time passed and the crying stopped, Jane took a deep breath and shared what was tearing her apart.

"It was a long time ago. Probably six years now. I was at a conference in New York, staying at The Plaza Hotel. You know how it is when you travel so much, you meet tons of people—strangers really. You're so happy when you run into someone you know. I was at the bar when I turned and saw Daniel. I thought, finally, someone I can talk to about real things. Not the kind of stuff you babble on about when you're at one of those conferences.

"Daniel came over and sat with me for hours. We drank… well, I can't tell you how many drinks we had, but it was a lot. By the end of the night, he walked me to my room. He was such a gentleman, but also a real charmer. Anyway, I went into my room, and he left. I crashed on the bed with my clothes on because I was wearing the same dress the next morning when I woke up.

"I was hungover of course. I needed coffee and possibly a bit of food, so I went downstairs to the hotel restaurant. When I got there, I saw Daniel sitting alone in a booth. He waved for me to join him, so I did. I remember at the time wondering how it was possible after all that we'd drunk the night before he looked so alert and handsome as if he'd just come in from a brisk walk in the fresh air. He looked amazing, and I think I looked like I felt. It didn't matter, though, because he was a perfect gentleman and was very attentive.

"I remember being so struck by him that when it was time for me to check out of the hotel, all I could think about was Daniel and that I wanted to see him again. I didn't know how or when, but I knew if there was a way to make it possible, I wanted to see him. Was I lonely? Of course, I was. Was I jealous of you? You bet I was. You had this wonderful husband, and I had nothing."

"But Jane, you always said that's the way you wanted it. You said you loved not being tied down with a husband and children."

"I did say that, and I meant it. At least I meant it at the time. Until six years ago, I was perfectly content with my life. For some ridiculous reason, I started to fall in love with Daniel. I took advantage of every opportunity to see him. Of course, it was only at functions when others were around. We didn't exactly hang with the same people. Those moments were brief, but I looked forward to them.

"When you talked about him at our get-togethers, I loved hearing about his days and what he was up to. It would hold me until the next time I could see him or hear about him. Even though I was jealous of you, I was so grateful that at least I had that. Through you I had a secret love affair with your world. I kept up the pretense that I didn't want a husband, but it was a lie."

Maggie was afraid to ask the obvious question, but it needed to be asked.

"Did you and Daniel ever…?"

"No. Not ever and not because I didn't try. If I knew I was going to see him, I dressed especially pretty. I flirted with him every chance I got, but he never seemed to notice. Finally, I half-jokingly said that I wouldn't say no if he ever asked. We were in Rachel's kitchen one time when we all had that Christmas party. Remember?"

Maggie nodded. She remembered the party and couldn't believe she'd never noticed Jane flirting with her husband. Once again, Maggie was clueless.

"What did Daniel say?"

"He looked me in the eye and said thank you, that he was flattered, but that he was in love with his wife."

Maggie refused to let the tears build. She didn't doubt that Daniel loved her, but to hear Jane say the words hit her hard. Daniel was in love with love and pretty women. Jane was a beautiful person inside and out, but even for him there were limits. Cheating on your wife with her friend was off limits. It baffled Maggie the lies people told themselves to live with their choices.

"It didn't stop me from loving him, Maggie. I've loved him for years."

Maggie understood Jane's pain. When you lose someone you love, it's devastating, no matter the circumstances. Maggie couldn't believe she was sitting here trying to console a woman who was in love with her now deceased husband.

"So, you've been grieving Daniel's death these last couple of weeks by shutting out the world and hiding in your house?"

Jane shook her head. "No. I haven't been grieving his death."

Maggie was confused. "I don't understand."

Jane ran her hands through her hair.

"I've been angry that he cheated on you. I've been furious with myself for living in a fantasy world, a world that I was prepared to hurt one of my dearest friends for. Have I been hiding? Yes, I guess I have been because I've been ashamed of myself and afraid to look you in the eye and pretend any longer. I didn't know about Daniel's cheating on you until recently. If I'm grieving anyone, it's the loss of our friendship. I should have been a better friend to you."

It seemed bizarre, to say the least, that Maggie should give any words of wisdom to her friend. She wondered how Jane would feel if she knew that Daniel had not only been unfaithful, but that he had fathered a child from one of his affairs. Maggie was far from enlightened, and anything she might say to Jane right now might come off as being insincere, but she wanted to ease her friend's pain.

"Daniel is gone, Jane, but I'm still here. You haven't lost your friend. You don't need to feel embarrassed or ashamed. You need to come out of the darkness and find joy again. There is absolutely nothing you can do about the past. I'm learning the hard way that's true for everyone. At some point, we need to make peace with it all and move forward. Trust me, if I can do that, so can you."

Jane smiled and nodded, pulling Maggie into a hug.

They agreed to see each other the following Friday when Jane would host their monthly lunch-bunch group.

"Let me know what I can bring. I'm looking forward to it."

Jane nodded and thanked Maggie for checking in on her.

As Maggie drove away, she laughed at the crazy events of the last two days. Daniel had been gone almost three weeks, and he was still creating havoc. This must be the wave her friend Rose had talked about. Maybe it was time to buy a journal after all.

An early morning call from Daniel's office woke Maggie.

"Hello?"

"Hello, Mrs. Wheeler, it's Brenda from the office. I'm sorry to call so early, but I wanted to reach you before you put anything else on your calendar for today."

"Yes, hello, Brenda. That's fine. What can I do for you?"

"Well, Mr. Patterson asked me to call you to see if you would be able to come into the office to collect items from your husband's office. You see we've hired someone new, and although Mr. Wheeler took some things from his office, he left behind several items that we just assumed he would come back in to retrieve. Of course, since his unexpected passing, that isn't going to happen. Mr. Patterson didn't want to just throw these things out without checking with you first."

The last thing Maggie wanted to do was to see Richard Patterson again, but she supposed there wasn't anything to be done about it. She was curious what things Daniel felt weren't important enough to take with him when he quit. Curious or not, Maggie wasn't certain she wanted to know the answer. She was surprised it had taken his office this long to get in touch with her.

"I can come in tomorrow morning, Brenda, if that works for you. How is nine o'clock?"

"Yes, thank you so much, Mrs. Wheeler. That would be great. I'll see you then. Goodbye."

Due to rush hour traffic, it was a slow drive into the city the next morning. Maggie marveled that so many people took this route twice a day. She thought it was no wonder so many struggled with stress due to their daily commute.

She parked her car in the underground garage and made her way up to Daniel's office. As she got out of the elevator, she could feel several eyes on her. To avoid the awkward stares, Maggie had hoped Brenda would be at the front desk to greet her. Unfortunately, she had to announce herself with the receptionist, who directed Maggie to a leather chair in the waiting area.

With every tick of the clock, Maggie became increasingly agitated. Her heart started to beat faster, and she thought it might have been less stressful for her had she told Brenda to throw everything into the trash. Instead, she felt exposed and awkward and was certain she was now the subject of office scrutiny and gossip. She was almost ready to leave when Brenda came around the corner, apologizing for making Maggie wait so long.

Maggie lied, "I understand. It's no trouble at all."

They walked to the end of the floor and to Daniel's corner

office. Floor-to-ceiling glass walls made Maggie worried she wouldn't be able to go through drawers in private.

Richard Patterson joined them. He approached Maggie and hugged her, giving her an air kiss.

"Hello, Maggie. How have you been?"

"I'm doing fine, Richard. Thank you."

Richard held on to Maggie's hands and kept nodding his head long after Maggie's response. He turned to Brenda and thanked her. Brenda left Richard and Maggie alone so that they could talk.

"I instructed everyone to leave Daniel's office exactly as it was when he left. He was a wonderful and important asset to this organization, and he deserves all the respect we can give him. It was the least we could do."

Maggie resisted the urge to slap him. She knew how awful Richard had been to Daniel over the years and hearing him now say things she knew he didn't mean made her angry.

"Maggie, if there's anything I can do for you, I hope you will come to me and let me know. I'm here for you."

"You're here for me?"

She had nothing to lose at this point and felt no desire to keep up any pretense. There was no way to explain how she knew, but something deep inside convinced her she was right. She couldn't explain it; she just knew.

"Just how much did you know about Daniel's extramarital hobbies, Richard?"

Stunned, he shook his head. "I didn't know anything at all. Daniel loved you, Maggie. I just assumed everything was fine between the two of you."

"Stop it. I've always felt that there was something about you I didn't like. I couldn't put my finger on it, but I think I know what it is now. Not only did you know about Daniel cheating on me, but I also have a strong suspicion that Lorna might be in the dark about your flirtations and affairs. You flirted with me and the other wives when we were in your presence. I think you covered for Daniel and who knows how many others. What is it? A club? I don't know what you had on Daniel, but I'm convinced whatever it was, you used it to make him miserable whenever you needed to. What do they call that, leverage?"

Maggie could tell she had hit a nerve. She knew in her heart that she was right about Richard, and she was glad she had the chance to speak her mind and give voice to what she had always suspected.

"I'd like to be left alone now. If you'd leave me to go through Daniel's things in private. Please close the door on your way out."

"Of course. Ask Brenda if you need anything at all."

And with that, Richard Patterson turned and walked out of Daniel's office.

Maggie pulled the blinds down to cover every glass wall so that prying eyes didn't have the chance to watch her go through her late husband's personal belongings. As she went through each drawer and cabinet, it was clear that what remained had no value to the firm, and before long Maggie came to the same conclusion. Daniel had taken everything that meant anything to him.

Golf clubs, an umbrella, a pair of shoes and a blazer hanging from the hook on the back of the door could all be discarded. There were books, and Maggie decided they all could go as well. She was ready to let Brenda know that she would be taking nothing when a travel book for Italy caught her eye. Maggie decided to take that with her. She didn't know when, but she was certain that it was only a matter of time before she would get there. If nothing else, this book would be her reminder.

Chapter Sixteen

MAGGIE

Maggie remembered everything about her wedding. The way Daniel's hair swooped down and to the side like a velvet ribbon. His blue eyes staring back at her as they said their vows. It didn't matter that thirty-two years had passed; she could remember every moment of that day with such clarity, it could have easily happened the day before.

Although her memory was clear, she remembered that their first few days of married life were not the happily-ever-after that most couples experience. Her heart raced, remembering the panic she felt when they were on the plane headed to Captiva and their honeymoon. The fear came on suddenly, and she naturally associated the terror with being on an airplane for the first time in her life. If she had looked closer, she would have understood that her feelings sprouted not from a fear of flying, but a shocking realization that she was now a married woman at eighteen years old.

Maggie couldn't understand how a seemingly joyous and well-planned event could rock her world so thoroughly, but rock it, it did, and she had no idea why. The flight attendant felt bad for the newlyweds and must have told the pilot about it because within minutes of Maggie's white-knuckles and stiff body language, he came out from the cockpit to offer his congratulations and a bottle of champagne. She didn't have the heart to tell him that she was pregnant, and her new husband would have to enjoy the bottle by himself.

Once in Florida, Maggie decreed that they would have to find an alternate way to travel home when the honeymoon was over. Since she assumed that flying was at the root of her panic attack, she would make certain that she would never again experience such an event. The decision was made that they would travel home by train. After all, what could go wrong if she was only a few feet off the ground?

As the honeymoon progressed and Maggie felt less stressed by it all, she decided that if God wanted her to get back home via airplane, then he was going to have to do something to prove it was his plan for her. It was only a few days after she made that decision that there was a nationwide train strike. No trains would be available on the day of their departure. Maggie was going to have to travel home by plane, and there was nothing she could do about it. Strangely, she felt at ease about it, declaring that if God wanted her to go home by plane, then who was she to disagree?

The trip home was much more relaxed, and Maggie didn't feel the same panic she felt on the way to Florida. Once again, she was certain it was the fear of flying that made her struggle so. The truth was that she had a few weeks to come to terms with her new status as a married woman, and it wasn't so bad after all. At least that's what she told herself.

Now a widow, Maggie hated the new status and the label. If Daniel hadn't died, she would have had the title of divorcee. Every time she had to fill out an application or form, she'd have to check off a new box, one that she had up to now always ignored. She wondered why it was so important to announce such things to anyone. She always thought it was insulting to list a celebrity's age after their name. She noticed it was a practice that was applied more to women than men. It was as if they had an expiration date, a 'Best Used By' date. She would never accept such labels. She was Maggie. A woman. Not a soon-to-be-fifty-year-old-almost-divorced widow. Simply, Maggie Wheeler.

Daniel's estate, which now had honored his latest will, was progressing quickly. Maggie was pleased that soon it would all be behind her. She had no desire to know Daniel's daughter Emily and hoped she wouldn't ever have to be confronted with that part of his life. The only thing that lingered on Maggie's mind was the realization that Daniel might have additional children he was unaware of before he died. At this point, nothing would surprise her.

She needed to get outside and breathe the crisp fall air. She ran upstairs to get a sweater and headed to the backyard. Looking over her garden, she was glad that she had found some time to tend to the area and prepare for the winter months. Her plants were bare, and she had covered her prized rose bushes with burlap. Maggie found the dirt pile beyond the fence and knew why it was there. Her friend the woodchuck was now hibernating. It was getting close to Thanksgiving, and the weather had turned especially cold. She smiled, remembering how irritated she was with the animal but now wished he was around so she could talk to him. How strange it was to see the world with new eyes. She was ready to make friends and accept her furry pal when he returned in the spring. She looked forward to it.

The sun had disappeared behind the clouds, and a blustery wind forced the leaves off the trees. Maggie pulled her sweater close and went back inside the house. It was the kind of weather that made you want to stay inside next to the fire with a warm cup of tea. She placed the tea kettle on the burner and selected her favorite cup. She had enough wood for the fire for now but made a mental note to get outside soon to collect more.

Somewhere inside her purse, her phone buzzed. Sarah always made fun of her for not selecting a ringtone, even though Maggie repeatedly explained she didn't like being startled by the sound. Instead, she was content to keep her cell phone on vibrate. Maggie struggled to find the phone among the assortment of mostly unnecessary items inside her purse. When she finally found it, she could see that the caller was Paolo Moretti.

"Hello?"

"Hello, Maggie. It's Paolo Moretti. I hope I haven't caught you at a bad time."

"No. Not at all. I'm glad to hear from you, Paolo."

"I'm sorry to have to share with you the news that Rose has passed away. She died yesterday."

Maggie had spoken with Chelsea a couple of times since returning from Florida, and although her friend hadn't been able to sit with Rose the way Maggie had, she was able to get updates on Rose's health. Maggie had known that this day was coming, but the news caught her off-guard, and she tried not to cry into the phone.

"Oh, Paolo. I'm so sorry. I'm just so sorry."

"I know. She was a wonderful woman, and I'm going to miss her."

Maggie could hear Paolo sniffling slightly. She knew he too was having a difficult time not crying.

"Maggie, I wanted to call you to tell you that Rose's funeral will be held in Connecticut, on the 17th. I thought you might want to attend."

"Yes, indeed I do want to be there. Of course. Can you send me all the information via email?"

"Yes. I'm going to do that as soon as we hang up the

phone. Ciara can't make it, but I will be there. I hope to see you then."

Maggie was happy to know that Paolo would be at the funeral. She felt close to Rose even though she hadn't known her for very long, and Paolo was the only other person who understood that.

"Thank you, Paolo. I'll see you on the 17th."

"Goodbye, Maggie."

Maggie hung up the phone and sat on the sofa thinking about her dear friend, Rose. She tried to console herself with the thought that Rose was no longer suffering with the cancer and was finally without pain. Rose was in a better place, and if she had her way, had probably gone looking for Anne Morrow Lindbergh. Maggie hoped that was the case, and if it was, that Rose told Anne about Maggie.

The drive to Connecticut was almost three hours from Maggie's home. Before getting on the road, she booked a room at a small hotel in the area and let her children know what was happening. All three of her girls offered to go with her, but Maggie wanted the time alone in the car to think. She had such fond memories of Rose and was so sad that she wouldn't get to talk with her again. Rose shared her stories and wisdom with Maggie and even though she would never get to sit with her friend, Maggie knew she would carry Rose's words with her for the rest of her life.

Timing her arrival at the hotel just in time to check in, Maggie parked her car in the hotel parking lot and carried her overnight bag to her room. There was little time to rest as the wake would begin in one hour. She had a change of clothes and had just enough time to freshen up before heading to the funeral home.

Rose and Maggie had never talked about religion when they were together. The obituary made it clear that Rose had been Catholic. A wake today followed by a church service and drive to the cemetery would be tomorrow morning. As soon as she was ready to go, Maggie stopped at the front desk to ask for directions to the funeral home. Fortunately, she wouldn't have to travel too far. The funeral home was only a few blocks to the west of the hotel. It was even possible to walk, and Maggie would have if the temperature hadn't been in the thirties.

There was a long line leading into the funeral home, and the parking lot was full. Maggie thought that she should have realized that someone like Rose would have a large gathering of friends to honor her life. Maggie was only one of Rose's most recent acquaintances, and she could see that her friend was much loved by many.

By the time Maggie reached the inside the funeral home, Paolo saw her and waved. She was happy to see a familiar face in the crowd. As he approached her, Maggie was signing her name in the funeral guest book.

They embraced, and Maggie could see that Paolo's eyes were red, most likely from tears.

"I'm so glad that you could come, Maggie. Rose would have been so happy to know that you were here to celebrate her life."

"I had to come, Paolo. She was a wonderful woman, and I'm only sorry I didn't get to spend more time with her. I have to be grateful that we got to know each other before she passed."

"Yes. I'm glad of that too."

The line approaching the casket moved, and Maggie stepped forward, Paolo standing with her along the way. When they reached the front, both Maggie and Paolo knelt and said prayers. Looking at Rose, Maggie's tears formed, and she reached out to touch her friend. Rose's husband and son, both gone before her, would be waiting for her. She had joined them in heaven, and Maggie was certain that nothing would have made Rose happier than that.

When they made their way out of the funeral home, Paolo walked Maggie to her car.

"Where are you staying, Maggie?"

"I'm at the Thayer Inn just for the night. I plan to drive back home right after the funeral tomorrow."

"Will you have dinner with me tonight, Maggie? There are a few things I need to discuss with you."

Maggie didn't have any plans for the rest of the day, and she was thrilled that Paolo wanted to spend some time with her. She was glad for the company.

"Of course. That would be very nice."

"The Crescent Inn, where I am staying, has a lovely restaurant. I think it would be very good and also quiet. How does that sound?"

"Perfect. How about seven o'clock? I'll meet you there."

"Very good. I will see you at seven."

Ever the gentleman, Paolo opened her car door and helped her inside. Closing the door, Maggie rolled down the window.

"Thank you, Paolo. I'll see you later."

As she drove off, Maggie watched Paolo in the rearview mirror. He stood in that spot watching her drive away.

Chapter Seventeen

MAGGIE

The Crescent Inn was a lovely hotel on the bank of a river. Although it was cold, Maggie walked around the property to take in the beautiful scenery. She was glad she was wearing her leather gloves, but her ears were starting to turn red from the wind. Looking at her watch, she decided she'd better get inside as Paolo was probably waiting for her in the lobby.

Once inside, she didn't see him in the lobby, but walked to the restaurant and found him sitting in one of the chairs near the hostess podium.

"I'm sorry, Paolo, I hope I didn't keep you waiting. It's just that this hotel and property is stunning. I had to walk around and check it out. I love how they decorated the place with pumpkins and fall colors. It's so charming. My hotel is nice, but it's nothing like this one. How did you find it?"

"Truly, I didn't have any idea of this place. I looked on the Internet and saw the pictures. I thought it was very pretty and booked it right away."

The hostess guided them into the restaurant and to a table in the back. The room was somewhat dark with low beams and candles. It reminded Maggie of The Brotherhood of Thieves on Nantucket Island. It was cozy and as Paolo had mentioned, very quiet.

Paolo was carrying a package, and once they were settled at their table and drinks were ordered, Paolo handed it to Maggie.

"What's this?"

"Shortly before she died, Rose asked me to give this to you. I was going to mail it but then, well, when she passed away and you said you would be here, I knew I would give it to you in person."

Maggie pulled the ribbon from the package and opened the wrapping paper. Cutting the tape off the box with her knife, she opened it and found three leather-bound books inside. An envelope sat on top of the books. A lump rose in her throat.

"Oh. I know what these are."

She looked at Paolo to see if he understood. He smiled and nodded his head.

"They're her journals. I can't believe she gave them to me."

"You must read the note, Maggie. Please."

My dear Maggie,

I don't know when you will receive my journals but there is a strong possibility that you will be reading this after I have passed. After you left Captiva, I thought about you often. I wondered how your life was back home with all your obligations and concerns about what had happened in your marriage. I wanted to give you my journals so that in those moments when you feel alone, you might hear my words and remember that every woman struggles at one time or another in their life. Anne taught you some of that, and now, I want to add my words as well. But this letter is not just an invitation to read my words, it is also an invitation to live on Captiva Island permanently.

I'm not thinking only about what you will gain by living here, but also what you might give. There is so much life awaiting you. I'm just passing the baton. I have put Paolo's name on the deed to my home on Captiva. I didn't want to wait until I was gone and have the lawyers, courts and even the island fight over what has been the stabilizing and constant joy and peace in my life. Paolo did not want to own this house or the land. I asked him to hold on to it for one year, after that he can do with it as he wishes. Why, you might ask, did I make such a request? Because, Maggie, I want you to own the house, and if you might grant another wish, perhaps you and Paolo might reopen the Key Lime Garden Inn as well. I know that might be too much to ask, so for now, Paolo has agreed to take the property for one year in the hopes that during that time, you will accept my offer. He will simply put the house in your name when, and if, that time comes.

I hope, in these next months, you find what you are looking for. A deeper understanding of who you are and what you want your life to look like. You have complete control over that. Remember this, Maggie. There is no perfect place, no perfect relationship. There is only life and how you choose to live it. Don't wait, Maggie. Live your life and share it with others.

Your friend,

Rose

It was a miracle that Maggie could see the words on the paper. She couldn't hold back the tears and wasn't embarrassed that she let them fall in front of Paolo. Looking at him, she searched for confirmation of Rose's proposal. Paolo nodded his head and took Maggie's hand in his.

"I've agreed for only one year, Maggie. Rose knew you weren't ready to accept her plan for the property. She wanted to give you time."

"Paolo, this is crazy. Why would Rose want me to have her house? Yes, we became quick friends, but surely anyone would dispute any claim I would try to have on it. The town, or maybe even distant relatives. I know her husband and son are gone, but there must be cousins, nieces, and nephews. Someone is going to come forward and fight this."

"Rose thought of that, Maggie. That's another reason she wanted first to put the house in my name while she was alive.

I've not inherited it but rather I've simply owned it while Rose was still alive. There's always a chance that someone might fight that as well. Whatever troubles it might present, a year will give us the time we need to deal with it. God willing, no one will come forward. For as long as I've worked for her, Rose never had any family come to visit or stay at the house."

"Yes, I understand that, but you'd be surprised how many relatives suddenly appear when there is money to be gained. Besides, Paolo, I never said I would come to live on Captiva permanently. I'll visit, maybe even often, but to live there? I don't think that's possible. I have a family that needs me back in Massachusetts."

Maggie suddenly felt sorry that by entering Rose's life, she had created turmoil in people's lives, specifically Paolo's.

"Maggie. You don't need to worry about anything at this point. I had some of the same concerns you have now. And as you know, I didn't want the property in the first place, but Rose, well, she was very hard to say no to."

They hadn't even looked at the menu, and by now, the waitress had hovered more than once.

"Maggie, why don't we order our dinner and enjoy the meal? There is much to think about, and no decision must be made today. You have an entire year to think about this. For now, let's just enjoy our time together."

The rest of the evening was spent talking about Maggie's children, Ciara's food pantry, and gardening. Maggie wasn't surprised that Paolo knew as much as he did about flowers, and she took this time to pick his brain about how best to care for her roses. Eventually, talk turned to Italy and Paolo and Ciara's home and family there.

"I've always dreamt of visiting Italy. One day, I'm going to get there."

"You should go, Maggie. It's a beautiful country. I was born in a little town called Gaeta, a coastal town that sits on the

Tyrrhenian Sea. It's a bit south of Rome. You would love it there. Maybe one day I will show it to you."

The thought of traveling throughout Italy with Paolo Moretti sent a shiver up her spine. Nothing would make her happier than to see the town where he was born. She wanted to know more about Paolo and his life and wondered how someone she had only known for a few months could make her feel that anything was possible. He smiled at her, and his ocean blue eyes stared into hers, making it difficult to look away. Worried he could read her mind, she looked down at the menu and tried to focus.

They ordered dinner, and Paolo filled their glasses with another pour of wine. The food was delicious, and it was evident to anyone who observed them that they enjoyed each other's company. Paolo had a wonderful sense of humor, and Maggie laughed more than once at his stories. It felt good to be able to laugh again, even as they shared the loss of their friend, Rose. Maggie thought more than once that Rose was looking down and watching them as they huddled close, whispering so they wouldn't be overheard by people at the other tables.

When dinner was finished, Paolo carried the box of journals and walked Maggie to her car. He put the box on the passenger seat instead of in the trunk because she wanted to touch the journals on her way home.

"Is that silly of me?"

"Not at all. I understand completely. So, I'll see you in the morning for the funeral. You should be back here at nine-thirty. There is a final goodbye and prayer and then the cars will drive in a procession to the funeral. If you want, you could join me in my car. We could drive to the cemetery together."

Maggie did want more time with Paolo but thought it would be better if she got on the road as soon as she left the cemetery.

"Thank you, Paolo. I think I will begin my drive back

home right from the cemetery. It's a three-hour drive and I'm not really a fan of driving so far on my own. I'll see you in the morning."

Paolo smiled and seemed careful not to show any disappointment in her response. There was so much to think about, and she wanted to spend time alone with her thoughts as soon as possible, starting tonight.

"Goodnight, Paolo, and thank you for a lovely dinner. I'll see you tomorrow."

"Goodnight, Maggie. Drive safely please."

She drove back to her hotel and couldn't wait to get into bed with Rose's journals. Rose had thrown Maggie off balance with her request. Her idea that Maggie should own the Captiva Island property was crazy. Who turns over a property to someone they barely know? She shook her head trying to understand what about her gave Rose the impression that she could run an inn? She'd never run a business in her life, let alone an inn fifteen hundred miles away from where she lived.

Not to mention that although Maggie was struggling with the events of the last few months, Rose's implication that taking over her property was a sign of moving on. As wise as Rose was, Maggie felt she was off the mark with that assumption. Accepting Rose's offer wouldn't be the only evidence of Maggie's evolving wisdom and strength. If she did accept the house, it would be a business decision only and not an indication that Maggie was or wasn't getting on with her life. She appreciated the gesture, but there was no way she was going to move to Florida.

When she got into her hotel room, Maggie placed the box of journals on the table across from her bed. She changed into her pajamas, pulling her bathrobe on to stay warm. She climbed into bed and sat staring at the box. On the drive back to the hotel, she was anxious to read Rose's words, but now that she was in her hotel room, she wasn't sure this was the best place to look at them. Settled in front of the fireplace at home with a cup of tea was a better plan. Reading the journals would have to wait until she returned to Massachusetts.

She found the remote and searched for something to watch on the television. A movie to distract her seemed like a good idea and so she clicked through the stations until Kevin Costner and *Field of Dreams* showed on the screen. Her favorite film of all time would do the trick. It didn't matter that she had seen the movie more than fifty times. It was like comfort food. The kind that hugs you and reminds you of a time long ago when life seemed simpler.

Maggie laughed when she thought about life being simpler years ago. Both her mother and grandmother had struggles of their own. They were different struggles of course, with worries that Maggie couldn't fathom. Her grandmother was poor and worrying about whether crops would produce what they needed to eat was a daily concern. Her grandparents lived on a farm in Scotland and her grandmother recalled several times when money and food was scarce. Women had different challenges than the men, but no one was immune from labor.

The events of the day had left Maggie exhausted and troubled. She longed to return to Captiva, but now she had more to consider than just visiting the island for vacation. Was it crazy to consider Rose's proposal? Living on the island had appealed to her more than once over the years and she even approached the subject with Daniel. They'd never considered making the island their full-time residence, but to have a vacation home on Captiva had been considered, although briefly. Now, the idea that Maggie would move permanently to Florida was a real possibility, if only she could find a way to make it work for her family. And what about the Key Lime Garden Inn? She would have to research its history to learn more.

Her eyes heavy, Maggie pushed the subject of moving to Captiva out of her mind. It was too much to consider, and if she continued to run it over in her mind, she'd never get any sleep. She turned off the television and the light and looked out at the full moon. She envied others who, somewhere on Captiva at this very moment, were looking at the same moon. She closed her eyes and fell asleep remembering the sound of Captiva's ocean waves.

Chapter Eighteen

SARAH

S arah and Ben had seen each other only a handful of times
since her father's funeral. The talk of marriage never
came up, and although she was grateful to not have the conversation, Sarah realized prolonging the inevitable was a mistake.

Her family was right: She had to confront Ben as soon as
possible. He had a right to find a woman he could build a
future with, but Sarah hated the idea of not ever seeing him
again. She enjoyed his company and wished things could stay
the way they were between them. She knew she was kidding
herself. Ben often talked about the family he would have in the
future. Sarah felt she had no right to keep those things
from him.

Promising to make dinner tonight, Sarah made plans for
Ben to come over to her apartment at seven o'clock. A chicken
was roasting in the oven, and the potatoes were almost ready to
mash. Sautéed green beans completed the dish, and she figured
since she would be delivering bad news, the least she could do
was bake Ben's favorite chocolate cake.

A bottle of their favorite Pinot Noir sat at the end of the
beautifully set table. Anyone would think she was planning a

romantic dinner. Romance was the furthest thing from her mind, and when the doorbell rang, she jumped, her heart beating fast.

When she opened the door, a delivery man stood in front of her with a long white box.

"Delivery for Ms. Sarah Wheeler. Sign here please."

Sarah signed the paper and thanked the man. Carrying the box to the table, she wondered who would be sending her flowers. Ben didn't usually do that. As a matter of fact, he thought flowers were, as he called it, "predictable."

He congratulated himself on being more creative than that, and he was right. Ben was famous for finding just the right gifts for her. She loved anything vintage, and her apartment reflected that fact. Among the items displayed several were from Ben over the years.

She opened the envelope and looked at the card inside.

"I know this isn't like me, but I figured the surprise was worth it. I love you, Ben."

While most boyfriends would send red, white, or yellow roses, Ben had found orange roses to satisfy Sarah's desire for individuality. Her eyes filling with tears, she started to cry but stopped herself.

Taking a deep breath, she looked in the hall mirror to make sure her mascara wasn't running. She was angry with herself. For a moment, she considered that there must be something wrong with her for not wanting to marry Ben.

She immediately stopped herself from thinking such thoughts. What was wrong with not wanting to get married? Nothing, that's what. She was tired of having to defend her position. The only problem was that no one was fighting her on this. The only person she was fighting with was herself, and she didn't know why.

Placing the flowers into a vase her mother had gifted her last year on her birthday, Sarah stood back and looked at the arrangement. Pleased with how the flowers looked, she carried them to a table in the living room. Before long, her doorbell rang again, and this time it was Ben.

They hugged, and Ben lingered in their embrace for a bit longer than usual.

"Your flowers just arrived. Ben, they're beautiful. Thank you so much. You didn't have to do that."

"I know I always say flowers are nothing special, but I thought tonight I'd be unpredictable for a change."

"Well, whatever you do, don't tell my mother that flowers are nothing special. You'd get a lecture on just how special they are."

"The last thing I want to do is upset your mother. She does like me, right?"

Laughing, Sarah didn't want to explain just how much his mother, and her family in general, loved Ben. It was going to be hard enough to say goodbye to him tonight, and the added burden of knowing how sad her family was about it didn't help matters.

"Something smells great. How about I pour us a glass of wine? I'll get the wine opener."

One thing Sarah hadn't considered was when to tell Ben how she was feeling. Should she approach the subject before or after dinner? It seemed the only right thing to do would be to enjoy their dinner and wine first, otherwise the talk would be strained, and the food might sit on the table, uneaten.

After a few minutes of enjoying their wine, Ben seemed distracted, as if he had something he wanted to talk to her about. It suddenly occurred to her that her plan to talk after dinner would fall apart because she hadn't considered Ben might have a plan of his own. As they sat on the sofa, Ben took Sarah's hands in his.

"Sarah, I've been wanting us to have some time alone so we could talk. We've been together now for a few years, and I think we have a wonderful relationship. There's no one else I want to spend my time with…my life with."

"Ben, stop. Please." She understood what was happening, and she was terrified what he might say next.

"Sarah, no, let me say what I came here tonight to say. I love you. I've known for months now that you were the only woman in the world for me. I can see what our life looks like in five years and beyond."

Sarah pulled her hands from Ben and got up from the sofa. She had to tell him now, before he got on his knees. Her heart beat fast with regret for having let things get this far.

"Ben. You're a wonderful man. Any woman would kill to be with you. I know how lucky I am to have you in my life. I want to be with you and experience things with you. But I can't do that as your wife. I can't marry you, Ben. It's not your fault. I've known for a while now that I don't think I'm the marrying kind. I don't want children. I don't want to be tied down like that. I should have told you sooner, but I've been confused and trying to make sense of who I am."

She wanted to say more, but the look on Ben's face made her stop. He was shocked, certainly, but he also seemed angry. Everything about Ben was usually calm and even-tempered. She had never seen him angry, and it surprised her to imagine this would be his reaction. She watched as he tried to regain his composure. When he spoke, he chose his words carefully but got right to the point.

"So, what you're saying is you don't love me."

"Ben. I never said that."

"Do you? Do you love me? Because, honestly, Sarah, you've never once said it in all the time we've been together. I've told you many times before that I loved you, and you never reciprocate. Answer my question. Do you love me?"

"Yes, Ben. I do love you. Of course, I do."

"Are you in love with me?"

Sarah was starting to sweat. The distinction of being in love rather than loving Ben wasn't anything she'd considered. It was ridiculous really because any other woman would have wondered about this months ago. She managed to be with a man for three years and never thought about being in love.

Now, confronted with the question, she realized that she'd ignored this aspect of their relationship because she didn't see its importance. Being in love meant you didn't think clearly. It meant clouding your decisions and reactions due to someone else. Things got messy and complicated when they didn't have to. It suddenly occurred to Sarah that she had approached her relationship with Ben as one would a business partnership, and she was unable to avoid that truth any longer with his question.

"No, Ben. Not like that. I'm not in love with you."

There was a moment between them where no one spoke. The silence was painful, and Sarah felt sorry for herself as much as she did Ben. Completely out of touch with her feelings, she thought she could logically and clearly explain her thinking to Ben, and they would make a joint decision how to move forward.

It hadn't occurred to her that emotions would get in the way and that the tension and hurt would overpower any plan she might have had. No one was crying, but no one was talking either. It was clear there would be no understanding between them. He was angry, of course, but now seemed resigned to the situation. There would be no mutual, respectful agreements between them. Instead, Ben got up from the sofa and walked to the front door. Turning, his last words to her stung.

"I don't know what it is that you're looking for, Sarah, but I know you won't find it if you're always running away."

Ben walked out of her apartment and shut the door behind him. There was no use in thinking they would mend their differences so that a friendship, at the very least, would remain. No, Ben was gone for good, and although he was hurt, Sarah was convinced, in time, he would see that ending their relationship was the right thing to do.

Of all her siblings, Sarah was the one who had the biggest reputation of being stubborn. The more someone pressured her or told her she was wrong, the more she dug her heels in and fought to prove that she was right. This time would be no different.

She walked into the kitchen and poured herself another glass of wine. Taking the chicken out of the oven, she mashed the potatoes, stirred the green beans, and plated her food. It was on the third bite that she had difficulty swallowing, and only then did she stop worrying about her mascara.

———

There was a message on her cell phone, and it wasn't until the next morning that Sarah realized it. Her brother, Michael, had left a message the night before.

"Hey, sis. It's me. I just wanted to let you know that we lost the baby last night. Brea is in the hospital, and I was wondering if you'd maybe meet me there. I came home just for a bit to make sure my mother-in-law would watch the girls. I'm heading back to the hospital. Brea had some complications, so they wanted her to stay overnight. It's just …I could use the support."

Sarah called her brother immediately.

"Hey, I just got your message. I'm so sorry, Michael. How is Brea?"

"She's going to be okay. It's going to take some time. It's hard right now."

Sarah knew her brother better than anyone, and she could hear it in his voice that he had been crying.

"Of course. You'll both be okay. Do you want me to pick you up or should I just meet you there?"

"I'll be at the hospital all day, so we better meet there."

"That makes sense. I'm getting in the shower right now, and I'll head over. Hey. I'm so sorry. I love you."

"I love you too. I'll see you soon."

She showered and dressed as fast as she could. Sarah worried about her brother, and although she knew in time the pain would lessen, the sadness would be overwhelming for a long time. She would be there for Michael and Brea and hoped they would be able to move forward and maybe try again to expand their family. Only time would tell.

When she got to the hospital, Michael was already in the room, comforting his wife. Sarah and Michael always had a special bond, and in the most difficult times of his life, he leaned on his sister. This time would be no different, and fortunately, her sister-in-law had come to be just as close to Sarah. Brea smiled when Sarah entered the room. With tears in her eyes, Brea reached for her, and they hugged.

Pulling a chair closer to her sister-in-law's bed, Sarah watched as her brother stroked his wife's hair and held her in his arms. The intimacy between them was so raw and vulnerable. Sarah marveled at what an amazing husband her brother had been to Brea. She watched the two of them complete each other's sentences over the years, and she was pleased to see her brother with the right person after a string of bad relationships. Brea was by Michael's side in everything he did, and their bond was the strongest display of what a good marriage should be.

As Brea wept, her husband consoled her and kissed her wet face. Sarah's heart broke for both of them, but she was comforted in knowing that their love for each other, and their commitment to their marriage would get them through this. They were in love with each other as much as ever, and it was a joy to watch such intimacy.

What Michael and Brea had was a beautiful thing, and for

the first time in her life, Sarah was jealous that she didn't have the same relationship with Ben. To know that it wasn't for lack of his trying but for hers made her sadness even more painful. Sitting before her was the best example of a true and beautiful bond, and for the life of her, she had no understanding of how she might experience the same thing with someone else.

In that moment, she understood that it didn't require a piece of paper to announce a commitment to another human being, but it wasn't commitment that Sarah was afraid of. She wanted a guarantee that whomever she gave her heart to completely would stay with her until the end of her life. She wanted assurances that no one would ever cheat on her, would ever want to be with someone else.

The fact that there could be no guarantees and that it would require a huge leap of faith was terrifying to her. No one was more committed to loving Sarah than Ben, and when that wasn't enough, she knew she wasn't in love with him. No matter her issues, letting Ben go was the right thing to do.

For the first time in her life, she was finally angry at her father. Sarah had never known that he cheated on her mother, but that didn't mean she didn't see that something was wrong in their marriage.

Maybe Lauren wasn't the only one who took after their mother. Refusing to admit the truth was starting to become a family tradition, one that she would have to challenge to stop the cycle. She wasn't sure she was strong enough to make that change, but she did know she was stubborn enough to do things her own way.

It was time to confront her fears and find the kind of love that her brother had. In that moment she promised herself that whatever road she chose to travel, it would never again be based on fear, and that was enough for now.

Chapter Nineteen

MAGGIE

Thanksgiving was two days away, and Maggie was busy getting the house ready for the holiday. Everyone, including her mother, would descend upon her, and she wanted this year to be as special as she could make it. It was their first Thanksgiving without Daniel, and Maggie planned to give the turkey cutting honors to her son Michael. He would sit at the head of the table for the first time, and she knew it would feel bittersweet.

The house was coming along, and her grandchildren had been over the day before to carve pumpkins. Names were given to each pumpkin, and Olivia insisted that her pumpkin, "Frankie," would sit on the top step at the front door, but Maggie explained that all the hard work of designing and cutting the pumpkins would be for naught if a squirrel got a hold of him.

The decision was made that all pumpkins would sit inside the house to keep them safe. Olivia's sister, Lily, agreed with her grandmother, and wrapped a towel around her pumpkin in case it got cold at night. Maggie was just happy to know she wouldn't have to pick up the huge mess any squirrel might make. Cora and Quinn copied everything their cousins did, so if the pumpkins were to stay inside, that was fine with them.

Once everything had been done, Maggie brought in as much wood as she could carry and stacked it inside the hearth firewood rack. A cup of tea and a blanket helped create her cozy setting. The box with Rose's journals sat on the coffee table in front of the fireplace. Maggie took the first of four journals out of the box and admired the worn leather. On the inside of the front cover, Rose had written her name and the beginning and ending dates of the words within.

Rose Johnson Lane
November 24, 1974 - May 28, 1975

How strange that the journal began on the same day as Maggie was reading it. What were the odds? She checked the other journals to see if there were earlier dates to read first, but no, the one in her hand was the first, and so, she began.

November 24, 1974

I'm not sure I know why I'm writing this down. It's not like this is a memory I wish to keep. Maybe when I'm done filling this book with my thoughts, I'll throw it into the fireplace and be done with it all.

Why is this happening to me now? I've struggled with this thought more than any other. After all, things don't just happen for no reason. I've always believed there was a purpose to everything. So, if that's true, that means this was supposed to happen and I'm supposed to learn something from it. I think that was my intention when I bought this leather journal. If I write it all down, I'll be able to understand the point of everything. So far, all I feel is anger and I'm worried I'll probably break this pen because of the white-knuckled pressure from my hand.

How does one write anger anyway? Should my letters look larger or darker? How can my pen scream onto the paper? That's what I want to do. I want to scream. I feel like I'm screaming already but no one can hear me. I made a promise that I plan to break already. I decided I wouldn't write his name in this journal. He doesn't deserve a place on these pages. But I can't keep that promise.

Robert.

It's funny how small, seemingly insignificant decisions have the power to change one's entire life. I remember the turtleneck he wore. It was olive-green. I remember thinking that color was perfect against his caramel-colored hair. His blue-green eyes staring back at me asking if I'd like to go to the school dance. I said yes, of course. It was destiny after all, and one doesn't mess with destiny.

My friend Ginny used to make fun of me for always saying that every-thing was pre-destined. She was quite right to tease me. Ginny has a wonderful marriage and husband now, so she must have known more than I back then. Ginny's never been confronted with a cheating husband. Gregory has never come home and asked for a divorce because of another woman. Leaving her without any choice about her future. Not like me. I've been left with no power to make any decision about anything. I've been left out of the conversation and presented with a fait accompli.

As I write these words, it suddenly occurs to me that there is something I can do. It's only a small decision but at least something that will make me feel like I have some control. I won't ever buy another piece of clothing in olive-green again. Today, a small decision, tomorrow I'll tackle some-thing else.

Maggie closed the journal and sat motionless, feeling stunned to find that Rose's husband had cheated on her so many years ago. He had asked Rose for a divorce because he was in love with someone else.

When Maggie confided in Rose, the thought had never crossed her mind that her friend could empathize with her struggles. Rose understood what Maggie had gone through and wanted to comfort and advise her the only way she could—by sharing her journals. These journals were a gift to Maggie in more ways than she had imagined.

Tears formed as Maggie realized the treasure she held in her hands. She had been disappointed to not have more time with her new friend. Rose had had a very full life, and Maggie would get to know that life better over time through her journals. She wanted to savor every minute and keep these minutes every day as her private visit with Rose Johnson Lane. Maggie didn't want to rush through each book, but just as she had done with getting to know Anne Morrow Lindbergh, she would discover these two women in her own way—quietly, with a cup of tea.

Thanksgiving Day arrived, and with it came the noise and laughter that Maggie had come to love about the holidays. Children always brought a special perspective on the day, and she loved to hear each of her grandchildren talk about their lives and what was new and exciting in their world.

No matter the visit, and Thanksgiving was no exception, Beth always managed to bring her laundry with her. According to her daughter, somehow her clothes smelled better when they were washed at her mother's house instead of her apartment.

Michael and Brea and their girls arrived after Beth, and Maggie was glad to see that her daughter-in-law was feeling much better.

Although she had no doubt that the sadness lingered and that it was too soon to think about having another child, Maggie watched her son and his wife appear upbeat and happy for the sake of their daughters. She felt their pain, and her heart broke watching how brave they had been through it all.

Lauren and her family arrived next along with their grandmother, who they picked up on the way. Maggie's mother still drove her car, but with it getting darker earlier these days, she didn't want to drive at night.

Sarah arrived shortly after Lauren, and Maggie was surprised she came without Ben. She didn't want to assume anything, but it didn't matter as her daughter Beth wasted no time getting to the bottom of her sister's relationship.

"Where's Ben?"

It was obvious to everyone but Beth that Sarah didn't want to talk about it. Maggie was about to step in and stop the interrogation, but Sarah indulged her little sister.

"We broke up."

Lauren was the first to respond.

"Oh, Sarah, I'm sorry. You know we all really liked Ben, but it was probably for the best."

"You're right. I feel good about my decision. After we all had that talk the night of the sleepover, I had to give it serious thought. You guys helped to get me to realize the truth. He is a great guy, for someone else."

Beth wanted details, and Maggie could see her daughter wasn't going to leave it alone.

"So, how'd he take it? When did you tell him? How did you tell him?"

Michael tackled Beth. "Really, Bethy. Can't you just leave it alone?"

Sarah stopped her brother. "No. Michael, it's all right. I figured I'd have to talk about it today, so we might as well get it over with."

Turning to her sister, Sarah continued, "I don't think Ben took it very well, actually. That's the part that's difficult. I mean, we'd been together a long time, and I think everyone, including Ben, just assumed we'd get married. Mom was right, though. It wasn't fair to keep dating when he wants marriage and kids. That's just not for me."

This was the first time Sarah's grandmother had heard of her granddaughter's aversion to getting married.

"Sarah Wheeler. What are you saying?"

Everyone knew how opinionated their grandmother was, but Sarah hadn't anticipated the conversation going in this direction. Maggie tried to stop the inevitable rush to judgment, but there was no stopping Sarah Rose McKinnon Garrison.

"I understand that perhaps Ben wasn't the right man for you, but you'll get married when you fall in love. The right guy is out there, Sarah, and once you decide to get married, the two of you will naturally want children. You've got plenty of time. You don't need to rush."

Even though Sarah was dead set against marriage and children, Maggie could see her daughter struggle to leave the possibility on the table, but she did so for the sake of peace.

"I'm sure you're right, Grandma."

Maggie marveled at the finesse of her daughter's response. She, like her children, had to constantly navigate the opinions and conversations of her mother. She was both proud and amused that her children had learned the art of talking to Grandma. That skill wasn't something you could teach; it came naturally to all of them over the years.

Not to be the only target of conversation, Sarah turned to her sister, Beth.

"By the way, weren't you going to do something about your little problem?"

Now all eyes were on Beth, and her grandmother didn't miss a beat.

"What's going on with you, missy? Do you have troubles in your love life too?"

Maggie watched her two girls go at each other and worried that an argument was about to ruin the day.

Beth glared at her sister but didn't want to make a bigger deal of things, so she answered her grandmother the best way she knew how.

"No, Grandma, I don't have troubles in my love life."

Beth looked down at her hands, and Maggie could see the sadness in her face. She turned to Sarah and shook her head.

As soon as Sarah saw Beth's face, she immediately regretted pressuring her.

Beth looked up at her siblings and continued, her chin sticking out in defiance. "Besides, there's nothing in my love life anymore. As soon as I realized his situation, I had no choice but to let him go. I don't regret it for a minute."

Sarah walked over to her sister and put her arms around her. "I'm so sorry, Bethy. I didn't mean to be such a jerk."

Beth smiled at her sister and punched her in the arm. "Yes, you did."

Maggie's mother looked confused. "No one tells me anything in this family."

Everyone laughed, and the tension evaporated as quickly as it began.

Maggie lit the candles on the table centerpiece and called everyone to the dining room. As they had done for many years before the carving of the turkey, each member of the family had a chance to say what they were thankful for.

One by one, with lumps in their throats and tears in their eyes, they shared what was in their hearts. When it was Maggie's turn, she looked around the table, and her heart was full.

"No one could have predicted when we sat around this table last year that this year would bring such change for all of us. Every year we share how blessed we are to have each other, and I know this year is no different. For me, what is different, is that I know that no matter what we all experience, we can always come home. In good times and in bad times, we can count on each other. We are a family, no matter where we are, and no matter what life throws in our path, we gain strength in that knowledge and will lean on it whenever we need to for the rest of our lives."

With tears in her eyes, Maggie looked at Michael and Brea.

"This year, we've lost two members of our family. It's been hard and a bit scary to think that we don't know what this next year will bring. But what I do know and what I'm most grateful for is that what this family can count on is our love and support for each other. No matter where we are."

As the family raised their glasses, Maggie remembered that months ago she'd decided not to allow Daniel to be part of her family anymore. She'd vowed to cut him out of her memories completely. Now that he was no longer with them, the loss of her husband brought more clarity and perspective.

She'd been foolish to think she could erase so many years and more foolish still to pretend he no longer had a right to be part of her family. Maggie realized that Daniel would always be with them, and that he would forever be a member of this family—her family, and that was as it should be.

Chapter Twenty

MAGGIE

B etween Thanksgiving and Christmas, there was much to be done. The lunch-bunch ladies always had their annual get-together to swap Christmas gifts. This year it would be hosted at Maggie's house, and she couldn't be more thrilled. She was worried that this year, after so much had happened, it would be impossible to enjoy the Christmas season, but she had been worried for nothing. Jingle bells and Christmas lights, as well as the smell of balsam fir, would beckon her into the holiday spirit.

The town center had a lovely Christmas celebration with local vendors selling their handmade items. The carolers sang near the gazebo on the town green, and the manger display was ever present throughout the month of December. The trees around the center shone with colorful lights, and this year there was no need for fake snow on the windows of the shops as a storm had dropped several inches of snow only two days before the annual tree lighting celebration.

Maggie stopped into the local coffee shop for a hot chocolate with marshmallows. Lauren asked her mother if they could meet at five o'clock because she wanted to talk to her about something that was on her mind. Maggie had noticed that she had seemed unhappy lately and worried that perhaps something was wrong in her marriage. Jeff was a great guy, and there didn't seem to be signs of trouble between him and Lauren, but experience told Maggie that appearances could be deceiving.

Lauren was bundled up in a coat accessorized with a large scarf, hat, and mittens, and for a minute, Maggie wasn't sure it was her daughter running toward her.

"Hey there. Are you really in there under all that? It's not that cold."

"Hi, Mom. Yes, it's me. And yes, I needed all this because I'm freezing. Don't worry, my eyes aren't covered so I'll be able to see the tree lighting."

"Well, let's get you inside. A nice cup of hot chocolate should warm you up."

The coffee shop was decorated with Christmas lights, and they had a fire going in the corner. The hot chocolate soothed Lauren, and her fingers warmed as she held her cup.

"Mom, I wanted to run something by you. I've wanted to talk to you about this for a while, but you've had so much going on I was reluctant to burden you with it."

"Lauren. You know you can talk to me about anything at any time. No matter what. It's never a burden to hear what's on your mind. I've always told you kids you can come to me whenever you need to."

"I know. Of course, you're right. I've just been wondering if I'm making too much of this. Here's the thing. I want to go back to work. I miss it. Part of me has been feeling like a terrible mother because I'll have to leave the girls in someone else's care, but I know that's absurd. Women who have children work outside the home all the time. It's just that I think Jeff has always said we'd miss so much of their lives if I didn't stay home. It's why I quit in the first place."

"Have you talked to Jeff about how you feel?"

"No. Not yet. I wanted to talk to you first because, well, it's possible we might need you to watch the girls more than you do now. I mean, we could pay someone, but..."

Maggie stopped her daughter mid-sentence. "Not on your life. Listen, I'm close by, and I'm sure we can figure something out. I think you should run it by your husband, though. Talk to him and see how he feels about it. You need to be sure it's not just the issue of who would take care of the girls after school."

Maggie heard herself talking and knew that even though she could convince Lauren that she would be able to help and that it was no bother, inside she was feeling something quite the opposite. For weeks, Maggie had been reading Rose's journals and found herself contemplating the idea of moving to Captiva and accepting her offer to take over Rose's property. She told no one of her feelings and as soon as she considered the possibility, she just as quickly pushed the idea away. Her family needed her here, not a three-hour flight away in Florida. Now, with Lauren's request, Captiva seemed to drift away as nothing more than a silly dream.

"Mom? Did you hear me? Where'd you go?"

"Oh, I'm sorry, sweetie. I was listening."

"Well, it would be a huge worry off our shoulders if you were there for the girls. I'm sure that would be Jeff's only concern. I'll talk to him tonight. I'm really excited about it. Thank you so much. You're the best."

Looking at her watch, Lauren got up from their table and grabbed her handbag.

"I've got to run. The girls are over at a friend's house, and I've got to pick them up. I promised them we'd make Christmas sugar cookies before dinner."

"What about the Christmas tree lighting ceremony?"

"Oh, right. Well, maybe you can use your phone and take a

video. I can't wait to get home and figure out how I'm going to talk to Jeff. I'll talk to you later and let you know how it goes."

Lauren bent down to give her mother a kiss and then walked out of the coffee shop and across the street, leaving Maggie sitting alone drinking her hot chocolate. When she was done, Maggie put on her coat, hat, and gloves and walked to the town square where the tree lighting was about to begin. She waved to people she knew and smiled at the children making a snowman. She dodged a few snowballs along her walk and remembered when her children were young and played in the snow. Snow angels had dominated her backyard, and there was the inevitable snowball fight with Daniel starting it before the kids realized the battle had begun.

When it came time for the tree lighting, they began counting backward from ten, and the crowd's excitement grew. Finally reaching one, the switch was flipped, and the lights came on, the people clapping as if something miraculous had happened. It didn't matter how predictable it all was; it was tradition, something you could count on, and that was what was being celebrated.

When it was over, Maggie walked back to her car and thought about what Christmas would look like on Captiva Island. It was now a punishment to think such thoughts, and so, just like in years past, she accepted what was, instead of what could be.

A call from Christopher was the last thing Maggie expected, but she couldn't have been more thrilled to hear his voice.

"Hey, Mom. Guess who's coming home for Christmas?"

"Oh, my goodness, Christopher. You're coming home? When?"

"I'll be flying back on the 23rd. The best part is that I'm going to be home for two weeks. I can't wait to see everyone."

Maggie started to cry, and she didn't care if her son could hear her. "I can't believe this. This is going to be the best Christmas ever."

"I've got to run. I've only got a few minutes to talk. I'll be seeing you very soon. Tell everyone I love them, and I can't wait to see them."

"I will. I'll tell them. I love you. Stay safe. See you soon."

When Maggie hung up the phone, she couldn't wait to call everyone to tell them that Christopher was joining them this year. The last two years during the holidays had been difficult for Maggie and Daniel. They wanted all their children home and safe, and it didn't really feel like Christmas without their son. After everything that they had endured these last months, it felt like the new year would be better for all of them now that they would end this year together.

She called Sarah first, then Beth and Michael, finally calling her mother. She wanted to save the call to Lauren for last since she had hoped Lauren's talk with Jeff would go well and they could talk uninterrupted. When she finally placed the call, she had an unexpected reaction from her daughter.

"Mom. That's great news. Thanks for letting us know."

"Lauren, is everything all right? Your voice sounds funny."

Lauren brought her voice down to a whisper.

"Everything's fine. It's just that we're in the middle of our discussion, and things are going in a very different direction than I expected. Let's put it this way: I didn't see this coming."

Maggie's timing had been off, and she hoped that her interruption hadn't made things worse for her daughter. It was hard to tell what was happening by Lauren's voice. She didn't sound upset, which was good, but there was something in her voice that told Maggie her daughter was surprised by Jeff's reaction. Maggie wouldn't be able to sleep tonight if she didn't get an explanation from Lauren about what was going on, but there was no way she would call her back and risk interrupting them again.

She knew her daughter well and figured that before the night was out, she would get a call from Lauren, and all would be explained. Lauren didn't disappoint, and about two hours after their first call, she called her mother back.

"I knew you'd call me tonight. I'm so glad. I was planning on staying up all night watching old movies and biting my nails."

"You know me too well, Mom. There's no way I couldn't call you back. I'd be up all night too."

"So, tell me. How did it go?"

"I hope you're sitting down, Mom."

"I'm sitting, and you're scaring me."

"Jeff hasn't been happy at his job for a while. I knew that because we've talked about it over the last several months. I wasn't sure where things were headed at his company, and even though I kept telling him to look somewhere else for a new job, he seemed reluctant to do it. I could never understand it except to think that maybe it was because he was so worried that he wouldn't be providing for his family, and it might be too big of a risk."

"Yes, I remember you telling me how much he hated traveling for his job."

"Oh, Mom. He hated that part of the job the most, I think."

"So, what happened? Did he finally quit?"

"No. Not yet. But get this. He wants to be a stay-at-home-dad. He was thrilled to hear I wanted to go back to work, because he wants to stay home with the girls. You know how much he loves all those cooking shows and is always preparing these gourmet meals? He wants to be the one to do all the cooking and cleaning and taking care of the children. He has no problem with my returning to work at all. In fact, it aligned with his dreams perfectly. Mom, I had no idea this would be his reaction, but it couldn't have been more perfect. We've both been thinking about this stuff for months and instead of sharing our ideas with each other, we've been terrified to approach the subject. Can you imagine?"

Maggie could hear her daughter smiling through the phone and was so happy for her and her family. Lauren was right: This would be a perfect fit for their family. It wasn't the traditional way many thought about what a family dynamic should be, but that was old thinking. It might have been different for her generation and the generations that came before, but families looked different these days, and there was no rule that said a man must go to work outside the home while the woman stayed at home to take care of the children. Times had changed, and Maggie was thrilled that her daughter had found happiness in her family life. She couldn't ask for anything more for her children.

As soon as Maggie hung up the phone, her mind started running a mile a minute. Was it possible? Could she really do this? Captiva Island had become an unattainable dream, and now, with Lauren's phone call, Maggie's world would change once more, opening the door for something else, a new beginning, and the hope for a life that she would design for herself, not one that fell into her lap based on other people's choices and needs. It felt right, and she wanted to celebrate her decision.

As the hours passed, the idea that she could not only move to Captiva but possibly run a business there began to grow. She didn't know a thing about running an inn, but surely, she would be able to learn. The fact that Paolo, Ciara, and even Chelsea were knowledgeable about the area and the local businesses would be a tremendous asset to her. She wouldn't really be running it all by herself since both Ciara and Paolo had an interest in the property. She would have to talk to them about it, of course, but Maggie was excited about the possibility of this new venture. The decision was made. She would move to Captiva and reopen the Key Lime Garden Inn.

Instead of her usual cup of tea, Maggie opened a bottle of Pinot Grigio, threw a few logs on the fire, and pulled the next of Rose's journals out of the box. Turning the pages to where she had left off, she settled into the corner of the sofa. Tonight, she, Anne and Rose would toast to the future—her future and hers alone. She raised her glass and thanked the two women who had become her best friends these last few months, and would no doubt be with her as she made the next step on her journey.

Chapter Twenty-One

MAGGIE

For the first time since she'd returned from Captiva Island, Maggie felt as if the weight of the world had been taken from her shoulders. The release of stress and tension about her life seemed to melt away, and a new reality had taken form in her mind. She was moving to Captiva Island after the new year, and she couldn't wait to share her news with everyone. Deciding who to tell first was her only concern.

She wasn't sure who would present any resistance to the idea, but she knew immediately who she could count on to treat her announcement as a declaration of independence. As soon as the decision was made, she wanted to video with Chelsea to let her know what her plans were for the new year. It was six o'clock in the morning when Maggie decided to call Chelsea.

"What's the matter? Are you okay? Who died?"

"Why are you always assuming the worst?"

"Because you never call me at six in the morning. Good news is typically delivered after the sun comes up, which won't be for another hour and fifteen minutes."

Maggie could barely contain her excitement.

"I'm glad you're horizontal because you might fall down when I tell you this. I'm moving to Captiva next month."

Chelsea sat up in her bed and almost dropped her phone.

"This has to be real because there is no way you would pull a trick on me like this so early in the morning. Oh, Maggie. I can't believe this. How did this happen? Have you been talking to a real estate agent behind my back?"

"Nope. You're probably not going to believe this, and I should have told you about this sooner, but I didn't know what I was going to do. Rose wanted me to take over her property, and she put Paolo's name on the deed before she died. He's going to hold on to it for a year and then put the house in my name if I want it. I didn't know how much I wanted it until the last few weeks. I've struggled with this decision. I mean, it's crazy, right?"

"Maggie, my love, I've come to believe that nothing is too crazy anymore. Besides, I think it's destiny. You were meant to come down here and meet Rose."

After reading Rose's journal, Maggie had some ambivalence about the word destiny, but the turn of events over the last few months made her believe there could be something to the theory.

"I don't know about destiny; all I know is that it feels right."

"How did the kids take the news?"

"I haven't told them yet. As a matter of fact, I haven't told anyone, not even Paolo. I'll probably call him next. I wanted to talk to people who would be supportive of the idea before I got any pushback or negativity from anyone. You were my first call. Now, aren't you glad I woke you up?"

"I'm honored, and excited, and now completely awake. I guess I'll get up and make coffee. My niece Kaitlyn is visiting, and seriously considering moving here permanently, which thrills me to no end. She's my sister Gretchen's daughter. She's a real fish the way she's in the water all day. My sister is furious with her because Kaitlyn doesn't want to go to college. Gretchen agreed to let her stay with me for a bit before she drags the girl off to school somewhere. I feel bad for the kid. I think my sister doesn't have a clue how to deal with her. She's always been closer to my nephew David and somehow, Kaitlyn's been ignored."

Raising three girls, Maggie had a lot of experience with female drama. When they were younger, her girls were much harder to understand and deal with than her boys, but over time she could see a shift in their personalities, and she found herself getting much closer to her daughters as they became adults.

"I'd like to smack my sister over the head about it, but I figure the best way I can help them is to let Kaitlyn stay here and see if we can figure out what it is that she wants. Getting away from her mother was the best way to go because I think if the girl stayed home much longer, they'd probably kill each other. I'm happy for the company."

"That's wonderful, Chelsea. I'm sure I'll get to meet her when I'm there next month. I've got to go myself. Lots to do. Wish me luck on telling my children. I hope they're supportive, but I'm prepared if they're not."

"It's your life, Maggie, just remember that. I'm so excited for you, and for me. I can't wait to see you again. Good luck and say hello to Paolo for me, and Merry Christmas."

"Merry Christmas, Chelsea."

Positive reinforcements would strengthen Maggie's resolve as the morning progressed, and by ten o'clock, she was ready to call Paolo. Her heart was racing as she placed the call. As soon as she heard his voice, she calmed down.

"Maggie. I'm so glad to hear from you. How have you been?"

"I'm doing well, Paolo. As a matter of fact, I'm doing great."

"I'm glad to hear it. You and your family must be getting ready for Christmas. I imagine you're looking forward to seeing your grandchildren open their presents."

"Indeed. I'm done with my shopping and all the presents have been wrapped and are hidden away. Paolo, I'm calling you because I wanted to let you know that I've changed my mind about Rose's property. I'd like to come back to Captiva right after the new year and live in the house. I'm certain I want to move there permanently, but I think the first step is to settle in there and see how it feels. I'm really excited about it. I think it's the right thing for me at this time in my life."

Maggie imagined Paolo's face at her words. She knew this was the news he was hoping for.

"Maggie, that is fantastic. I'm thrilled you've decided to come back. I've been praying that you would change your mind. This is the best Christmas present. I know you're making the right decision. Are your children supportive of the idea?"

"I haven't told them yet, Paolo. I wanted to call you and Chelsea first because I knew the two of you would be on my side. I'm not so sure about my children. I can only hope they'll be as happy about this news as you are, but something tells me I may have to convince them."

"If they want you to be happy, and if this is what will make you happy, then I have no doubt they will support you in your decision. Have faith, Maggie. I will be praying for you."

Paolo's soothing voice and his gentle demeanor was music to her ears. She was excited to see him again and was content to allow herself to feel that way without putting any pressure on herself to defend her feelings. He was her friend, and she wanted to be around him more and more as time went on.

"Thank you so much, Paolo. That means a great deal to

me. I will be in touch and let you know my plans after the holiday. Merry Christmas, Paolo."

"Yes, yes. That's wonderful. I will look forward to it. Merry Christmas, Maggie."

Maggie ended the call to Paolo and sat with her thoughts for a few minutes. She decided the best way to tell her children was to explain everything to them at Christmas Day dinner, which was only two days away. She wanted to wait for Christopher, who was flying in later tonight. It was important that all her children be present for the announcement, and hopefully, there would at least be a couple who would be on her side. Lauren, Michael, and Christopher would probably support Maggie's decision, but Sarah and Beth were the two she was most concerned about. Regardless, Paolo had made a good point when he'd said that if her children wanted her to be happy and if moving to Captiva would do that, then they should support her. That's what she would pray on, and she had two days to prepare her speech. Hopefully, two days would be enough.

The hours passed, and Maggie would now and again doze off in front of the fireplace only to hear a noise and wake, thinking it was Christopher. She had gone through much of the wood for the fire and needed to go outside to get more if she wanted to continue to stay up waiting for her son.

She put on her coat, boots, and gloves and opened the door to beautiful falling snow. Maggie loved the peaceful feeling of quietly falling snow. It was hard to describe, but there was an actual sound to it. She stood in place for a few minutes sticking out her tongue to catch the flakes. No matter your age, it was the kind of thing you did. Smiling at her inner child, she gathered up several logs and started to make her way back to the house when a taxi pulled up in front.

Christopher got out of the taxi and paid the driver. He ran to his mother as she dropped the wood, extending her arms out to reach for her son. Tears fell as they laughed and hugged. Maggie couldn't let go of him.

"I'm not letting you go, so stay with me here for a minute."

She squeezed harder before pulling back and looking at her son's face. Christopher, or as his siblings preferred to call him, Chris, was a handsome man. With light brown hair and crystal blue eyes, he had a smile that would light up any room. As many girlfriends as he'd had over the years, he never got serious about any of them, preferring instead to keep things casual. It was a good thing, too, because he'd always known he would go into the Marines at some point, and leaving a girlfriend behind would be difficult.

"How about I put my bag inside and help you with this firewood, Mom?"

He didn't wait for an invitation. He threw his bag into the foyer and ran back to pick up the logs Maggie had dropped. Maggie grabbed some too, and they made their way back into the house.

"You must be hungry. I made a lasagna earlier; would you like some?"

"Are you kidding, Mom? I love your lasagna. Absolutely, but let me get upstairs and take a shower first if that's okay. It's been a long day, and I'm really beat. My stomach is growling, though, so I don't care if I head to bed with a full stomach. Give me a few and I'll be right down."

Nothing made Maggie happier than to feed her children. She loved the sound of forks clinking against plates. Talking over one another and laughing was the best noise coming from either the kitchen or the dining room. She had known that her children would leave her one day, but until they did, she was determined to create memories that would stay with them their entire lives. Those memories were the ones they would share with their own children, and new traditions would be built around them.

Christopher inhaled the lasagna and a tall glass of milk. He was the only one in the family who loved drinking milk, and no matter how many times his sisters tried to get him to try almond or other nut milks, he refused. Maggie too had been a milk convert and loved to use almond milk for many things, but it was impossible to get her to change her tea-drinking habits. A splash of milk after pouring her tea into her cup without sugar was her preference. With Maggie's love of British royalty and its history, she was pleased to hear that Queen Elizabeth liked her tea prepared exactly the same way.

She had hoped to get a few minutes to talk to her son, but as soon as he was done eating, he headed straight to bed.

"I'm sorry, Mom. I'm tired. Is it okay if we talk at breakfast?"

"Of course. I'm just so glad you're home."

Maggie hugged her son and watched him climb the stairs to his bedroom. She was getting tired too, but she waited for the embers in the fireplace to turn black. Shutting off the Christmas tree lights, she walked back into the kitchen to put the lasagna into the refrigerator. She always hated going to bed with dishes in the sink, so she washed her son's dish and glass before turning off the rest of the lights. She would spend time with Christopher tomorrow, and the day after that, the rest of the family would arrive. Beautiful chaos would fill her heart once again, and she prayed that her announcement wouldn't ruin the family's holiday spirit.

Chapter Twenty-Two

MAGGIE

Christmas morning arrived with the usual excitement and anticipation. As Maggie lay in her bed, she remembered the many Christmases that had come before, and how her children couldn't wait to wake her and Daniel to come downstairs to see what Santa Claus had brought them. Luckily, they had a fireplace, so the chimney made it easy to convince them that Santa had really been there. Daniel would make sure to eat the cookies and drink the milk left for Santa the night before.

Now Daniel was gone, and her children had families of their own, but that didn't stop the excitement in her home. Soon they all would arrive with stories about the gifts under their trees. Maggie would explain that Santa had dropped off some gifts for them at her house as well. Those packages, combined with the gifts from their grandmother, were sure to make the visit an exciting one.

The house smelled of balsam fir and all the cooking that she had done the day before and early that morning. Christopher was up early, just like he had done when he was a little kid.

With a stern voice, Maggie yelled out to her son, "Christopher Edward Wheeler! If you're thinking about shaking those presents, you better think again."

Most everyone arrived at the same time, and there were screams of happiness to see Christopher was home safe.

Michael was the first to hug his brother.

"What time did your plane land?"

"Oh, man. It was a long flight. By the time I picked up my bag and got a taxi, it was around ten by the time I got home. Of course, the time didn't matter to Mom, who had a pan of lasagna waiting for me. I think she must have been cooking all day."

"Yeah, well, it's obvious you needed it. You're too skinny. I plan to fatten you up in the next two weeks."

Lauren let loose her two kids, and Michael's followed, running to check out the gifts under the tree.

"Two weeks? How did you manage that?"

"I'm not sure how I got so lucky, but I'm not complaining. I'm not the only one who got so much time off. Everyone is pretty much in the same situation as me. Not going to question it."

Beth and Christopher were the youngest and had been close growing up. She jumped into her brother's arms and tackled him to the ground.

Michael tried to pull them apart.

"Hey, stop it. This is a peace zone. No fighting here."

Maggie loved all the noise and activity but shook her head at the way some things never changed no matter how old her children were. Watching Beth and Christopher tussle on the floor as adults made her laugh. The next generation had a different focus; they were already shaking some of the packages to guess what was in them.

The table was set with Maggie's finest china and crystal, and a second table was covered with appetizers and chocolate for the children. An eggnog bowl without alcohol was placed on the buffet with bottles of rum and cognac to the side if anyone chose to add them to their glass.

Maggie decided to wait to make her announcement until after everyone had opened their gifts and finished eating. If things didn't go the way she had hoped, she didn't want to spoil the traditions of the day. After the food was consumed and the wrapping paper stuffed into a plastic trash bag, everyone settled in the living room. Her grandchildren were preoccupied with their toys, so Maggie decided it was time.

Hitting a spoon against the side of her eggnog glass, Maggie asked everyone for their attention.

"I have some news I want to share with you all, and I want you to hold off asking questions or making comments until I'm finished saying what I have to say. I've been thinking about this for some time, and an opportunity was presented to me about a month ago that I've been considering. If you all remember, I told you about the woman I met in Florida who passed away last month. It seems that it was her wish for me to take over her property in Captiva. It was called the Key Lime Garden Inn. I've been researching it, and it has quite a history. It's a beautiful property. She was hoping that maybe the inn could be restored and reopened as well, and I'm considering that as a real possibility."

Sarah moved forward and looked as if she was about to speak, but when she saw the look on her mother's face imploring her to wait, she sat back into the sofa and crossed her arms over her chest.

"Rose didn't want the courts and lawyers to go through a long-drawn-out estate settlement, and since she has no living children, she decided to put the house in a friend's name for a year. By putting the house in someone's name who only will keep it for one year, it was Rose's wish that I would take it over in time. She felt allowing a full year would give me time to accept her offer. Her friend doesn't really want to own the property; he is just doing it as a favor to Rose so that I might take it over from him, sooner rather than later, that is. After one year, if I don't take over the property, he has the right to sell the house and use the proceeds as he sees fit."

Sarah couldn't hold back any longer. "Then let him sell the house. You're not bound to take the property just because this woman wants you to, Mom. Are you thinking about running an inn in Florida? Tell us you're not seriously considering this."

Beth was next. "You're going to sell this house, the house we all grew up in? Is it because of Dad and what he did?"

Christopher looked confused. "What did Dad do?"

Lauren shook her head and gave her brother a look that said, *Not now.*

"This has nothing to do with your father. For once it doesn't have a thing to do with anyone else but me. This is something I want. No one is forcing me to move to Florida. And by the way, I haven't said I was going to sell this house. I don't need to sell it to move. The house on Captiva is paid for, and there are plenty of funds that Rose has left to pay the taxes on the property for quite a while. But I might add, if the time comes that it feels right to sell this house, then I will do it. That is my choice as well. For now, I'm not selling."

For a few minutes, the room went quiet, and then it seemed everyone was talking at the same time.

Sarah asked, "What about this house? You can't leave it empty."

Michael was next. "When would you go? How long will you be there? Are you going to come back here at all?"

Beth wanted to know who else Maggie had told. "What does Chelsea think about this? Did you call her? What about your lunch-bunch ladies? Have you told them?"

Sarah again voiced her opposition. "I don't understand how you can pick up and move to Florida just like that. I mean, why not just go down for the winter months and then come back here? People do that all the time. They call them snowbirds, I think."

Only Lauren and Christopher kept their opinions to themselves. Maggie didn't answer any of the questions but stood firm in her decision. She'd expected some resistance and wasn't surprised by her children's objections, but she would address everyone's concerns in the coming days. After all, she didn't have all the answers just yet, and she also knew this would not be the last discussion on the subject. That was fine with her. She was prepared to deal with each of her children as the questions came. But the one thing she would not do was change her mind. Maggie was determined to do what she wanted and not let anyone create a speck of doubt in her mind. This was something she knew was right for her, and after everything she had been through, that was all that mattered.

It was Maggie's mother who spoke next.

"I think it's a wonderful and brave thing you're doing, Maggie. I wish I'd had the guts years ago to do what you're doing. If you want to run an inn at the North Pole, I'd support you. You can do anything you set your mind to. I believe in you, and I'm very proud of you."

Maggie wanted to cry but did everything in her power not to fall apart in that moment. Those words meant everything to her. No matter how old she was, she would always seek her mother's approval, and now hearing her mother tell her that she was proud of her made the decision to move to Florida that much sweeter.

"Thank you, Mom."

Smiling, her son Christopher joined his grandmother in supporting his mother's decision. "I think it's great, Mom. When will you go?"

"I want to go next month. I've got a few things here I want to settle, but I'm pretty sure I can make it happen soon after the new year."

Lauren got up from the sofa and put her arms around her mother. "Looks like we're both starting a new journey soon. I'm so happy for you, Mom. I know you've wanted to make a change, and now you're doing it. It's not easy to fulfill a dream, but when you do, it's life changing. I know it will be that way for me too, and I couldn't have done it without your encouragement and support."

Sarah was the only one who was still skeptical. Ever the cautious one, she reluctantly joined the others in supporting their mother. "I'm glad you're not selling the house. It's good to have a fallback just in case Florida doesn't turn out like you expect. I think between Beth and me we should look at any contract you sign. Don't sign anything until we've had time to look things over."

Sarah looked confused and turned to Lauren.

"And what new adventure are you embarking on, may I ask?"

Lauren looked at her husband, and he nodded his head, encouraging his wife to share their news.

"I'm going back to work, and Jeff is quitting his job to stay home with the girls."

Michael smiled and extended his hand to his brother-in-law.

"Sounds like a sweet deal to me."

Brea looked at her husband and said, "Don't get any ideas."

Beth had a different response. "I want to live here. I want to move back home. Can I stay here while you're in Florida?"

Maggie was surprised. "Beth, honey, you don't have to ask me silly. This is your home. Of course, you can live here. In fact, I love the idea. You can take care of the house and the plants. I'll have my mail rerouted to Florida, so you won't have to deal with that, but otherwise, I think it's a great idea."

Christopher couldn't help but tease his sister.

"Seriously, Mom? You're going to trust your plants to her? She'll kill them all."

Beth paid him no attention. "As it happens, I'm actually getting more interested in gardening these days. I'd like to keep the garden going and grow and eat organic vegetables. I'm considering becoming vegan. You don't have to worry about the plants or the garden, or the greenhouse for that matter. You'll see."

Maggie had no doubt her youngest daughter would take good care of her garden. Like her other children, Beth succeeded at everything she tried, and it made Maggie happy to know that at least one of her children might have inherited her green thumb.

Michael filled his eggnog glass to the top and announced it was time to toast the new year and their mother's new adventure.

"To Mom. Here's to the best mother in the world. May she find this new journey to be everything she dreams it will be. We love you, Mom."

Maggie was proud of her children. She knew that change was difficult for all of them, but they weren't the type to shy away from a challenge. She looked at each of them and realized she had half-expected she would have gotten a lecture from them about her responsibilities. She'd anticipated the need to defend her choice but instead found that it was not necessary because in the end, all her children really wanted for their mother was for her to be happy—and she was.

Updating Christopher on the days leading up to his father's death would be difficult, but it had to be done. She had moved beyond the events of the last few months, and explaining everything to him would only bring her back to relive it all. Maybe it would be best coming from her daughter Lauren. Maggie was flying high on a cloud of joyous anticipation, and the truth was she didn't want to lose that feeling. She made a mental note to talk to Lauren about it tomorrow. For now, she and her children would continue to enjoy the holiday. She decided that everything else would fall in place as it should.

The ebb and flow of Maggie's life was changing because for the first time she made the decision to put herself before anyone else. She was secure in her choice. Everything she would do going forward would be with the singular focus on creating the life that she had always wanted. She knew she couldn't forget the past—that would be impossible. In fact, she knew it was important to remember every detail of the past. It was the only way she would be able to move forward.

She was in large part, a new person, one who wouldn't give regret a minute of attention. That was the old Maggie. That was the Maggie who questioned her choices, who worried what others might think of her. Now a confident woman, Maggie Wheeler would live her life the way she pleased, and no one was going to stop her.

Chapter Twenty-Three

SARAH

The letter had a return address of a Ms. Emily Wheeler, 21 Craven Court, Hull, MA. Sarah's heart began to race, and she was already angry before she opened the envelope. It was from her half-sister, and although Sarah was not happy to see it, she wasn't surprised. She'd known it was only a matter of time before the young girl reached out to the family.

Inside was a Christmas card with a typed letter folded inside it. A photograph of a young blond woman stared back at her. Emily was striking, and to Sarah looked like a Wheeler. There was still disbelief in her mind, but in her heart, she could tell that the girl was her father's daughter—her half-sister. Sarah unfolded the letter and took a deep breath.

Dear Sarah,

I know that I don't have to explain to you who I am, as a lawyer told me that you and the rest of your family have been made aware of my existence. I'm sure it came as a shock to all of you that we have the same father. I'm writing this letter to you without my mother's knowledge, because, well, I think she would disapprove of what I'm doing.

As difficult as this is for all of you, the fact that I was born isn't my fault. I hate that your family has suffered not only the loss of our father but any security you had about his life and your own. It may be crazy for me to ask this of you all, but I very much would like to be in your lives. I know my mother would probably be upset that I want to get to know you, but I'm 19 years old and I can make my own decisions. Legally, she can't stop me.

You probably don't want anything to do with me and I can understand your feelings, but I am hoping that you all might understand mine. I'm an only child and always wanted to have a brother or sister in my life. When I found out about all of you, I was so happy because I felt my dream was coming true.

I'd love to meet with you and the rest of my siblings one of these days and I'm open to anything you might suggest. We could all meet at a coffee shop, or I can come to your house. I'd like to make a promise to you that if you tell me to go away and leave you all alone, I will. I have no desire to push myself on any of you. I only want to be in your life if you want the same. Otherwise, there is no point in continued communication.

I will give you my email address and cell phone number so you can get in touch. Please don't contact my mother because I don't want to have to explain all this to her and end up arguing about it.

I look forward to hearing from you.

Emily Wheeler

Sarah wasn't surprised at all that Emily had contacted her. She knew what her mother did not: that it was only a matter of time before the young woman reached out to one of them. The letter sounded like Emily wanted nothing more than to have a relationship with her siblings, but Sarah still didn't trust the situation.

She considered throwing the letter away. After all, if she did, Emily would take it as a sign that they wanted nothing to do with her. The only problem was she couldn't trust the girl to stay away even though she'd stated that she would. No. She would have to contact her siblings to get their opinion. She figured the best way to get everyone involved was to have a video chat. She sent a text to her siblings, and everyone agreed to meet online later that day. She decided to call her mother to let her know what was happening.

"Oh, Sarah, I'm not sure about this at all. How do you feel about it?"

"To be honest, Mom, there is a part of me that wouldn't mind getting to know her, but I also am afraid to open that door. I'll feel better once I get everyone else's opinion on the matter. More importantly, I really need to know how you feel about it because if you'd rather we politely explain we can't meet with her, then that's the end of it as far as I'm concerned."

Sarah hated how her father had created such a mess, but it wasn't Emily's fault, and she shouldn't be punished because of it. Still, her mother would have to come to terms with her father's other family, and Sarah would have to help her if Emily came into their lives.

"I think that it's up to you and your siblings to decide. If you all would like to meet with her and after you do, you feel she is someone you want to get to know better, I'll accept that. I trust all of you to use your gut on this and get back to me on how it goes. Try not to put too much emphasis on how I'll feel about it because truthfully, as long as you all are happy, then I'll be happy too. I'm not ready to meet her, and honestly, I don't think it's at all necessary. She wants to have brothers and sisters, and I can't argue with that."

Sarah marveled at how brave and strong her mother was. She couldn't imagine dealing with everything her father had put her mother through. Maggie Wheeler was tough, and Sarah was incredibly proud of her.

"That sounds right. I'll get back to you after our video call."

"Good luck, honey. I'll talk to you later."

Instead of a video call, they all decided to meet at Lauren's house. It was impossible for Michael to get away from work, so he sent a text with a quick answer to the question of whether to meet with Emily.

Beth had something to say about that. "Are you kidding me? For such an important decision he gives a thumbs-up emoji? That's just lazy."

Lauren corrected her sister. "Not lazy, Beth. Busy. There's a difference. The guy is working around the clock these days. Cut him some slack."

The coffee pot was full, and Sarah was the first to pour herself a cup. "Anyone else want a cup of coffee? I had an early morning meeting, and I swear I'm still not awake."

Lauren and Christopher each grabbed a cup out of the cabinet and added cream and sugar in their coffee.

Sarah started the meeting. "So, what do we think of this situation? Anyone think it's a good idea to meet with her or should we just say no, thank you and close the door on this? Mom seems open to whatever we agree to, which surprised me. I don't think I would be as forgiving as she seems to be."

Both Beth and Christopher, being the youngest of the siblings, were intrigued and wanted to give Emily a chance. Christopher offered his opinion first. "I think it can't hurt just to meet her. You can't force a relationship with someone. It has to grow slowly in time, but she is our sister, after all."

Beth corrected him. "Half-sister."

"That doesn't make her any less our sister. It sounds like she wants to be not just in our lives, but a part of this family. I think she sounds sad, to be honest. How can we turn away someone who is just asking to connect with her brothers and sisters? I say we at least give her a chance."

Lauren spoke next. "You all have to remember that it isn't just Emily who will be in our lives. It's inevitable that her mother will somehow end up coming face to face with Mom. I don't want that to happen."

"Exactly what I was thinking," Sarah said.

"Listen, Mom isn't even going to be here pretty soon. Maybe we plan to meet Emily after Mom has left for Florida. At least that way she won't be subjected to either Emily or her mother, at least for the foreseeable future."

Lauren nodded her head. "Christopher makes a good point. Mom will be gone in a few weeks. Why not set a date to meet with Emily after Mom's left for Captiva?"

"Wait. What about Christopher? He won't be here in January. We have to do it while he's home," Beth said.

They all looked at him, but he just shrugged. "C'mon guys, It's no big deal. I'll support whatever you decide. I have no problem letting her into our world if you all don't. I think it's more important to do it after Mom leaves for Florida."

They all agreed that they would meet with Emily, but also made a promise not to commit to anything other than giving her a chance to talk to them. Once the siblings were onboard, it was Sarah who would get in touch with the young woman and set a date sometime toward the middle of January. It looked like the new year held more surprises for every member of the Wheeler family, and most of it relied on faith to move forward. That and a desire to protect the family and their mother no matter what.

Sarah decided to email Emily instead of calling her. Since Emily lived south of Boston, everyone agreed to meet at The Scarlet Oak in Hingham. Sarah thought it best to reserve a room where they would have privacy to talk. It was also a way to let Emily know that they were invested enough to travel to her, and to give her a chance to be heard without the noise of other patrons. They set the date for the first week in February to be certain their mother would have left for Florida.

Within minutes of her hitting the send button, she received a response.

Hi Sarah,

Thank you so much for agreeing to meet with me. I know exactly where that restaurant is, and I think it's a perfect location to meet. I can't wait to meet you all. Please stay in touch and let me know if anything changes.

Emily

Once the meeting was set, Sarah put Emily out of her mind for the time being. She had other, more important issues to deal with. There were things happening at her job that she had no control over that could impact her immediate future. Rumors about a layoff had been spreading in the last two weeks. At first, she'd ignored them. It wasn't the first time she'd heard talk of a layoff. Eventually, she came to believe the rumors were credible and her counterparts in other departments were already being let go. It was only a matter of time before she would be out of a job. Sarah was certain that although she had been with the firm for several years, the cuts were more to align the organization with changes by department, and there was nothing she could do about it.

She wondered if it was time to look for another job. It couldn't hurt to put feelers out to see what was available in her field. She had worked so hard for years to get the position she currently held, and the thought that she would have to start over pained her deeply. Her father was the person she'd admired most when it came to understanding money and how to invest. Her father had built a reputation in the business for always beating the market, and Sarah wanted to be just like him. Until now, she'd never worried about losing her job. Her reputation as Daniel Wheeler's daughter had gotten her in the door, but it was her keen eye for buying and selling stocks at the right time that had garnered her the most respect. How she could be let go after all these years was impossible to comprehend.

She had a meeting first thing in the morning with her boss, and she had a feeling the meeting was a bad omen. She hadn't talked to her boss in a few weeks. He had been traveling and was out of touch during that time. It was impossible to know exactly what the meeting was about since he was vague about the agenda. Worrying about it would do her no good and would probably keep her up half the night. The only thing to do was to turn in early and try to calm her nerves. Tomorrow would come soon enough.

———

Her boss was almost always late, and today was no different. Sarah remembered reading somewhere that people who were late all the time were arrogant. Being late meant that you wanted others to not only wait for you but to schedule their lives around your schedule. An image of small planets circling one larger planet immediately came to mind, and if she wasn't so nervous, she'd have probably laughed at the thought. As it was, she sat in her chair like a child waiting for the principal to scold her for doing something wrong.

"Good morning, Sarah. I'm sorry for keeping you waiting."

John never apologized or explained himself. The fact that he was doing so now, was not a good sign.

"No problem, John. How was your trip?"

"Productive. We've got Jameson and Clark Corp. It was touch and go there for a bit, but I got them."

Jameson and Clark Corp. was a big get. Her boss was the head of an institutional investment firm and he had just landed a major client. There would be talk on the street about it for weeks.

"That's fantastic. Congratulations."

"Thank you. Listen, Sarah. The reason I wanted to meet with you this morning is because there are going to be some major changes here, and it's going to impact every department, yours included."

Sarah's heart beat faster, and she was starting to sweat. She could hear the words before he said them and thought for a minute, she might have her first ever panic attack.

"You've been an incredible asset to the firm all these years, but there really is nothing to be done at this point to save your position. I've thought about you more than some of the others, to be honest. I've wracked my brain trying to find a way to keep you onboard, but there just isn't anything I can come up with that wouldn't be a step back and possibly a cut in salary. I'd hate to put you in the position of having to make that choice. You're too good for that. I've consoled myself thinking that leaving here will give you a chance to flourish somewhere else. I have no doubt that another firm will hire you in a heart-beat. My assistant Paula has a file with all the information you'll need regarding your severance package. You'll get six months full salary, so you'll have plenty of time to find another job. Think of this as a positive thing."

Somewhere halfway through John's speech, Sarah could only hear noise. She couldn't focus on what he was saying until his last words. "Think of this as a positive thing." Was he kidding? Did he just say those words? How could this be anything other than a disaster for her?

Her soon-to-be ex-boss moved toward her to assist her out of the chair and out of his office. Not because Sarah's legs couldn't support her, but because their meeting was over. It was over because he decided it was over. To remove her from his office as soon as possible would prevent there being any further discussion about her situation. Arrogance was certainly one way to describe John Corbett, but there were a few other words to describe what she thought of him in this moment. She was too stunned to speak, but she had no doubt that in the coming days she'd find her voice again, and it wouldn't be pretty.

Chapter Twenty-Four

MAGGIE

A get-together with her lunch-bunch friends was planned by Rachel, who wanted to do something special for Maggie as a bon voyage party. They were sad to see her leave Andover but were happy to see their friend beaming with happiness and joy.

Maggie wasn't the only person who was beaming. Her friend Jane seemed particularly upbeat, and Maggie was happy to see that she had managed to come out of her depression to enjoy life again.

"Jane, you look gorgeous. What's different?"

"I decided to start wearing more colors instead of just white. What do you think?"

Jane twirled around, and Maggie applauded her outfit.

"I approve. Those colors are perfect for you. I've always wanted to get a personal analysis of my colors and style. I have no idea what I'm supposed to wear, but I've always loved pink, so I decided pink must be my color."

"Maggie, I'm going to confess something else that is making me happy these days. I've met someone on one of those dating apps. He's wonderful. I never thought I'd find someone like him. I thought it was too late for me, you know, too set in my ways. It's funny what can happen when you open your heart, isn't it?"

Maggie wasn't surprised to hear this news. The truth was that after their last encounter, Maggie felt Jane was able to release the guilt she was feeling. Jane had finally allowed herself to admit that she wanted someone to share her life with.

"I'm glad, Jane. I'm truly happy for you."

"Thank you, Maggie, and thanks for being such a dear friend."

The day was a perfect send-off, and Maggie promised her friends to attend future lunch-bunch get-togethers with Chelsea via video.

The holidays had passed, and her son Christopher returned to Iraq. After the blessed chaos of the holidays, Maggie both loved and hated the quiet that returned. She had no idea what next year's holidays would bring, but she didn't want to think that this last Christmas was the last time they all would celebrate at the house at 12 Willow Lane. Beth would be living there, and it was very possible that Maggie would return to celebrate with her family, but she couldn't be sure what Christmas in Captiva would look like. For now, it was enough to take one day at a time and let the days and months ahead develop as they would.

Her children helped her pack, and they were with her the day the moving truck came. Even Michael was able to take a little time off to be there for his mother. Amongst the activity, Michael pulled his mother to the side and whispered, "Mom. Before you get on the road, I wanted you to be the first to know. Brea is pregnant. It's really early, and honestly we don't want to tell anyone else at this point, but we couldn't let you go without telling you."

"Oh, Michael. I'm so happy for you both. Of course, I

won't say a word to anyone. Promise me you'll keep me updated on how Brea is doing. I don't care what time of the day or night it is. You call me, okay?"

"Absolutely. I have to say it's a strange feeling."

"What do you mean?"

"Of course, we are thrilled about the baby, but it's also bittersweet. Brea talks about the baby we lost, and I can see the sadness in her eyes. I worry that maybe this is too soon."

"To lose a child is the most heartbreaking thing a woman can go through, Michael. It's hard on the father as well, but when you carry life inside you, there is a bond that is only between a mother and her child. Brea will feel that sadness for the rest of her life, but it won't stop the joy of living and of celebrating a new life. Focus on the new baby but always give her whatever time she needs to talk and cry over her lost child. Things will get better; you just have to give it time. Be patient with her and with yourself."

"Thanks, Mom. You always know the right thing to say."

The movers stacked the boxes into the back of the truck and then added a few pieces of furniture that Maggie wanted to keep with her in the Captiva house. They would leave for Florida right away, getting there a day before Maggie and Sarah. Since Maggie had marked the outside of the boxes, Paolo would have no trouble knowing where to place them inside the house. He promised to text Maggie when they arrived.

Now that Sarah wasn't working, they'd decided that she would accompany her mother on the road to Florida. Maggie was happy to have the company. Sarah's disappointment with her job was all-consuming these last few days, and it was Maggie who had the idea that Sarah should join her. It didn't take much convincing, and before she knew it, Sarah was already packing her bags. She would fly home after Maggie was settled in her new house and then would begin the task of actively looking for a new job.

There were tears and lots of hugs before Maggie and Sarah began their journey. They wanted an early start, so the goodbyes would have to happen at dinner.

"Listen to me, all of you. I'm not the only one taking a journey. Each of you have so much to look forward to in this new year. I want to hear from all of you, and often. Send texts or emails or, and I say this with all the love in my heart, make a phone call. I know, I know that might be asking too much, but I want to hear your voices."

Lauren hugged her mother and tried not to cry.

"You know you're going to hear from me. I'm used to talking to you every day. That's not going to stop just because you're fifteen hundred miles away."

Maggie handed the keys to the house to Beth with a warning that if she killed all the plants, Maggie would come back and take the keys away.

"You don't have to worry about a thing. You're going to be pleasantly surprised when you see how well I do with the garden. All kidding aside, Mom, please don't worry about anything. We've got this."

Maggie didn't want to take one last look at her house. She was ready to begin her new life in Florida, and there was nothing about the Andover property that needed to be preserved in her mind. It was all there, memories carved into her heart that she would take with her as she traveled south. For Maggie, the only real thing of value was her children, and they would be with her every step of the way.

The women got on the road at six o'clock the next morning. It was still dark out, but with so many miles to travel they needed an early start to get to Richmond, Virginia before dinnertime. They decided that Sarah would drive for the first leg of the trip, alternating every four hours. To drive straight through to Captiva from Massachusetts would be exhausting, so they decided to do the drive in two days. Sarah made the hotel arrangements for each night. It was cold in Massachusetts, and there was snow on the ground. They would see a change in the weather the farther south they traveled, and Maggie couldn't wait until the warmth of the Florida sun was upon them.

The long drive gave Maggie the time she needed to talk to Sarah about her job. She was a captive audience, after all, and although she had been complaining all week about getting laid off, she'd never talked about what her plans were going forward.

"Honey, I know it's been a difficult week, and I'm not trying to put any pressure on you, but I thought maybe since we have all this time together, you might want to think about what's next. Have you thought about what you might want to do?"

"I don't really know, Mom. I mean, have you ever felt like your identity is tied up in what you do and not who you are?"

Maggie thought her daughter was smart enough to already know the answer to that.

"Well…"

"I'm sorry, Mom. I wasn't thinking. Of course, you understand what I'm talking about. It's just for so long I've seen myself through Dad's eyes. I can honestly say that until this happened to me, I hadn't even considered that. I'm sure you already knew this, but I doubt I would have listened to you if you told it to me. It's like my world has been upended, and I don't have a clue what to do about it."

She empathized with her daughter and could only give her the advice she wished someone had given her years ago.

"Sarah, I'm starting to believe that things do happen for a reason. We may not understand what that reason is, and that's okay. When you don't know what to do, it's best you don't do anything except stop, take a break from any major decisions, and figure out what makes you happy. I wish I had done that myself. Here I am at my age finally getting around to doing that very thing. I have tremendous faith in you and your decisions. I know if you take some time, you'll feel better about whatever decision you make. It's why I suggested you drive to Florida with me."

Laughing, Sarah said, "So the idea that I come with you to Florida was your way of stopping me from making a rushed decision before I was ready? Nice move, Mom. I'm impressed. I didn't see that coming."

"Of all my children, you are the most stubborn. You might have said no to me and went headlong into a mess you'd regret. I didn't know what you would do, but I'm glad you said yes."

Maggie could tell that her daughter was considering everything she had said. They rode for many miles in silence, feeling no need to talk. Eventually, Maggie shut her eyes and fell asleep, only waking when it was her turn to drive.

"How long was I out?"

"About an hour and a half. It's your turn to drive and maybe my turn to nap."

Maggie gave her daughter a tired smile and yawned. She was surprised she was able to sleep since her adrenaline had been working in overdrive ever since they got on the road. They swapped seats, and Maggie pulled the car out onto the highway as Sarah settled in on the passenger side.

"I've been giving a lot of thought to what you said earlier. I loved working toward a goal. I think it's the competitive spirit that I have, but I'm not certain it's the industry I love. I think I loved Dad and wanted him to be proud of me."

"Sarah, your father was incredibly proud of you. He was proud of all his children."

"I know, Mom. That's not what I mean. What I'm trying to

say is in some small way, I think I was trying to compete with him. I wanted to not just do the same work he did; I wanted to beat him at it. Remember when I was little and how I'd challenge Dad to all kinds of competitions? It didn't matter whether it was a card game or touch football. I thought he'd respect me if I beat him. There were times I wished I was a boy."

Maggie was surprised to hear her daughter say those words. "For heaven's sake, why?"

"Because he never pressured Michael or Chris to be anything like him. He was thrilled with them no matter what they did for a living or what paths they took in life. But with us girls, it always felt like we had to do that one more thing to get a positive response out of him. Once we got that one more thing, it was off to the next one more thing. It wasn't easy to believe he was proud of me no matter my choices."

It was hard to hear Sarah talk this way about her father, but Maggie had to admit, she understood exactly what Sarah was trying to say. She was right. Daniel never pushed the boys the way he did his daughters, and it never seemed as if they had finally arrived at the place where he was satisfied.

"I'm sorry, honey. I always felt that he wanted only the best for you girls. I always believed everything he did and said was with that in mind, but I can understand how you feel. How do you think this knowledge will affect your career plans?"

Sarah smiled at her mother and placed a hand on her shoulder.

"I know that Dad did the only thing he knew how to do. I don't believe he ever wanted to hurt Beth or Lauren or me. It's just that I've spent so many years chasing something that I never stopped to see if I truly wanted it. I wanted Dad to love what I did, I never considered whether I loved what I did."

"And so?"

"And so, I'm going to take some time to figure out what I

want. I want to love what I do. I'm going to take after my mom for a change. I think she's a pretty smart woman, and I only wish we'd had this talk years ago."

"I'm happy for you, Sarah. You are doing what I should have done a long time ago. I can't wait to see what you come up with. Whatever it is, you've got my complete support. On another subject, have you seen Ben at all recently?"

"No. Not since the day that I told him I wasn't in love with him. I'm pretty sure I won't hear from him ever again, and I wouldn't blame him. Trying to be 'just friends' with someone who wants to marry you never works. I'm sorry about that too because we were good friends, and I'd love to support him in whatever he does in the future. Instead, I have to be happy for both of us that we didn't make a serious mistake by marrying."

"Speaking of marriage, I heard you say that you don't want to get married or have children. Have I understood correctly?"

Sarah rolled her eyes. "I'm assuming Michael talked to you."

"Well, that and you've mentioned this before. Is this something you'd like to talk about? After all, we've got plenty of hours ahead of us."

Maggie could see that Sarah was starting to regret accompanying her to Captiva. It was not Maggie's style to interrogate her children, but she worried that Sarah was making another rash decision.

"Mom, please don't take this personally, but Dad's behavior and your marriage in general has had a strong impact on me. Not to mention what Luke put me through. His cheating on me didn't help. I'm still trying to work this out in my head, and I'm not there yet. Honestly, when I'm ready to talk, I'll come find you, but for now, let me figure this out in my own way."

Maggie tapped her daughter's knee. "You've got it. No more talk about marriage and babies. I'm hungry. How about you? I've got some sandwiches and bottled water in the cooler in the backseat. Why don't you pull them out, and we'll eat while I drive?"

If nothing else, the food would keep them from talking for a while, and her daughter could once again be at peace with her decision to be Maggie's travel buddy. She made a mental note not to pressure Sarah about anything for the remainder of the trip. This was precious time with her daughter, and she wanted nothing to spoil the mood.

Chapter Twenty-Five

SARAH

The next two days were more relaxed than Sarah expected. She couldn't remember the last time she took a vacation and the tension that she usually felt in her shoulders was already gone. She had mapped out the directions, with stops along the way to stretch their legs and breathe the fresh air. Bathroom breaks almost always had Sarah coming out with bags of chips and her beloved chocolate covered raisins. She would worry about gaining weight some other day, but she let the drive to Florida be justification for snacks.

With a stop in Virginia and then Jacksonville, Florida, the women arrived at their hotels close to dinnertime. Room service in Richmond was all they had energy for and with a long hot shower and an early to bed evening, they had more than enough energy to begin again the next morning.

Maggie's phone vibrated and Sarah laughed.

"That's got to be Lauren. We've been gone only one day and she's already checking up on you."

Maggie looked at her phone.

"No. It's Paolo. The movers arrived this morning. He just wanted to let me know."

Her mother's face lit up and she was smiling.

Sarah wondered about this man who had made her mother blush.

"So, Mom, tell me about Paolo. You haven't really said much about him other than his relation to Rose and her property."

"What? Oh, there's really nothing to tell. He's just a very nice man, that's all."

Sarah decided not to press, but she couldn't wait to see for herself what is was about him that made her mother smile the way she was.

When they made it to Jacksonville, they were surprised by the number of restaurants and shops along the road leading to the hotel. After checking in, they decided to eat at the Italian restaurant across the street. The hostess grabbed two menus and Sarah and her mother followed her to a booth toward the back of the restaurant.

"How about we get a bottle of Merlot?"

"That sounds great, although I expect I'll fall asleep the minute we leave this place if I drink too much."

"That's a good thing, Mom. If we get to bed early again tonight, we can leave for Captiva around five or six. If we do, we can get there before noon. How does that sound?"

Her mother's smile broadened, and she nodded her head.

"I'm game. The sooner we get there the better."

Sarah had no problem adding garlic bread and a salad to their order. She was starving and it was hard to decide what to eat with such an extensive menu. Sarah finally decided on the gnocchi and her mother selected the risotto alla Milanese. Everything was delicious, and the women took their time to fully enjoy the food.

By the time they returned to their hotel, it was eight o'clock and they were much too sleepy to bother with showers. Instead, they decided to get up early and take their showers before getting on the road again. Sarah set her iPhone to wake them at five o'clock the next morning.

When the alarm went off, Sarah called for room service, and they ordered coffee and bagels to go, showered and checked out of the hotel. The last leg of the journey was little more than five hours and would get them to their destination before lunch.

Within hours, they were on MacGregor Boulevard which would lead them to the Sanibel Bridge. Except for a stop to get a smoothie at the Sanibel Outlets, her mother only allowed one short stop as soon as they were over the bridge. Sarah wanted to get out of the car and take a few pictures with her iPhone. There was enough wind to entice several windsurfers to venture out on the water, and they glided along the white caps at record speed, with Sarah taking videos of their adventure. She took several pictures of the landscape and then got back inside the car.

"One of these days I'm going to try windsurfing. I would live on the beach if I could. That's what I'll do for work. I'll be a beach bum. Sound like a good idea?"

"Sounds like fun but not a good idea. Wait until you see Rose's house. You're going to fall in love just like I did."

"I'm sure I will, but I need to correct you, Mom. The house is going to be your home. You've got to start thinking that way."

Until now, her mother hadn't talked about the property as if it were her own. Sarah wondered if, by not admitting her ownership, she might be leaving the door slightly ajar to keep alive the possibility of returning to Massachusetts. She could hear the concern in her mother's voice.

"I know you're right, Sarah, but I'm so happy, and I'm worried if I say the words out loud, I'll jinx myself. Not to mention there's a certain truth to the fact that I've made such a big deal about this I'm going to look foolish if it doesn't work out."

"Is that all? I thought maybe you were having second thoughts."

"Not on your life. I'm certain this is the right thing to do. The moment I decided this was the life for me, I never looked back."

"Then why care what anyone else thinks? So many people have dreams that are never achieved because of fear. You've already succeeded because you put yourself out there and let the universe do the rest. That's the best way to approach it. Everything after that is just icing on the cake."

Her mother smiled and nodded her head. "You're right. No more negative thinking."

They decided to drive to Chelsea's house first. Her mother sent Chelsea a text letting her know that they had reached the island. Chelsea and her niece Kaitlyn were sitting on the porch when their car turned the corner into the driveway. Chelsea came running down the stairs with her arms outstretched and screaming.

"Woohoo! You made it! You both must be exhausted. That's a long drive."

Sarah stretched her arms and legs and then ran into Chelsea's arms. "If I'm stiff, imagine how Mom is feeling."

Hugging Chelsea, Maggie made a face and said, "Hey, I'm not that out of shape."

Kaitlyn extended her hand to shake Maggie's and then Sarah's. "Nice to meet you both."

Chelsea clapped her hands and then put her arm through Maggie's.

"I've made a nice lunch for us. It's all set up on the lanai. I'm sure you want to get over to the house but relax and have a bite to eat before you go over there."

Kaitlyn said to Sarah, "I've been at the beach and left my

stuff there. I'm headed back to the beach right after lunch if you'd like to join me."

Sarah looked at her mother. "What do you think? Do you need me to go with you?"

"No. Don't be silly. I'm sure Chelsea can bring you over to the house later, and if you're still at the beach and I feel like it, I might join you. Just stay in touch via text to let me know where you are. Take whatever you need out of the car before you go, though."

The ladies enjoyed their sandwiches and lemonade. As soon as she finished her food, Sarah changed into her swimsuit and pulled a few things out of the car. Kaitlyn and Sarah headed to the beach, leaving Chelsea and Maggie alone.

Sarah loved the beach, and just like she had done on previous visits with her family, began collecting seashells as soon as she dropped her stuff off on a beach chair.

Kaitlyn was rubbing suntan lotion on her legs and looked over at Sarah. "You're going to love it here. Captiva is beautiful. I don't think I'm ever going home."

"Oh, I've been here lots of times. I used to come here with my family almost every year since I was a kid."

"Oh. I didn't realize that. Lucky you. I wish my parents took me with them when they traveled. I used to think their travels were nothing more than an opportunity to get away from my brother David and me." Kaitlyn thought a minute and added, "Correction. They wanted to get away from me, not my brother."

Sarah remembered being nineteen and figured Kaitlyn was exaggerating just a bit.

"Oh, I'm sure that's not true."

"It certainly felt like it. These days we disagree on everything. Right now, our biggest disagreement is about college. I don't want to go, and my mother is forcing the issue. I don't understand why. I mean, college is so expensive. Either she has no concerns about me having tremendous school debt or she has no qualms about paying through the nose for my education. I just don't get it. I'd have thought she would be thanking me for saving her, and possibly me, tons of money."

"What does your father say?"

"Oh, he's on Mom's side. I don't stand a chance unless I refuse to go home and just stay down here with Aunt Chelsea. Even then, I'm not sure I'll get my way."

Sarah never imagined that she'd ever give advice to a nineteen-year-old, but for what it was worth, she felt she had some experience with her sister Beth that might come in handy in this situation.

"You know, Kaitlyn, running away won't solve anything. If I had to guess, I'd say that your parents want you to have a good education and a chance for job opportunities you wouldn't get without a degree. There are plenty of kids who would love to be in your shoes, kids who would be thrilled to have the chance to go to college. It isn't just about the books and what you'll learn in class. It's also about living away from home for the first time, learning how to prioritize your time, testing your ability to work as part of a team and taking your first steps at adult responsibility. Not to mention some fun parties you'll attend. If you don't go to extremes with either working hard or partying hard, four years from now, you'll be a completely different person. I know that's how it was for me."

Kaitlyn considered Sarah's words. It was rewarding to think that she might be making a real difference in the young woman's life. She wasn't interested in becoming a mother, but Sarah wondered if this experience was anything like what it would be to talk to her own daughter. She pulled her beach chair closer to Kaitlyn and poured suntan lotion into her hands. Rubbing her palms together, she motioned for the girl to turn with her back facing Sarah. She rubbed the lotion on to Kaitlyn's back and gave her one more piece of advice.

"When I was young, I had a period in my life where my mother and I didn't get along at all. I think I was around seventeen. I pretty much thought that she not only didn't understand me, but that she didn't understand what it was like to be a young girl of seventeen. Trust me when I say this. My mother and your mother both were young once, and they haven't forgotten what that time was like. As I grew older, I was surprised to learn just how smart my mother was, and how much we had in common. My advice to you is not to push your mother away. It's hard to talk to someone who doesn't want to listen. When two people only want to be heard but don't want to listen, nothing gets accomplished. You want your mother to hear you. I get that, but you need to listen to her as well. Give her a chance."

Whether Kaitlyn would take her advice, Sarah couldn't be sure, but she hoped some of what she said had gotten through to the girl. They spent the next couple of hours getting sun and swimming in the ocean. An occasional good-looking guy would walk by their chairs and Kaitlyn would point them out to Sarah. Although several years older than Kaitlyn, Sarah had to admit that the girl had a good handsome guy radar, and fortunately she only selected guys that were about her age. When the opportunity presented itself, the young girl walked toward the water to get a closer eye on them. Before long, Kaitlyn would strike up a conversation, leaving Sarah to enjoy the solitude for a bit. A few minutes of peace and a chance to drink in the surrounding beauty was all Sarah really wanted.

Chapter Twenty-Six

MAGGIE

M aggie was happy to spend some time with her friend, and Chelsea couldn't wait to show Maggie a couple of new paintings that she had created since Maggie left the island.

"These are beautiful, Chelsea. Are you planning on selling them?"

"I'm not sure. I have a friend in Sanibel who has a gallery and asked if I'd like to show my work there. I hadn't considered it, but ever since she offered, I've been thinking of nothing else. Do you think I should?"

"Oh, definitely. Are you kidding? Do you realize how many tourists stop in galleries on their vacation? Landscape art like yours sells like hotcakes. Trust me, my friend, you'll be a big hit."

Maggie kept looking at her watch, anxious about seeing Paolo. Talking to him about her ideas for the inn was making her excited and nervous at the same time. *What if he thinks it's a bad idea? What if he likes the idea but doesn't have time to help?* She could never run the place alone. Her nerves were getting the better of her, and she figured she'd better talk to Paolo before she chickened out.

"Chelsea, I've really got to get over to the house. I've got a few things I need to talk to Paolo about. I've got to send him a text to let him know I'll be there in a few minutes. Thank you for lunch. I'm so happy to be back here and thrilled we'll be neighbors."

Chelsea put her arm through Maggie's and walked her down the steps to her car.

"Listen, if there's anything you need, you let me know. I'll come by tomorrow and see how you're getting along."

Maggie got into her car and waved out the window at Chelsea. She knew that there was no way her friend could wait until tomorrow to see her place. Maggie fully expected Chelsea to come sometime later that afternoon and wouldn't be at all surprised if she walked over with Sarah and Kaitlyn when they were done at the beach.

Maggie sent a text to Paolo to let him know she would arrive shortly. When she got to the house, the gate was already open, and she was able to pull her car onto the shell-lined driveway to the back near a separate carriage house with three doors. Paolo was standing in front of the building waiting for her.

He ran to the car and opened her door. They embraced, and it was the first time Maggie had been so physically close to him. With his hand on her back, she could feel its strength and ruggedness. He carried her luggage into the house and offered to show her around the property, but Maggie declined.

"Paolo, would you mind if I explore a little on my own first? I'll come find you after I walk the grounds and a bit of the house. I'm not sure I can explain, but I want to be very quiet and listen as I walk."

"Of course, if you wish. If you need me, I'll be near the shed."

She wasn't sure any words would make him understand her meaning, and she didn't want to offend.

"I want to feel the history of the place, maybe even Rose's voice."

Paolo smiled at her but said nothing, just nodded his head.

She felt slightly embarrassed by her request. "You must think me silly, or maybe a little crazy."

"Not at all, Maggie. There have been many people in this house over the years. Family and friends, some famous people as well. I understand the need to remain quiet so those voices can be heard. If it helps you even a little, I have heard some of those voices myself."

It made her heart happy to know that he understood her meaning, and that he wasn't offended. She should have known that Paolo would have had many moments like the one he described over the years. Perhaps when they had time they would sit and talk about those moments.

"Paolo, there is something I need to discuss with you. If you'll indulge me these few minutes alone, maybe there is somewhere we can sit and talk after?"

He nodded and said, "How about we meet inside in about an hour?"

He left her to walk the grounds alone. From her time with Rose, Maggie had been able to see a few plants and shrubs, but there was much more that she couldn't see. Rows of key lime trees lined the property, and beyond the house near the fence there were several more fruit trees. Maggie ran her hand along the branches, and although there was no fruit visible, she was stunned when a thorn cut her finger. Maggie knew a lot about gardening, but she had no knowledge of the Florida key lime tree. She would have to educate herself about her newly acquired garden, and she was grateful that she had a willing teacher in Paolo.

After licking her cut, she continued her walk among the shrubs and fruit trees. It was a glorious place, and she had to pinch herself to believe it was really hers. The only thing that would make it more perfect was if she could share it all with her family. She didn't linger on that thought too long because she didn't want her journey to begin with regret of any kind. This was what she wanted, and Maggie knew how important it was to be grateful and to thank Rose for believing in her when she could barely believe in herself.

It was time to go inside. She wanted to first stop at Rose's chair. The woman had passed only two months ago, but her spirit was still very present. Tears brimmed in Maggie's eyes as she moved around the room, her fingers lightly touching picture frames—memories of people long since passed. Rose's books were the jewels in the room. It was the area that Maggie had yet to explore. Nothing in this room would be changed, she promised herself. It would be the only way she could preserve what was gone. She knew it was a promise made from desperation, the kind one makes to oneself to keep things from changing. She was planning only minimal changes throughout the property, but this room would stay untouched.

She climbed the stairs and walked through several bedrooms, all decorated in a combination of Victorian lace and seashells. Every room had a vase filled with flowers, she assumed cut from the garden. Small cedar chests sat at the foot of each bed, and the lace curtains moved gently, letting the ocean air fill the rooms.

The floors creaked, and the fragrance of lavender and chamomile was strongest in Rose's bedroom. The windows were closed, and the shades lowered. The room stayed in darkness, which was so unlike the rest of the house. Maggie made a mental note to ask Paolo about it. Perhaps it was Ciara's idea, but Maggie was certain that Rose would have wanted the outside light to permeate her room.

It was a little more than an hour later when she heard Paolo come into the kitchen from the back door.

"Have you had enough time, Maggie? Do you need more? I can come back in a little while."

"No, Paolo. This is fine."

They sat across from each other at the kitchen table. Maggie's nerves had passed, and she was anxious to hear Paolo's opinion of her idea.

"Paolo, I've given this some thought, and I'd like to reopen the Key Lime Garden Inn."

There, I said it. No going back now.

Paolo sat motionless for a few minutes. She could see him struggling to answer her non-question.

"Maggie, I'm not sure you understand what something like that would take. It's a very difficult and exhausting business. You need many people to help you."

"Yes, I know. That's why I'm talking to you about it. I want you to help me re-open the inn."

She could tell that she might not have calculated the pressure she was putting on the man. It never occurred to her that he might feel he had been forced into a corner. He had feelings for her, she knew that. But she never wanted to take advantage of those feelings, and she certainly didn't want him to feel she had manipulated him. Looking at his face, she was suddenly sorry she'd ever brought up the subject.

"I'm sorry, Paolo. Of course, it's a crazy idea. I've been looking at pictures online of what the inn looked like, and I guess I got carried away."

"No. Maggie. It isn't that."

"Then what is it?"

It was obvious that she had touched a nerve somehow. She wasn't sure what was upsetting him so, but clearly, something was wrong. She had worried about jinxing herself, and Paolo's reaction convinced her that she was right to worry. This house might be hers one day, but today, right now, it was Paolo's, and she had no right to push him this way.

"Maggie, when you called me to say that you decided to move to Captiva and move into this house, my heart practically jumped out of my chest. But as fast as I was to get so excited, I had to remind myself that your coming here might be a temporary thing. You've already been through so much, there was a good chance that within a few months you would regret your decision and move back to Massachusetts. I couldn't let myself believe you would stay here, and that you would see that this is your home. This is where you belong."

Paolo wiped his eyes with the back of his hand. "Now that you tell me you would like to reopen the inn, I'm going to let my heart not be afraid to hope…"

"Oh, Paolo. I didn't realize. Of course, I want to stay here. I should have trusted that this is the right thing and made you aware of my commitment to this place."

Watching Paolo's reaction broke Maggie's heart. She'd never wanted to bring him one minute of worry, and she could see that perhaps his feelings for her were growing faster than she was ready to think about, but maybe now it was a good idea to address the elephant in the room.

"Paolo. I want to make sure you understand how I feel about you. I must admit there is something between us. I think we both know that to be true. It's just that I'm not ready to think about starting another relationship with anyone just yet. It's too soon for me. As you said, I've been through a lot in the last year. I'm still processing that. With all my heart, I want to stay on Captiva Island and reopen the Key Lime Garden Inn, and I want to take ownership of it, just like Rose wanted. Beyond that, all I can promise is that I will take it one day at a time, and you can be certain that I wouldn't entertain the idea of living here and reopening the inn without you. I can't promise anything more than that right now."

Paolo was smiling, and Maggie wondered if he believed her words. He certainly acted as if he'd heard her, but the twinkle in his eye spoke of something more. A confidence maybe that, in time, she would come to feel for him what he felt for her now. She was fine with that.

"Maggie, I understand everything you say. And yes, I will help you reopen the inn. It's going to take more than just the two of us, you understand. I have several people on the island that I can call to help us. But first I will need to speak to people at the Town Hall. Of course, the property is zoned for business, so that is not a problem. I would expect that there might be one or two people who would take issue with the reopening, but in general I believe the plan will be well received. Many were disappointed when the inn closed down."

Maggie was beyond thrilled to hear that Paolo was on board.

"I understand. Thank you so much, Paolo. I can't wait to get started. Although I haven't a clue what comes next."

"What comes next is you entertain your guests. I forgot to close the gate, and if I'm not mistaken, you have three women coming up the driveway as we speak."

Chapter Twenty-Seven

MAGGIE

Maggie got up from the table and looked out the window. She knew that Chelsea wouldn't be able to wait to see the property and would most likely walk over with Sarah and Kaitlyn when they came back from the beach. Sure enough, after only a few hours, the three women arrived at Maggie's front door.

"Mom. This place is beautiful. You've got a tropical secret garden here. You'd never know what was beyond the gate from the street. I can't believe this is where you're going to live."

"Paolo, this is my daughter, Sarah. My friend Chelsea you've met, and this is her niece, Kaitlyn."

"Very happy to meet you all. If you will excuse me, I've got to speak to my sister."

Turning to Maggie, he said, "I will talk with you tomorrow, Maggie."

"Thank you, Paolo."

Sarah watched Paolo walk out of the house and to the rose bushes at the back of the yard before she turned to her mother and smiled. Maggie tried to ignore her daughter, but Sarah wasn't having any of it.

"What?"

"So, that's Paolo? The gardener? I thought he was some old guy. Mom. He's gorgeous. I mean, like movie star gorgeous. Why didn't you ever say anything?"

"What exactly do you think I should have said? He's my friend and he's not just the gardener, he's a huge help around here, not to mention the actual owner of this property at the moment."

Her daughter rolled her eyes at her mother and decided to leave the topic alone—for now.

Maggie gave them a tour of the property, both inside and out, and laughed when Sarah decided right away that one of the bedrooms would be hers.

Watching Sarah flop on the bed, Chelsea agreed it was a perfect bedroom for Sarah.

"Well, you certainly can't go wrong no matter which room you choose. What I can't get over is how many bathrooms this place has. I'm truly jealous of that."

Maggie looked at Chelsea and asked, "For heaven's sake, what do you need four bathrooms for?"

"I don't. I just want them. There's a difference."

Ciara came into the room to see if anyone wanted something to eat or drink.

Maggie introduced the group to Paolo's sister.

"Oh Ciara, thank you, but we're fine. This is my friend Chelsea and her niece Kaitlyn, and this is my daughter Sarah."

Ciara nodded her head and said, "Pleasure to meet you all."

Turning to Maggie, Ciara said, "I'm heading over to the community soup kitchen. I wasn't planning to go there today but apparently there have been so many people in line, they really need more help. We also have so many deliveries, they need more people to help accept the items as well as distributing the food. It's been crazy busy lately. We need all the hands we can get."

"Would you mind if I go with you? I'd be happy to help out if it's hands you need," Sarah asked.

Kaitlyn spoke up, "Me too. I'd like to help if you don't mind."

Chelsea looked at her niece in astonishment.

Ciara nodded and said she was thrilled that she'd have two more people to help.

"That would be wonderful, thank you. Just so you know, we'll be working until seven o'clock. If that works for the two of you, I'll pull the car out front, and we can go."

Sarah smiled and nodded her head.

"Yes, that's fine. I'm ready."

Kaitlyn wanted a few minutes to put makeup on. Sarah hardly ever wore makeup. She was blessed with beautiful clear skin with only a hint of freckles over the bridge of her nose. She had the same cornsilk-colored hair as her mother, and it was straight and just below her shoulders. She figured it was easier at the beach to keep her hair in one long braid and thought there was no reason to change it just to do a bit of volunteer work.

Maggie pulled Ciara aside. "Ciara, before you go, there is something I'd like to talk to you about. I was wondering if Paolo talked to you about our plans for the property?"

"Yes, and I think it's wonderful."

"Do you think you'd like to stay and help us get this place up and running? I don't want to assume anything, and I know how busy you are with your volunteer work, but I know we'd love it if you could find the time."

"Absolutely, I want to help however I can, and I'm sure I have a few friends who would be happy to help us as well. I think it's fantastic what you and Paolo want to do, and I think many people on the island will be happy about it too."

Maggie was thrilled to hear that Ciara would join them. Chelsea looked as though she was about to faint watching the three women leave them.

"Did I imagine it, or did my niece just volunteer to help out at a food pantry?"

"You did not imagine it. Both girls are on their way to Ft. Myers with Ciara. Why so surprised?"

"Maggie, my dear, Kaitlyn has barely moved off the lounge chair since she's been here with me."

Maggie was a little surprised that Sarah wanted to spend her vacation time volunteering at a food pantry, but she wasn't as shocked as Chelsea was. Maggie was proud of her daughter and knew that Sarah always had a desire to help people, be it with financial advice or any other kind of assistance. Maggie made the connection between Kaitlyn offering to help because Sarah offered first, and she didn't rule out the possibility that Sarah's act of kindness and generosity was rubbing off on her.

Putting her arm in Chelsea's, Maggie smiled at her friend. "How about I show you the rest of the property and we have ourselves a lovely cup of tea? It just so happens that I packed my favorite tea kettle, teacups, and tea, and I know exactly which box they're in. We can drink it in the garden."

"Sounds like heaven. Lead on."

Maggie made tea and carried the tray to the table under the pergola. The sun was getting stronger every day, and she was happy to have a shaded area in the garden where they could sit. Maggie guided Chelsea to the table and remembered the time, not that long ago, when she'd sat at this very table, meeting her dear friend Rose. It was the spot where Maggie had received Anne Morrow Lindbergh's book *Gift from the Sea*. She would also remember that day as the beginning of her belief that the woman who came to Captiva on vacation so many years ago might hold the key to a greater understanding of herself.

It wasn't just the last seven months that beckoned Maggie to the island. She believed in her heart that Captiva was always meant to be her home. Meeting Rose and learning about Anne Morrow Lindbergh convinced Maggie that the three women were kindred spirits. They encouraged her along her journey to island life and deep introspection. This was exactly where she was supposed to be in this moment, and she felt her entire body align with this truth.

Chelsea admired Maggie's tea set and the quiet peacefulness of the garden.

"This place has a magic about it."

"You feel it too?"

"I do. I can understand how you were drawn to it."

Changing the subject, Chelsea was interested in what was new in Sarah's life.

"I'm so happy that Sarah came with you. I understand she lost her job recently and she broke up with Ben. What happened there?"

"Yes, she's trying to figure out her next move. I told her to take a break from making any decisions right away and just enjoy a small vacation down here. As far as Ben goes, while I was sad to see that relationship end, I think she did the right thing. She wasn't really in love with him, not the way you should be if you plan to get married. Although that's another story for another day. Apparently, she's not certain she wants to ever get married or have children. I think there's more to it than her thinking she's not the marrying kind. Only time will tell."

Chelsea was as direct as usual. "I'll tell you what she needs. When she falls head over heels in love with someone, she'll get married and have children. She just hasn't found the right guy yet. When you know, you know. So what if it wasn't Ben? She's got plenty of time. She's young yet. There's no rush. I say she should play the field and enjoy herself before getting tied down."

"I'm sure you're right. These next few days, she's going to enjoy the beach and won't worry about anything. When she gets back home, her first plan is to find work that she will truly enjoy. That's what I wish for her. What do they call that? Meaningful employment?"

"When we were young and looking for work, we were happy just to get a job. We weren't raised to think of work as meaningful. It was plenty meaningful if we got a paycheck."

Chelsea always made Maggie laugh, and she envied her friend's directness, unfiltered as it was.

"So how about you tell your friend what's going on?"

Maggie was getting up the courage to talk to her friend about the idea of turning the house back into an inn. "Chelsea, I haven't told you everything. I mean I've been thinking about the history of the house."

"You mean that it was an inn years ago?"

"You knew? Why didn't you say anything about it?"

"What was to say? It was an inn, so what?"

"Well, one of Rose's wishes was that the property return to its glory days. She tossed out the idea that maybe I would consider reopening the inn."

"Are you kidding me? She wants you to turn the house into a bed and breakfast?"

"Well, actually, there's a difference between an inn and a B&B."

Chelsea rolled her eyes. "You know perfectly well what I'm talking about. Is running a business like that something you want to do?"

"Truthfully, until Rose's proposal, it had never entered my mind, but when she wrote to me about her wishes, I couldn't stop thinking about it. I mean, the property is huge. I'm not sure it's even practical for me to live in such a big house all alone. It almost begs to be something more than someone's residence."

"Now, Maggie. Don't start thinking that Rose will haunt the house if you don't turn it back into an inn."

Maggie laughed. "Don't be silly. I'm not thinking that at all. At least I wasn't until you brought it up. I talked to Paolo about it, and he's agreed to help me. I couldn't do it without him and his sister's help." Maggie looked down and sheepishly added, "And yours."

"How did I know that was coming? Listen, my love, I'm here to help you in any way I can. You know you can count on me. Besides, think of all the fun we'll have, and how much I love to cook. By the way, what is the difference between a bed and breakfast and an inn, anyway?"

"Well, from what I've been able to research, it seems that inns provide more food and are a bit larger than a bed and breakfast. I'm not sure breakfast is required, but dinner generally is. The best thing we could do is research the industry and the Key Lime Garden Inn specifically. It might be nice to recreate what it used to be, along with some more modern touches."

They got up from the table, and Maggie walked Chelsea to the gate.

"Stay in touch. I'm ready to jump right in whenever you need me. By the way, I'm sorry I never got to see Rose before she died. Every time I called Paolo to see if Rose wanted company, he said she wasn't really having people come by other than hospice."

"I understand. Thank you for trying, Chelsea. I really appreciate it. I'll talk to you tomorrow. You are the absolute best, you know that?"

Chelsea nodded her head in agreement. "I am, aren't I?"

Chapter Twenty-Eight

SARAH

The food pantry was about a forty-minute drive from Captiva, and while Kaitlyn sat in the front passenger seat due to anticipated car sickness, Sarah sat in the back asking a million questions about where they were headed and how she might be of service.

"You don't need to worry about having something to do. No matter how many volunteers we get, we can always use more."

As they made their way through downtown Ft. Myers, the image of tourism and beach shops were nowhere to be found. Sarah remembered leaving Captiva to go to Ft. Myers beach a few times, but Ciara was driving through a part of the city she had never seen before.

"How often do you work at Coastal Community Outreach, Ciara?"

"I'm there every day, actually. I only come to Captiva in the early morning and stay until one o'clock. I have more time at the food pantry now, of course. I only stayed at Rose's place to make sure she had her breakfast and lunch, and I would prepare a dinner for her and leave it in the refrigerator so it would be easy to heat up. I have longer days at Outreach now."

She could hear the sadness in Ciara's voice.

"You must miss her very much."

Ciara nodded her head. "I do. She was like a second mother to me and my brother. But I'm happy that she isn't suffering with the pain anymore. It seemed unbearable at times, and she wasn't one to complain, but I could see the pain on her face."

They turned into a parking lot, passing a long line of people waiting to pick up their food.

Kaitlyn gasped. "My God. The line goes down the street. Is it always like this?"

Ciara smiled at her. "You can't see from here, but the line goes around the block. And yes, it's always like this."

Sarah could tell that this was the first time Kaitlyn had ever witnessed people standing in line for food.

Ciara continued, "You have to understand, for some of these people, without us, they wouldn't eat at all. People from all walks of life rely on us. We have seniors and children and in some cases people who had a good job and a home who for whatever reason now find themselves without those things. For some, poverty is only one medical crisis or a lost job away. For me, the hardest part is seeing children go without food. Many of our volunteers are teachers who have had to feed their students because the parents are unable to."

Sarah was happy she'd decided to volunteer today. The image of starving children was overwhelming. Her heart broke for these people. The plan to spend the day here instead of tanning on the beach was a good one, and she wished she had more time on the island to volunteer more than just one day. It felt good to be useful, to be needed.

They got out of the car, and a volunteer unloading boxes onto a truck waved at Ciara and her friends.

"Hey, Ciara. The donation from Misty River Farmstead finally arrived today. Look at this haul. It's amazing."

Ciara peered inside one of the boxes. "This produce looks fantastic. Trevor, I'd like you to meet Kaitlyn and Sarah. They're friends visiting Captiva for a few days. They asked if they could help by volunteering today."

Trevor looked at Sarah and smiled. "So, you decided to forgo the beach for a day? We don't serve drinks with umbrellas in them here."

Sarah took an immediate dislike to the guy. He was handsome, with long brown hair that was in a bun on the top of his head. He wore a bandana around his neck, a pair of cut-off jean shorts that were frayed, and a T-shirt with a peace sign on the front. She felt the need to respond in kind to his comment.

"Nice of you to appreciate the gesture. I didn't know being a snob was a requirement for the job."

Trevor wasn't offended, although Sarah had hoped he would be. Instead, he just kept smiling at her as he continued to unload the truck.

As they walked by him, Sarah turned to Ciara and said, "Is he always so rude?"

"Who? Trevor? He's a sweetheart. He was just teasing you. Kaitlyn, why don't you help Trevor and the others unload the truck and Sarah, you can come with me inside. I can use some help stacking items on the shelves."

Sarah turned back to watch Kaitlyn join the others at the truck. Trevor was still looking at her. She was immediately angry at herself for looking back at him. Why was he so smug? She thought volunteers were kind and caring people. He might be wearing a peace sign on his shirt, but nothing about his demeanor said anything but arrogant.

They worked for several hours distributing food and organizing the inventory. Occasionally, Trevor would come inside to speak with Ciara, and when he did, from the corner of her eye,

Sarah would catch him looking at her. It was unnerving, to say the least. As the hours passed, the line was considerably shorter than when they first arrived at the food pantry, and Sarah's legs were getting tired. It wasn't difficult work, but her body could feel the strain. She made a mental note to get back to the gym as soon as she returned to Massachusetts.

The remaining items were to be put on the top shelf, and without a ladder, there was no way she'd be able to finish her work.

"Need a hand?"

Sarah turned to see Trevor standing in the doorway. She was happy to have someone taller to reach the shelf, but that it was Trevor made her wish she had found a ladder instead.

"Sure. Thank you."

He lifted the remaining items from the box and stacked them neatly above.

"Looks like that's the last. I guess you can go back to your vacation now."

Sarah fumed. "Are you always this rude, or is there something about me that brings out the worst in you?"

Trevor smiled and stared into her eyes. "There is definitely something about you." And with that, he walked away, leaving her flustered and without an appropriate comeback.

Shortly after their exchange, Kaitlyn came looking for Sarah.

"I think I should check my birth certificate. I can't be nineteen years old. My body feels like it's at least sixty."

Sarah was surprised to hear Kaitlyn pick a senior number. She half expected her to say something more insulting, like thirty.

Kaitlyn stretched and said, "I'm ready to go home. How about you?"

Sarah wanted to leave as soon as Ciara was ready. Although happy that she had spent the afternoon helping out, she wanted distance from the insulting volunteer who had made the day more stressful than she'd expected.

As soon as Ciara was ready to drive Sarah and Kaitlyn home, she came looking for them.

"So how was your first time volunteering?"

Kaitlyn was the first to speak. "First and last for me, I think. I don't mean to sound like a spoiled kid, but I think I need the kind of volunteering that lets you sit down all day. Got any jobs like that?"

Ciara laughed. "As a matter of fact, I do. This is only one department within the Coastal community. There is so much work to be done to help, both volunteering and salaried positions."

This information piqued Sarah's interest. "Is there a list of jobs online that one can apply for? I mean, are they all in Ft. Myers?"

"Yes, many are in the Ft. Myers area. Our outreach extends to much of the Southwest Florida region, however. There are positions in Cape Coral, for example. I can text you a link to the information. Is this something you are thinking about, Sarah? Would you move here like your mother did?"

Sarah wasn't sure what she was thinking about, to be honest. What she did know was that she loved the way today had made her feel. When she was growing up, she knew that she would have a job helping people in some way, but her relationship with her father had dominated her career moves. She told herself that helping people make money was the closest she would ever get to making a difference in people's lives. Frustration by the constant need for her father's approval had set her on a path that was not entirely hers. She didn't consider losing her job to be a blessing, but after today, she wasn't quite sure about that.

"Oh, I'm not sure really. I guess it wouldn't hurt to look."

Kaitlyn had a very different perspective, however. "I'm

glad we could help a little today, but I have to start thinking about college."

Sarah laughed. "Whoa. That's a serious pivot from this morning. Did volunteering do this to you?"

"Sarah, if I didn't get to meet a super handsome and friendly guy, today's experience might have been a bummer. I mean, I'm exhausted."

"Wait. You met a handsome guy while we were there? I swear you can find a good-looking guy no matter where you go. How exactly did you manage that?"

"What? Don't tell me you didn't see him. That guy Trevor. I was working with him all afternoon. What a sweetheart. Too bad he's so much older than me."

Sarah was stunned. How in the world did Kaitlyn think that guy was a sweetheart? She fought the desire to know more about him, but it didn't matter because Kaitlyn had no problem giving them all the details.

"I actually had fun because of him. He's quite the talker too. His name is Trevor Hutchins. He's thirty-four. Too old for me. He's from Alaska. Can you imagine? I've never met anyone from Alaska before. His family moved to Sanibel just before high school. I think his dad is in the military. I think the Navy, but I forget what he told me. He really loves the ocean, says he's really a fish. He's a real good surfer too. He said he's been in lots of surfing competitions. He has two sisters and two brothers, a big family. They all live down here. Trevor owns his own home on Sanibel. He moved into his house a couple of years ago. When they lived in Alaska, they lived in some kind of community place where everyone farmed and home-schooled. I think they're vegetarian or vegan. One of those diets. He's traveled a lot too. He's been to Bora Bora, Australia, and Hawaii. His parents have a place on the island of Maui, so they go there a lot. He's really smart. He was so kind and helpful to me today. Seems like a real gentle spirit if you know what I mean. I can't understand why he doesn't have a girl-friend. I guess he had something serious with a girl from Naples, but it didn't work out and he's been single ever since."

Sarah was dumbfounded. "You got all that from being with him for just a few hours?"

Kaitlyn shrugged. "I guess so. Don't you ask a lot of questions when you meet someone for the first time?"

Ciara was smiling, and all Sarah could do was nod her head. It was impossible to believe that Kaitlyn was talking about the same guy that had made Sarah so angry. Maybe there was more to Trevor Hutchins than met the eye. One thing that the two women could agree on, however, the man was easy on the eyes.

As they walked to the car, Sarah looked around to see if Trevor was still working. She couldn't find him anywhere and assumed he had already left for the day. As they pulled out of the parking lot, Sarah saw him. He was standing against his Jeep, his long hair no longer in a bun, but rather being doused with bottled water. He wiped his face with a towel and turned to see Ciara's car passing. Trevor saw Sarah sitting in the back-seat and smiled at her once again, this time extending his thumb and pinkie and moving his hand back and forth.

Sarah recognized the gesture. It was a Hawaiian hand expression of friendship signifying anything from "Hang loose" to "Take it easy." But to make his point, he yelled to them, "Until we meet again."

This time, Sarah was glad she was sitting in the backseat instead of the front, where Kaitlyn was. It gave her the chance to look out the back window to see Trevor watching their car drive down the street, and she smiled at the handsome but rude volunteer.

Ciara dropped the women off at Chelsea's since Sarah wanted to walk to her mother's place from there. They waved to Ciara as she drove off.

"I had a lot of fun with you today, Kaitlyn," Sarah said. "I hope I get to see you again soon. I have to return home to attend a meeting, but I'm going to come back afterward. I've decided to stay with my mother for a bit more. Help her get settled."

"Thanks, Sarah. I had fun too. I'm going to call my mother and let her know I'm coming home. I've thought about what you said this morning. I want things to get better between my mom and me. Maybe this is the first step."

Sarah smiled and extended her arms. The women hugged, and it warmed Sarah's heart to see Kaitlyn trying so hard to find her place in the world. She knew it would take many years before the young woman understood some of what Sarah was just learning herself: that the journey never ends, it just keeps getting better as long as you get out of bed every day and put one foot in front of the other. Most of what Sarah was coming to terms with was accepting things she couldn't control and taking control of what she could. If anyone was going to define Sarah Wheeler, it was going to be Sarah herself. That was the true beginning of the journey, after all.

She found her mother sitting in the middle of a room full of boxes.

"Hi Mom. Wow, it didn't seem like that many boxes when they were in the truck."

Her mother threw her hands up in the air.

"It's going to take me weeks to get through all this stuff. I'm glad you'll be here a few more days to help with this mess."

"Actually, Mom, I've been meaning to talk to you about that. I have to get back to Massachusetts tomorrow. I've got a meeting I have to attend. I'll be back right after the meeting, but it's important I do this."

"Of course, honey. I understand. You don't have to come back to Captiva, Sarah. I'm sure I can manage this. How about a cup of tea?"

"Leave it to Mom to bring out the tea to make any situation better. Sure, I'd love a cup."

Her mother couldn't wait to ask about Sarah's day.

"So how did it go?"

"It was hard work, but Mom, you should have seen all the people there who needed food. It was heartbreaking, especially the children. It's astonishing how many people are hungry in this country. It's shocking. I had no idea. Anyway, it's one of the things I wanted to talk to you about. I want to come back after my meeting. I want to stay with you for a while. At least until I figure out what I want to do with my life."

"I'd love it, but are you sure? I mean, there's a lot going on here and if I haven't emphasized enough about my plans for the property, I should tell you that there's going to be a lot of work ahead of me to reopen the inn. Is that why you want to come back—to help me?"

"It's only part of my plan. I didn't know how much I would enjoy being at the food pantry today, and it's made me think differently about what I want to do for a living. I mean, it's only one afternoon, I get that. But it goes deeper than that. I don't want you to think this is some phase I'm going through, and I haven't taken this seriously. The truth is that today I felt like myself, my true self, more than I have at any other time in my life. I think I should explore that further. I want to help you with the inn, but I also want to discover who I think I am, if that makes sense."

Her mother had tears in her eyes. "Sarah, it makes tremendous sense to me. If anyone can understand what you are going through, it's me. I'm just thrilled that you aren't waiting until you're my age to figure out who you are. It's a lot scarier the way I did it."

Sarah was happy to hear her mother's words and to know that she supported Sarah's plans.

"The other thing I wanted to tell you is the reason I'm

returning home. Michael, Lauren, Beth, and I plan to meet with Emily Wheeler. We wanted to wait until you were down here so that you didn't have to worry about her or her mother showing up on your doorstep. I'm not sure if I mentioned this before, but apparently, she didn't tell her mother that she reached out to us. I have no idea how this is going to go, but we thought Dad would want us to extend ourselves here. I hope you're not upset with us for meeting with her."

The tea kettle whistled, and her mother went to turn it off.

"As I told you before, honey, I'm not upset about this. In fact, I figured it was only a matter of time before you all would meet her. She's your sister. It's only natural that you all want to meet."

Sarah handed her mother Emily's letter and the photograph.

Her mother put her hand over her mouth.

"*This* is Emily Wheeler?"

"Yes. Why? Do you think she looks like Dad?"

The shocked look on her mother's face told Sarah that there was something more.

"I saw her."

"What do you mean, you saw her? When?"

"At your father's funeral. She was there. I saw her and … Oh my God. I'm so stupid. I thought maybe she was someone your father had an affair with. I remember thinking she was so young. I was angry and assumed the worst, of course. It never occurred to me that she was his daughter. I remember her crying. She was pretty upset, and instead of feeling sorry for her, I was angry."

Sarah put her arms around her mother. "Oh Mom. You couldn't have known. Of course, you would be angry. After everything you found out about Dad. It must have been awful. You have nothing to feel bad about. I think if I were in your shoes, I might have felt the same way."

"Sarah, when you all meet with Emily, try to understand that she's lost her father, too. I know it's only natural to think that you have more of a claim to grieving for him than she does, but that's not how it works. There's no way to quantify grief. It is what it is. She's in pain, and I think you all need to appreciate how strong and brave she must be to reach out to us."

Sarah nodded and smiled. "Sounds like a Wheeler to me."

Chapter Twenty-Nine

LAUREN

Lauren picked Sarah up at the airport, and they headed down to Hingham to meet with their half-sister, Emily. They would meet Michael and Beth at the restaurant. Before Sarah boarded her plane to Boston, she sent Lauren a text telling her that she had some news she wanted to run by her sister.

"What time is it? Are we going to be late?"

"No, we're fine, as long as the traffic isn't a problem. It takes almost an hour to get there. So how was Captiva? Mom sent me some pictures. Is it as beautiful as it looks on my iPhone?"

"Honestly, Lauren, it's paradise. I'm serious. The landscaping is incredible. Paolo—that's the guy who works the garden—is amazing. He's done so much with the place. He has an incredible gift with plants, not to mention he is incredibly attractive."

"Are you telling me that your news is that you've fallen in love with a gorgeously handsome Italian?"

"Actually, that's not my news. But now that you mention it. It isn't me who's falling for the guy."

Lauren's mouth dropped open. "No! No way. You can't be talking about Mom."

Sarah nodded her head. "Yup. I really think something is going on there. It's obvious to anyone with eyes that he's crazy about her, that's for sure. You know Mom, though; she'll probably think and re-think about it forever before anything goes on between them. He's definitely looking out for her interests, which makes me happy to leave her there with him and his sister, Ciara, and of course, Chelsea."

"So, if that's not your news, what is it?"

Sarah took a deep breath before speaking.

"I only flew home to meet Emily, but I'm going back. I want to stay with Mom for a while. I can help her with promotions, and you know how technologically challenged she is. I'm sure she's going to need help organizing and developing a computer system. I'm at a crossroads in my life and I'm trying to figure out what I want my future to look like. I'm tired of caring so much about what other people think. I know I can help Mom, and there's also my volunteer work."

Lauren was surprised at how much had developed in one week.

"Your volunteer work? Since when do you volunteer?"

"It's a long story, but yes, I've found a way to be useful and I'm enjoying it. At some point, I'm going to have to find a paying job, but I'm not sure what that looks like at the moment. I've got some ideas brewing, but I need time to formulate them. Staying in Florida helping Mom seems like a good place to start. That's what Mom says all the time. Paradise is a good place to start over."

"Did you tell Mom about us all meeting Emily today?"

"I did, but it wasn't until I was booking my flight. I waited until the last minute."

"And?"

"She was fine with it. She thanked us for waiting until she

left Massachusetts. She said she just isn't ready to meet Emily but didn't rule it out completely. Who knows when that will be, but I think she's open to it in the future. Depending, of course on how today goes."

They were almost at the restaurant when Lauren decided to ask Sarah how she really felt about Emily.

"To be honest, I haven't been thrilled about meeting her today. I'm doing it because it's probably the right thing to do. I'm trying to keep an open mind about it. How about you?"

Lauren had given Emily a great deal of thought and had finally come to the realization that if their father was alive, he'd be happy about what they were doing today.

"I think Dad would be happy about it. Don't you?"

Sarah shrugged. "I guess. I mean if he truly wanted us to know her, I think he wouldn't have kept her a secret for so many years. I mean, the girl is nineteen years old. That's a lot of years to keep lying to your wife and family. I don't know. I fluctuate between being angry and letting the anger go. I think Mom has done the best out of all of us. She's set a truly incredible example. One more thing you should know. Apparently, Emily came to the funeral. Mom saw her and thought she was one of dad's girlfriends."

"No. Poor Mom. I can't believe it."

Sarah continued, "Well when I showed Mom a picture of Emily, that's when she remembered her. She said she felt so stupid to think that since Emily was obvious very young looking."

Lauren was proud of the way her mother had handled everything considering.

"I think Mom has mastered the art of forgiveness but to never forget. I don't expect that our mother will ever again live her life the way she did when she was married to Dad. She talks about being mindful now. I've never heard her talk that way before. I hope I can continue to learn from her example, not just for myself but for my daughters."

They made their way into the restaurant and saw Beth and Michael sitting at the bar.

Beth announced, "She's not here. At least I don't think she is."

Beth took the picture of Emily from Sarah and looked around the restaurant.

Lauren said, "I'm sure she'll be here any moment."

Michael hugged Sarah. "So how was Captiva? Mom all settled in?"

"She is indeed. She couldn't be happier, that's for sure."

A tall young woman with long, wavy blond hair approached the group. "Hi. Are you the Wheelers? I'm Emily."

Sarah stood and shook her hand. "Hi, I'm Sarah. This is my sister Beth, and this is Lauren and my brother Michael. Our brother Chris is in the military and stationed in Iraq."

Lauren could tell the young woman felt nervous and awkward. "Would you like something to drink?"

Emily nodded. "A Coke, please. Thank you."

The hostess called out to the Wheeler party and as soon as Emily's Coke arrived, they followed the woman carrying menus to a room in the back of the restaurant. The restaurant was packed, and Lauren was happy they had been smart enough to reserve a private room for the meeting.

A gas fireplace in the corner of the room surrounded by Christmas decorations that had not been removed after the holiday, made for a cozy winter scene. Everyone took a seat at the table and placed their menus down on the table.

Emily was the first to speak. "Thank you all for agreeing to meet me today. I was nervous to contact you at first, but my friend Alison convinced me to reach out. I think she's watched too many Ancestry commercials."

They all laughed, and Beth spoke next. "Emily, I hope you understand that the hardest part of this was first finding out that our father was unfaithful to our mother and then of course his sudden death was devastating. To find out he had another family was hard on all of us. Speaking strictly for myself, the more I thought about it, the more I realized that you lost your father, too. I mean you weren't even at the funeral with us."

Emily looked directly at Beth. "Yes, I was. My mother told me that my father had died. I asked if we could go to the funeral, but she said no, that they had ended their relationship years earlier and that it wouldn't be proper to attend. I was pretty upset and looked up the obituary online. I have my own car, so I drove myself to the funeral. I remember seeing my father a lot when I was little, but he stopped coming around a long time ago. I don't think my mother hated him, but she wasn't happy about it. At least he took care of us financially over the years. He always provided for me, at least that's what my mother told me."

Lauren's heart broke for the young girl. It wasn't her fault that she had been born or that her father had basically abandoned her. The child support was one thing, but money was no replacement for a father's attention and love. She and her siblings could attest to that. She looked around the table and was certain every one of them were thinking the exact same thing. She wanted to comfort Emily, and so she apologized for her father's behavior.

"I'm so sorry you went through all of that growing up. I think it was incredibly brave of you to go to the funeral all by yourself. And then, to reach out to us was amazing. I hope you know how much we wish we could have known you all these years."

Lauren looked at Sarah. They chose to keep what they knew about that day to themselves. It was their mother's story to tell, and they didn't feel right sharing what their mother had told Sarah with anyone, not even their siblings.

"Absolutely. I wish we could have shared our lives with you as you were growing up."

Beth responded next. "I'm sorry too. You and I are probably the closest in age, with Chris not far behind. I bet we could have had a lot of fun."

Sarah corrected her. "You mean more like you two would have gotten into a lot of trouble together."

Taking a cue from his sisters, Michael went out on a limb and welcomed Emily. "We might have missed lots of years with you, Emily, but you're here now. I think I speak for everyone when I say that we'd like to get to know you better. Welcome to the family."

Beth laughed and said, "Don't listen to him, Emily. He just wants another babysitter in the family. Kidding aside, I agree with Michael. We've lost a lot of years, but we can start today."

Lauren was concerned and asked, "I think I remember you saying that your mother is unaware of you reaching out to us. Don't you think you should talk to her and let her know we met with you today? She is your mother and has a right to know what you're doing. I know you are legally allowed to make such an important decision and you don't need her permission, but I still think you should give her a chance to be a part of your choices. I'm a mother myself, and I know that's how I would feel."

Emily shrugged. "My mother and I haven't been getting along lately. It seems like she is unhappy with everything I do these days. We were close when I was growing up, especially because she was both mother and father to me. I'm tired of fighting, but I'll think about what you say. It hurts me that I can't share some of my life with her, especially something as big as this. I have to admit I do like having big sisters to give me advice, though."

Sarah laughed and added, "You say that now. Wait until you get unsolicited advice from us. You'll be telling us to mind our own business and leave you alone."

Emily laughed and shook her head. "I don't think so. I've hated being an only child. I always wanted a brother or a sister. I had no idea you all existed until last year, and now, with Dad's will, I have money I don't know what to do with. Although my mother is aware of that and is already giving me advice and trying to control what I do with the money. She says I'm too young to have that much money and wants to put it away in some sort of investment. I don't mind that, but I was able to convince her to let me trade in my old beat-up car for a new one."

The waiter came and took everyone's order. The menu was rather eclectic and had several amazing dishes to choose from. All in all, the lunch was a success, and Lauren was pleased that her siblings were all amenable to welcoming Emily into their family. In time, she would probably share in their annual celebrations and would get to know their mother as well. The more she thought about it, the more she was sure that her mother's ability to forgive would extend to Emily's mother as well.

As impossible as it was to imagine, Lauren was coming to terms with the fact that her family was growing and changing to include people near and far. A chosen family—one that would make a real difference in the world, and she couldn't wait to see what the future had in store for each of them.

Chapter Thirty

MAGGIE

M aggie was stunned at the number of people on
Captiva who supported and encouraged her and
Paolo to reopen the Key Lime Garden Inn. True to his word,
Paolo was able to enlist the help of several of his contacts.
Ciara surprised Maggie with the news that a few people who
volunteered at the food pantry wanted to offer their help as
well and would be meeting with Paolo this afternoon to learn
more about the project.

There wasn't a need to do major reconstruction, but there
were several areas in the house that needed updating as well as
painting over a couple of prior water leaks that had left stains
on the ceiling. The bathrooms were old, and Maggie felt that a
newer, more modern design would attract more guests. It
would be a challenge to preserve the history and charm of the
establishment while updating the property to welcome a new
generation of tourists.

Everyone in town was talking about the project, and if the
gossip was to be believed, Maggie could depend on a strong
demand for bookings right after the Grand Opening in the
spring. The Key Lime Garden Inn's reopening was listed on

the agenda of the next Town Hall meeting, and Maggie, Sarah and Paolo attended. Paolo was right. No one at the meeting objected to the plans, and they were pleasantly surprised at the support of not only the committee members but those in attendance, with many thanking Paolo and Maggie for granting Rose Johnson Lane's dying request.

After her visit back home in Massachusetts, Sarah returned to Captiva with a renewed sense of purpose. Maggie was happy that her daughter was content to continue her volunteer work while helping Maggie get the house ready to open to the public. She was impressed with her daughter's desire to spend more time working with Ciara to learn more about Coastal Community Outreach and the various departments within the organization. For the time being, Sarah would have to drive to Ft. Myers using Maggie's car, and either Paolo or Chelsea would drive Maggie wherever she needed to go if it was necessary. Ciara offered to let Sarah go with her, but Captiva was so far from Ciara's apartment, it just wasn't practical.

What Maggie did notice, however, was that on the days when Sarah would volunteer at the food pantry, she would come home mumbling to herself. Her days were divided among the various departments within the organization, but it was always the food pantry day when Sarah was her most flustered. Maggie tried to talk to her daughter about it, but she would just shake her head and say that it was no big deal. Maggie knew that whenever Sarah's mood turned grumpy, it was usually best to steer clear of her for a few hours until she calmed down.

Sarah sat at the kitchen table in front of her laptop. Her furrowed brow was an indication that something wasn't right.

"You seem deep in thought. Having trouble with your technology?"

"I'm working on setting up a website for the inn. I'm also looking into whether it's worth it to have an affiliation with third party travel groups that would add the inn to their list of recommended vacation spots. The idea is for you to not only get reservations, but to have a way to get reviews from your guests. I'm trying to get a handle on what it entails, but what I'm finding is that there are several places online with contradicting information."

Sarah closed her laptop and focused on what her mother was doing.

"I think I'm done for now; I can't look at another thing online. What are you up to today?"

Maggie stepped up on a small ladder and lifted curtains above her head. "Help me with this, will you?"

Sarah held one end of the curtain rod while Maggie set it in place and waited for her mother to move the ladder to the other end.

"So, no volunteering today?"

"No. I thought I'd see what I could do to help around here. We're getting close to opening this place, and while the contractors are working around the clock, I feel like I haven't been around to help you as much as I should. What's left to do?"

"Well, I've already spent a small fortune on all new bedding for every bedroom. Amazon and I have become very good friends. All those boxes are downstairs piled up in the living room. It would be great if you could help me get everything out of the boxes and laundered. Then we can make the beds. I'm loving how everything is turning out."

Sarah laughed at her. "Yes, not only have you made friends with Amazon, but I'm pretty sure you and HGTV have a close relationship. Mom, you always had a knack for decorating long before those shows, but now I'm starting to think you're hosting your own house decorating show. Is there a hidden camera somewhere that I can't see? Kidding aside, you've done an amazing job. Everything is so light and open. It feels like an ocean breeze has come up from the beach and now flows through the house. It's perfect."

"Sarah, that is exactly the reaction I was hoping for. That's how I see this place. I want everyone to appreciate the inn's history, but I also want them to love the place so much that they'll return again and again. Just like it used to be for us, remember? We always stayed at that cute cottage near the beach. And you're right: I have decorated the rooms with a sense that the house is an extension of the beach. Seashells everywhere, and light blues and greens with smatters of pink, yellow, and peach colors here and there was my plan from the start, and I think it works."

"Especially with the light beige walls. I can't believe what an incredible painting job you and Chelsea did."

"Chelsea's a hard worker, and honestly, I think she wanted the company. Ever since Kaitlyn went back home, I think she's been a little lonely. This project came at a really good time for her. I think she likes to feel needed, and boy, do I need her help."

Maggie could tell that there was something on Sarah's mind, but she had decided some time ago that with Sarah, it was always best to wait until she was ready to talk, and it looked to Maggie like today was the day that her daughter needed her mother.

"So, Mom, I've been thinking. What do you think about the Key Lime Garden Inn hosting a benefit for Coastal Community Outreach, specifically their shelter for battered women? They provide housing, food, and support for victims of domestic abuse. The more I learn about the organization, the more impressed I am with the work they do in Southwest Florida."

"A benefit? Honey, we're not even open yet. When were you thinking of doing this?"

"Oh, not right away. I was thinking maybe May or June,

after we've been open for a bit. I thought it would be a great way to not only help the community, but also get the word out that the inn was open. There are plenty of media outlets I can reach out to, and I can create fliers and go around Ft. Myers, Sanibel, and Captiva to distribute them. Paolo said Sanibellia will promote it too. You'd be surprised how many people from all over the world come to Paolo's nursery. I didn't realize it, but since it's in such proximity to the farmer's market, it's a natural stop for tourists. Plus, there are tons of places that Paolo and Ciara think we can promote the event. What do you think?"

"I think it's a great idea, but I've got enough on my hands just getting the place up and running."

Her daughter continued, "I've talked to Chelsea about it. She loves the idea. So does Ciara."

"Why am I the last to know about this?"

"Well, I figured if everyone else was on board, you'd be easier to convince."

Maggie hugged her daughter and laughed. "Of course, you did. You little sneak. But really, I do think it's a great idea. You and Ciara can run with this, I have no doubt. Just let me know what you need me to do, and I'll do it. I gather this will be a catered affair, with a tent and outdoor table and chairs, so you'll need my credit card."

Sarah smiled at Maggie and nodded her head. It wasn't the first time her daughter had used her credit card. She remembered a time when Sarah had memorized her credit card information and ordered pizza for her girlfriends and her during a sleepover. It wasn't that Maggie didn't want to pay for the pizza, but she was stunned when she asked her daughter if she needed the information to place the order, and her response was, "No. I've got it." Fortunately, Sarah never used the card inappropriately, but Maggie was shocked, nonetheless.

"What? You don't still have my credit card information memorized?"

"Mom, that was years ago. I've slept since then."

"Do me a favor, Sarah. Get all the information and the cost before you place any orders. First, I need to better understand what a benefit entails, the financials and such. I'll need to spend time with Ciara on the organization's profit and loss statements. I'm going to have to know whether this qualifies as a 501(c)3 or not. I assume it's a non-profit so there are tax consequences we need to be aware of. When it's promoted, you need all that information ahead of time. It's not like just throwing a party under an umbrella. And one more thing. I'm happy that you're working with Ciara at Coastal Community Outreach, but I feel it's important before I commit to this that I get a better understanding of everything the organization does and what their mission statement is. I don't want to host a benefit I'm not one hundred percent committed to myself."

Sarah let Maggie go on and on about her concerns before she interrupted her. Touching her arm, she said, "Mom. Have you forgotten what I've done for a living these last several years? I've got this."

Maggie rolled her eyes and threw up her hands. "Oh, Sarah, I'm sorry. Of course, you've got this. I think I'm a little overwhelmed with everything. My brain can only handle so much, you know."

Neither woman said anything for a few minutes. Maggie was adjusting the curtains to make them look *Architectural Digest*-perfect.

"Are you happy, Mom?"

Maggie was taken aback by Sarah's question. She'd been juggling so many balls in the air, she hadn't stopped to think about whether she was happy or not. Now that her daughter posed the question so directly, Maggie had to sit down and reflect before she answered. Looking at her daughter, she smiled.

"I don't know how to explain how I feel. I've got energy to spare. I know I'm dealing with a lot, but the truth is, I can handle it. Remember how I used to have this knot in my right shoulder? I used to ask you kids to massage it all the time."

Sarah sat next to her mother. "I remember."

"It's gone. That stiffness and constant pain is gone. I don't have a clue when it left me, but it's not there anymore. I feel like my posture must have been the reason—well, that and maybe some stress that I didn't know I had. I don't think I've been standing tall but rather hunched over for years. It must be that, although I never noticed it before."

Maggie looked down at her hands. She used to get manicures and would wear gloves whenever she did work inside the house. Garden gloves were on her hands when she worked outside or in the greenhouse. A slather of hand lotion several times a day kept her skin soft and her manicure preserved. Daniel always commented on how soft Maggie's hands were.

Now, her nails unpolished, she admired the roughness of her skin and the depth of the lines that traveled across the inside of her palm. There was something about her hands that made her proud. She'd worked her property these last weeks, both inside and out, sometimes forgetting her gloves because she couldn't wait to dig her hands deep into whatever project she was working on. She forgot to protect her skin from the elements, and it was this simple act that convinced her that she was beyond happy—she was content and at peace with her new life.

Maggie looked up at her daughter and smiled.

"You asked me if I'm happy? I am. Profoundly. I've never known this kind of happiness before. I feel safe and secure but vulnerable at the same time, and it feels wonderful. I wake every day excited about what new thing I might encounter, what new friend I might meet. I listen to the ocean and the waves at night, and I feel my heart beating in rhythm to everything around me. Like I'm part of something bigger than myself. I can't explain it, but I feel like I'm the missing piece to this big puzzle, and now that I'm here in this place, the puzzle is complete. Oh yes, Sarah. I am happy."

The women sat in silence for a few minutes. It wasn't awkward, but rather seemed necessary to appreciate Maggie's words and to let this new realization wash over them. Maggie was especially happy to share this moment with her daughter, who was on a path of her own. They would always have this memory, a memory that would carry each of them on their separate journeys for the rest of their lives. As soon as she had a minute to herself, Maggie would make a pot of tea and sit in Rose's chair to write about it in her journal.

Chapter Thirty-One

MAGGIE

Never, as far back as Maggie could remember, was any member of the Wheeler family able to keep a secret. It was impossible to hold surprise birthday parties or special news because someone always leaked the details before the event.

So, it came as no surprise to Maggie when a family member leaked the news that her children had organized a trip to Captiva. They wanted to be with their mother on opening day at the Key Lime Garden Inn. She didn't want to ruin their plans, so she kept the fact that she knew her family was coming to Captiva to herself.

Sarah worked with Paolo, Ciara, and Chelsea to plan the trip, all the while helping to get the inn ready. The promotions announcing the event to benefit the shelter had been circulating for weeks as well as the Grand Opening announcement, and so far, the news was well received all over town.

Because of the promotional work, including the Key Lime Garden Inn's website design, Sarah had done an amazing job getting the word out. So much so, that the inn already had reservations for two couples.

Two young women who were the daughters of a friend of

Chelsea's applied for the kitchen position. Riley and Grace Cuthbert had been running a food truck business in Ft. Myers for the last two years. Sales were slow, and their business was proving more difficult than they anticipated. Joining the Key Lime Garden Inn family in March was a blessing for them and for Maggie.

Sarah surprised no one when she showed herself to be resourceful with marketing and event planning. Her daughter had always been successful with whatever she put her mind to, and Maggie told her daughter as much.

"I'm serious, Sarah. I think you have a career in event planning. I mean, that's a real job. You should think about it."

"Mom, I promise to consider it if my plan falls through."

"What do you mean? What plan?"

"I want to stay in Florida. I applied for the position of Director of Community Relations. They called me, and I interviewed with them the other day. They offered me the job. I think Ciara might have had a hand in it. I asked her about it, but she said all she did was tell them that I deserved an interview. She said she was hands off after that and that it was the interview that sealed the deal."

Maggie clapped her hands in excitement. "Woohoo! I knew it. I just had a feeling you were going to stay."

Chelsea entered the room just as Maggie and Sarah were raising their champagne glasses.

"Well, ladies, what are we celebrating?"

Maggie handed Chelsea a glass and poured champagne into it.

"Sarah just accepted a job down here. She's staying in Florida."

"Congratulations. Way to go, Sarah."

"Not only are we celebrating Sarah's new job, but apparently you guys have been keeping a secret from me, which I'm still stunned about."

Chelsea's innocent look wasn't fooling anyone. "Who us? Keep a secret? Impossible."

Sarah shook her head. "Give it up, Chelsea. She knows. I'm not sure how she knows, because she's not talking, but trust me, she knows."

Maggie laughed. "Well, the truth is I promised not to tell on the person, or I should say, persons, who told me. So, sorry, but their secret is safe with me."

Since it wasn't necessary to pretend any longer, Sarah and Chelsea had to give Maggie the details. Everything was in place for the big day, and the only thing left to do was welcome her children, who were to arrive this afternoon. No one needed to pick anyone up at the airport, because two vans had been rented to bring her children and grandchildren to the island.

Maggie was overjoyed to think that she would share her love of Captiva with her family once again and would introduce a new generation to the secrets of the island. Her first order of business would be to distribute the plastic buckets that she had personalized with each of her grandchildren's names on them. Quinn, Cora, Olivia, and Lily would all have their very own seashell collections, and Maggie would be right in the middle of the hunt with them.

Paolo and Ciara as well as a few volunteers from the food pantry scurried around the property, making sure any last-minute touches were attended to. Maggie noticed Sarah talking to one of the workers out by the pergola. They had been talking for quite some time, and it didn't look like they were talking about the inn.

Maggie moved closer to the inside of the porch door so that she wouldn't be caught eavesdropping. She couldn't hear what they were saying, but it appeared as if the conversation was more personal and intimate. Before they parted, the man reached out and pushed several strands of Sarah's hair away from her face. Her daughter looked around to see if anyone had witnessed their exchange. Maggie moved back inside the house and smiled. Something exciting and new was happening to her daughter, but she would wait until Sarah felt ready to share that information.

Chelsea was talking to Paolo in the garden and noticed Maggie going into the house. She ran across the lawn and waved, calling out Maggie's name.

"Maggie, I've made the prefect Key Lime Garden Inn signature drink. Come into the kitchen. You must taste this. It's perfect if I do say so myself."

On the kitchen island, Chelsea had two martini glasses filled with a green liquid.

"I looked it up on the Internet. It's a Key Lime-tini. Isn't this the most perfect drink for the inn? It will be our signature drink. Taste it. Go on."

Maggie was impressed with Chelsea's enthusiasm. "What's in it?"

"Well, first you put lime juice and sugar around the rim of the glass. Then you mix rum, vanilla vodka, melon liqueur, pineapple juice, lime juice, and simple syrup. You shake it up and pour the strained liquid into the rimmed glass, then you add a piece of lime on the side. See for yourself."

Maggie lifted the glass to her lips and tasted the tart but delicious drink. She had to admit that Chelsea had created not only a tasty beverage, but a visually appealing one as well.

"It's really good. I like it. I'm curious, though. How many of these have you had today?"

"Only two. It took a few sips to make sure I had the right mixture. You have to watch what you put in these things. It's not equal parts, so I had to do some tweaking here and there."

Maggie wasn't buying the "few sips" story, but she let it go.

"I don't think you need to taste it any more today, Chelsea. It's perfect just as it is."

Chelsea was pleased with herself and with Maggie's reaction. Her excitement over the Key Lime Garden Inn signature drink was bordering on giddiness, and Maggie thought it best that her friend take a brief nap before the rest of the family arrived.

"I agree. I am a little tired. I think I will take a rest in your room if that's all right with you."

Maggie tried not to laugh at Chelsea, who was clearly feeling the effects of the inn's new signature cocktail.

"No problem. I'll come get you later when everyone is here. Be careful going up the stairs and hold on to the railing."

Maggie cleaned the kitchen, wiping down the counter where Chelsea had made a small mess. She walked through the house, making sure that she hadn't missed anything. Everything looked perfect, and she couldn't wait for her family to see what had captured Maggie's heart and soul.

The Key Lime Garden Inn would be open for business shortly, and her family would be there with her to see her dream come true. A text from Lauren an hour ago said that they had landed, and Maggie figured they would arrive within the hour. Paolo left the gate open so that the vehicles could drive through. The crunch of the shell-covered driveway signaled their arrival, and both Maggie and Sarah ran to greet everyone.

Throwing her arms out to reach for her family, Maggie gathered her grandchildren into a group hug.

"You're finally here. I'm so excited to see everyone."

Sarah glared at her siblings, focusing on Beth. "So now that everyone is here, it's time someone here confesses. Who told Mom that you all were coming?"

Beth took offense immediately, "Why are you looking at me? I didn't tell her."

Sarah looked at Michael and Lauren. "Well?"

In unison, they both shook their heads. "Not us."

"Ah, I get it. It won't take me long to finally ferret out the guilty party—or in this case should I say, parties?"

Maggie's granddaughters all ran away from Sarah as she chased them.

Lauren finally understood and looked at her mother.

"How in the world did the girls tell you we were coming?"

"You know that contraption you all bought for me so that we could video whenever we wanted to? Well, Olivia and Lily called me on it last week, and while we were talking, they happened to mention that they couldn't wait to see me soon. It was all downhill from there. They spilled the beans easily."

Sarah was tickling Cora when they ran back to the house, and Maggie tried to corral the group into their respective rooms.

Sarah showed everyone upstairs and heard something coming from her mother's room.

"Mom. I think there is someone snoring in your room."

Maggie had forgotten about Chelsea.

"Oh. That's just Chelsea. She was creating a Key Lime Garden Inn signature cocktail, and I think she went a little overboard on the taste testing."

Michael corrected his mother. "They don't call them that anymore, Mom. They're sensory evaluators now."

Maggie shook her head and shrugged. "Well, whatever you call them, Chelsea evaluated herself right into an afternoon nap."

Maggie was stunned when Paolo knocked on the back door. "What are you doing knocking on the door, Paolo? You don't have to do that. Come in and meet my family."

"I didn't want to intrude."

"Everyone, this is Paolo Moretti. He is the man I told you about."

Lauren was first to speak. "Very nice to meet you, Mr. Moretti. My mother speaks very highly of you."

"Thank you very much. Your mother has done a wonderful thing here. I'm sure you all are very proud of her."

Turning to Maggie, Paolo said, "I've got to get over to Sanibellia, but I wanted first to welcome your family to Captiva. I'll be back tomorrow for the festivities."

"Thank you for everything, Paolo. Tomorrow is a big day, and I couldn't have done this without you. Thank you for helping to bring my family here. It means a lot to me."

Maggie could tell that he was embarrassed by all the attention, but he deserved all the credit for the inn's successful transformation, and she wanted Paolo to know how much she appreciated him. He turned and waved to everyone. "I'll see you tomorrow. Very nice to meet you all. Enjoy your time with your mother."

Quinn had picked a flower from the garden and gave it to Maggie. "Grandma, I got this for you."

Maggie picked up the little girl and gave her a kiss. "Why thank you, Quinn. It's a beautiful flower. Can I wear it in my hair?"

Quinn pushed the flower into her grandmother's hair, but it kept falling. Maggie helped to stick it back in so that it would stay.

"How about we all go outside and get something to eat? Our chefs have prepared a delicious lobster meal for us, and they've set an amazingly long table out in the garden near the pergola. Let's celebrate and then tonight we can all walk down to the beach and watch the sunset. How does that sound?"

Michael spoke first. "Great, because I don't know about everyone else, but I'm starving."

Beth made fun of her brother. "When aren't you starving?"

Everyone walked out to the garden, and Riley and Grace carried out trays of lobsters, corn on the cob, mashed potatoes, salad, and mac and cheese for the girls. Once again, Maggie's children were with her at the dinner table. She was sad to miss her son Christopher, but she knew that in time, he too would visit Captiva when he was able.

Maggie jumped up from the table.

"Oh, I almost forgot. I want to get some pictures of every-one, and this gorgeous table too. I'll be right back."

She ran up the stairs and into the house to get her phone. She found it on the kitchen island and laughed when she heard Chelsea snoring all the way from the bedroom upstairs.

Heading back outside, Maggie stepped out onto the porch and looked out over the lawn and garden, the ocean not too far in the distance. It was another perfect day on Captiva Island without a cloud in the sky. A slight wind blew her hair in front of her face, and she pushed it back and behind her ear. She looked down at her family. Everyone was having a good time, and she was overwhelmed with emotion. Only a year ago, her world was completely different. It was almost as if she now was living someone else's life. But she wasn't, it was her life, and she was excited to see where her journey would take her.

Maggie thought about the events of the past year, and her life before Captiva. Every move she'd made over the years had been greatly influenced by her marriage. She could see things so clearly now. Daniel had control over the lives of so many. Jane, Beth, Lauren, Sarah, Emily, and Maggie, six women whose lives had been greatly impacted by one man.

Jane struggled with her attraction to Daniel, so much so that she was willing to throw her friendship with Maggie away. Their relationship on solid ground, Maggie and her friend were able to navigate the choppy waters of guilt and regret. Now, Jane was finally allowing herself to be open to a committed relationship with someone, and it pleased Maggie to know that Jane would continue to share her adventures with her and the other lunch-bunch ladies.

Maggie's daughter Sarah was terrified by the idea of marriage and motherhood to such a degree, she was unwilling to imagine ever wanting those things herself. Maggie could see a softening in Sarah and was happy to know that her daughter was taking the steps needed to find herself.

Her daughter Lauren had chosen to stay at home with her children while her husband went to work outside the home, just as her mother had done before her, because she thought that was the way it should be. Lauren had made decisions based upon something that wasn't true for her. Finding what worked best for her family was the only thing that mattered, and she did that. She kept the good times with her father in her memory and let herself move beyond the role of daddy's little girl.

Beth had suffered more than any of them. She was a child when her fantasy of the perfect father was destroyed. Learning to trust would be the one thing Maggie worried her daughter would struggle with. There was a lightness that was starting to shine from Beth that wasn't there these last years. Maggie could see that her daughter had all the strength needed to find her way, and Maggie would be there for her daughter every step of the way.

Emily was an unknown to Maggie, but she couldn't help but be impressed with the young woman. Emily had reached out to her siblings and asked to be a part of their lives, which, to Maggie, seemed a brave thing to do. Growing up with a father that she barely saw, this young woman refused to let Daniel choose her life. Understanding where she came from was the first step. What she would do with her life was still to develop, but wherever she landed, it was obvious to Maggie that it would be on her terms and no one else's.

For Maggie, she no longer worried where she belonged. She was where she was supposed to be. The past was the only thing that kept her from feeling confused. She knew where she had come from. It was easy to know where she was headed once she had a clear view of her life. Rose and Anne had done that for her. They held a mirror in front of Maggie and all she had to do was to take a good hard look at it.

Coming to Captiva wasn't running away. She had come to this island to find herself, and she did. This was her home, and for the rest of her life, she would remain grateful to the two women who had come to this house and left their mark. She would now leave hers and knew deep in her heart that Anne and Rose would be pleased about that.

THE END

Thank you so much for reading. I hope you enjoyed this story. Stay tuned for many more books in this series.

Read on for a sneak peek at Book 2
A Captiva Wedding

A Captiva Wedding

S arah Wheeler navigated around the lumber piled up beside the carriage house. She came to Captiva Island to help her mother open the Key Lime Garden Inn only a few months ago. The establishment's popularity in such a short amount of time surprised the women. The inn was so successful both Sarah and her mother, Maggie, needed to find other accommodations to free up all six bedrooms for guests.

Paolo, the inn's co-owner, came up with a solution. They would renovate the carriage house to provide the necessary room while keeping the women close enough to take care of guests of the inn, no matter the hour.

Construction was well underway. Maggie talked non-stop about her plans for the new apartment. The arrangement wouldn't work for Sarah, however. She needed to speak up before the work continued much further.

As Director of Community Relations at Coastal Community Outreach in Fort Myers, the daily drive from Captiva exhausted Sarah. Even traveling against the traffic both ways made for a slow ride. As soon as she decided to stay in Florida and take the job, she bought a car— a cute blue Prius. She sold her old car in Massachusetts to her sister Beth who whined until Sarah gave in.

It wasn't practical for Sarah to live on Captiva. She found an available condo to rent rather than buy property. She wanted to take her time and make that decision after being on the job for a few months. Sarah didn't tell her mother until she was sure she got the place.

Paolo was working in the garden and waved to Sarah. "How is work going? Ciara says you're doing a great job."

"Hi, Paolo. It's been busy for sure, but I love it. Have you seen my mother? I need to talk to her about something."

"She should be back any minute. She went over to Chelsea's to pick up a painting for the front room."

Sensing Sarah had something important on her mind, Paolo asked, "Is there something I can help you with?"

Sarah considered the question. Paolo's opinion on Maggie's possible reaction might help.

"I know my mother was planning on us living in the carriage house, but I don't think that's going to work. I decided to see what I might be able to rent and found a condo not too far from the bridge, on Summerlin. It's perfect for me to get to work and to Captiva. I just don't know how mom will feel about it."

"Your mother wouldn't want you to be unhappy. It can be difficult to travel back and forth. My sister complains about it all the time. Don't worry. I'm sure your mother will support whatever you want to do."

"I'm feeling a little guilty."

"About what?"

"I came here to help her with the inn. Then I go off and get a job and a condo, which takes me away from here."

"Don't be silly. We never could have managed the computer program you set up. You've done so much on top of your work at the outreach center. Besides, your mother isn't alone. She has a staff now to help run this place."

At that instant, Paolo spotted Maggie walking up the driveway carrying a large, framed painting, and ran to help her.

"Oh, thank you Paolo," Maggie said. "This thing weighs a ton."

"Let me get this inside and hang it up. I think Sarah wants a few minutes with you."

As Paolo walked inside, Maggie turned to her daughter.

"Is everything all right, honey?"

Screwing up her courage, Sarah said, "Mom, I know how much you want the two of us to live in the carriage house but driving back and forth to work is too much for me. I need to live off island."

Maggie smiled and nodded. "That makes sense. I wondered how long it would take you to come to that conclusion. I know how difficult traffic on the island can be. Why don't we see what's available and go look at some apartments?"

"We don't have to. I already did and I found a place. I signed a one-year lease this afternoon."

The speed of the decision took Maggie aback, but she supported Sarah's choice. "Oh, wow. That's great. So, you'll be moving right away?"

Sarah looked down at the broken shells in the driveway. She moved them around with her foot.

"Mom, I feel awful about this. I mean, you know I'll be over here all the time when I'm not working. I'll help you with whatever you need. Call my cell and I'll come right over."

Her mother put her arms around Sarah and tried to reassure her. "Don't worry about me. I have plenty of help. It's not your job to look after me. I love that you want to, but you need to care for yourself. I'll call you if I need you. Just come to visit. You don't always have to help with the inn. I can't wait to see your place. We'll help you move into your apartment if you need us."

"Thanks, Mom. You're going to love it. It's modern and has a super open-concept look. I've got a pool, too. It's really a house in a gated community, but it was listed as a condo."

"It sounds amazing. I'm sure I'll love it. I'm glad you're going to have your own place. You need your privacy. After all, you don't want to bring a date back here."

Sarah knew that was her mother's way of opening a conversation about her dating life. A life that was starting to pick up, even though she kept that information to herself.

"We're not going to discuss that, Mom, no matter how many times you try."

"Oh, come on. I've been good. I haven't been that nosey. You know I've been waiting for you to tell me what's going on between you and Trevor. Give me something. Please?"

Sarah laughed. "All right, all right. Don't beg. What do you want to know?"

"You seem happy. Can I assume that's because of Trevor?"

"I'm happy about a lot of things, and yes, Trevor is one of them."

"How about we go inside, and I'll make us some tea? You can tell me about him."

Sarah rolled her eyes, "There isn't a conversation that happens in this family without a cup of tea."

"A cup of tea helps people relax and feel comfortable. What's wrong with that?"

"If you ask me, I think it's your way of getting people to tell you things they wouldn't otherwise share. That's not going to work this time."

Inside, Maggie started the flame under the kettle. She used her bone china teapot and covered it with a warmer. When they settled in her mother's favorite room, Sarah admired one of Chelsea's paintings. "She certainly is talented. Is she going to show her work at the gallery?"

"That's the plan. Chelsea's been painting for months and has several pieces ready. I'm her biggest fan. She generously donated this piece to the inn. I love it."

Her mother poured their tea and sat back. "So, tell me about Trevor."

Careful not to say too much, Sarah had to think for a minute. A sip of her tea seemed a good way to stall.

"We've only been on a few dates. There's so much about him that I don't know. He comes from a wealthy family. They own lots of commercial and residential real estate all over the country, but especially here in Florida. They have properties overseas as well."

"So, Trevor has money."

"He could have all the money he wants, but he decided to go a different way. He's worked at Oxfam International and America. He's volunteered at several non-profits focusing on poverty and hunger. He's a real humanitarian."

Sarah tried not to gush and watched her mother closely to gauge her reaction.

Maggie smiled, but Sarah knew her mother wanted more information. All Sarah would give her was what she felt in the moment. She didn't share that the very man she found rude and irritating at first, had captured her heart and invaded her every thought.

"He sounds like a nice guy," Maggie said. "I hope I get to meet him one of these days."

"Stop pushing. This is why I don't tell you stuff."

"What did I say?"

"You know what I mean. We've just started seeing each other."

"Fine. I'm just saying when the time is right, bring him around."

"As it happens, he's coming to pick me up in an hour. We're going to Sweet Melissa's for dinner. You'll get a chance to say hello."

Sarah got up and kissed her mother's forehead. "I'm going to take a shower, thanks for the tea, and for being so understanding about the condo. I love you, Mom."

"Love you too, honey."

Looking through her closet, Sarah tried to find something to wear, selecting a white blouse and a skirt with a tropical design. Her cell phone rang, and Trevor's name appeared on the screen.

"Hi. I was just getting in the shower. Everything all right?"

"Sarah, I'm sorry, but I'm going to have to cancel our dinner tonight. Something's come up and I can't make it."

She didn't want Trevor to hear the disappointment in her voice. Staying upbeat, she tried her best to act like it was no big deal.

"I understand. Don't worry about it. I'm sure we can do it another time."

She was about to hang up when Trevor stopped her.

"Wait. I really wanted to see you, but I'm at the hospital. It's my son. He's been in an accident. I don't know what's happening. I'm waiting for the doctor, but no one has come out to talk to me, and I'm about to lose my mind."

Stunned, Sarah didn't know what to say. She wanted to ask a million questions, but this wasn't the time. "Do you want me to come to the hospital? I can leave right now."

The connection fell silent. She didn't know if he was still on the line. He might not want her there and couldn't find a polite way to say no. Sarah didn't know what to do, so she waited.

When he finally answered, Sarah's heart jumped out of her chest.

"Please come."

"I'm on my way."

Other Books by Annie Cabot

THE CAPTIVA ISLAND SERIES

- Book Two: A CAPTIVA WEDDING
- Book Three: CAPTIVA MEMORIES
- Book Four: CAPTIVA CHRISTMAS
- Book Five: CAPTIVA NIGHTS
- Book Six: CAPTIVA HEARTS
- Book Seven: CAPTIVA EVER AFTER

THE PERIWINKLE SHORES SERIES

- Book One: CHRISTMAS ON THE CAPE
- Book Two: THE SEA GLASS GIRLS

For a **FREE** copy of the Prequel to the Captiva Island Series, **CAPTIVA SUNSET** - Join my newsletter HERE.

Reviews are tremendously important to an author, and so, I hope you will leave a review of **KEY LIME GARDEN INN** on Amazon.

I read every review because I want to hear from my readers. You can click the following link to be brought directly to the review page. https://amzn.to/3sxWKzc

About the Author

Annie Cabot is the author of contemporary women's fiction and family sagas. Annie writes about friendships and family relationships, that bring inspiration and hope to others.

Annie Cabot is the pen name for the writer Patricia Pauletti (Patti) who, for many years, was a co-author of several paranormal mystery books under the pen name Juliette Harper.

A lover of all things happily ever after, it was only a matter of time before she began writing what was in her heart, and so, the pen name Annie Cabot was born.

When she's not writing, Annie and her husband like to travel. Winters always involve time away on Captiva Island, Florida where she continues to get inspiration for her novels.

Annie lives in Massachusetts with her husband.

For more information visit anniecabot.com

Printed in Great Britain
by Amazon

40016859R00162